Mills & Boon
Best Seller Romance

A chance to read and collect some of the best-loved novels from Mills & Boon—the world's largest publisher of romantic fiction.

Every month, six titles by favourite Mills & Boon authors will be re-published in the *Best Seller Romance* series.

A list of other titles in the *Best Seller Romance* series can be found at the end of this book.

Margery Hilton

THE HOUSE OF STRANGE MUSIC

MILLS & BOON LIMITED
LONDON · TORONTO

First published 1974
Australian copyright 1982
Philippine copyright 1982
This edition 1982

© Margery Hilton 1974

ISBN 0 263 73991 0

Set in 9 on 9 pt Plantin

02-0982

Made and printed in Great Britain by
Richard Clay (The Chaucer Press) Ltd,
Bungay, Suffolk

CHAPTER ONE

THE young farmer handed down Linzi's case, said cheerfully, 'Half a mile down the lane there—you can't miss it,' and gave her a parting grin as he pointed. The little country bus trundled away down the winding road, its friendly lights beginning to wink intermittently as it entered the tree-lined stretch beyond the bend. Finally they were lost in the black billowing shapes and Linzi was left with a suddenly daunting sense of being the last living entity in this part of the world.

With a town-bred girl's practicality she shrugged away the thought and turned her steps towards the dark, uninviting shadows of the narrow lane the farmer had indicated. There could be several reasons for her new employer's failure to turn up to meet her at the station as arranged. Anything could have stopped him, especially in an out-of-the-way place like this, tucked away in the heart of the North Riding, and with a crippled child ... All the same, Linzi felt some of her earlier confidence ebbing away and she could not help wishing she was driving instead of walking along this eerie country lane with its rough pitted surface underfoot, to say nothing of a case which was proving a much heavier burden than she had suspected when she packed it last night in readiness for her long journey north.

She paused to change hands and with the cessation of the gritting sounds of her own footsteps the silence of the countryside at night closed round her like a curtain of dark transparency in which even the stars seemed to have vanished. Night and the dark in the city were never like this.

Once again she refused to allow imagination to take over and moved on as briskly as she could, but for the first time the doubts were no longer as easily dismissed as they had been in London. Had she been wise to commit herself to a month on trial in the employ of a man she had never met? Even though the agency was highly reputable, and in this case had appeared to place greater stress on references of character than technical qualifications? Mark Vardan's own references had been impeccable—there was no malarkey about this job where she would be living in strange and isolated surroundings—but he had wanted to know a great deal about his prospective employee. Almost too much.

But that was understandable when the care of a child was involved, Linzi told herself. He wanted a girl who was kind, loyal, patient, affectionate, and sensible to care for his crippled daughter, and a girl who was, moreover, prepared to take herself and all her sterling qualities to a lonely house in the heart of the Yorkshire moors, two miles from the nearest village and twenty from the nearest market town. She must also be capable of supervising the child's education for an indefinite period. For this he was prepared to pay generously, extremely generously, and, once she had proved her suitability, allow the right girl to get on with the job free of any niggling supervision and with full authority, or so Mrs Mead, the rather aristocratic woman to whom Mark Vardan had entrusted the task of selecting a suitable applicant, had assured Linzi.

It seemed quite a tall order, considering that three well-qualified predecessors had failed to last the trial month, but to Linzi, fresh from college and her first disastrous love affair, it offered escape as well as challenge, a beginning to the future she had to build without Ian in it. They'd had it all planned. They wouldn't have a long engagement. They'd marry, she would go on with her teaching career, they could afford to postpone starting a family for at least three years. Ian himself had been the first to point out that it would be foolish and unfair to waste her training by plunging into parenthood straight away. It had all seemed considerate and logical, and Linzi had been too carried away on the wings of a wild new emotion to pause to reflect that his logic was suddenly a trifle cool, a trifle cautious ... She'd been blind to the tiny warning pointers, until the evening when Ian went unusually quiet, before he had told her of the Canadian job that was the chance of a lifetime, that he was afraid they'd been too hasty, that he wasn't sure and he wanted to be fair to her, and perhaps they ought to wait, not tie themselves down ... Oh, Ian ...! Even to whisper his name started the ache again, the bruising that pride couldn't cover when she sensed his relief after it was all over. He was free of entanglement and she—she was at the end of the most wonderful six months of her life, with an eternity of bleakness stretching greyly into the future.

Linzi blinked fiercely at the darkness. She had to keep her vow to put Ian out of her mind. She had to look forward, not back, think only of a new life among strangers. But even so there was a tenuous link with Ian, in which she could not

6

find even a bitter satisfaction at its irony. If only Ian knew she was going to work for Mark Vardan ...

But she had not known herself, not until the last minute, the identity of her employer. She had never connected the Mr Vardan of the agency's advert with *the* Mark Vardan, of whom Ian had often talked. Composer, conductor, virtuoso, and a name to be conjured with in the musical world. A man who had turned his back on the lotus world of celebrities and had, rumour whispered, become virtually a hermit. Rumour had whispered other things, of tragedy and a scandal concerning his dead wife, scandal hushed up, and that Mark Vardan was a man with a broken heart, that he had vowed never to play or conduct in public again until his adored daughter was able to walk again.

Which might be never, or so Ian had said, culling gossip from the circle of dilettanti in which he moved. Thinking back, Linzi could remember clearly one evening when Ian had lamented the loss to music of a man destined to attain the highest pinnacle of brilliance. Yet what of the child's loss? Linzi had wondered. How could the most successful of careers be weighed against a child's loss of the ability to walk, run, skip, play ...? Not for the first time she wondered what kind of a man was Mark Vardan. It seemed that he had sacrificed everything else he held dear to devote himself to his little daughter, and yet he had delegated the choice of an employee to others, and if that choice appeared suitable he was prepared to allow a stranger full authority over the welfare of his child. He wished more time for a composition on which he was working. Did that mean he intended to return to the world of music after all, leaving the child in the care of a stranger?

Linzi quickened her steps, conscious of a rush of travel weariness and impatience to reach her destination. Soon she would see for herself and——

Her thoughts were shattered by a blast of sound. The lane was dropping steeply into a sharp S-bend, and the shrill warning and brilliance of headlights overtook her long before her wandering senses had registered the approach of a vehicle. Startled, she spun round and blinked, instinctively springing back to the verge. Her heavy case impeded her and she stumbled, the glare outlining her face. The next moment her foot plunged into nothing and she sprawled helplessly across the unseen drainage ditch under the hedge.

For a horrifying moment she thought the car was on her,

then she realised it was passing and slowing to a halt. She began to struggle up, aware of stinging pain in her knee and one hand, and heard the door slam. Feet came running and a male voice said sharply: 'Are you all right?'

'I—I think so.' Her handbag seemed to be missing and she experienced a stab of panic as she groped beside her case. 'I didn't hear——'

'Look out! You'll be in that ditch again!' Hands reached out to steady her and draw her back on to the gravelled surface. In the light from the car a concerned pair of blue eyes looked down at her. 'Sure you're okay? I'm most terribly sorry, scaring you like that.'

The clean-cut features under ruffled fair hair were friendly and genuinely worried, and Linzi managed a smile. 'It was my own fault. I was daydreaming—or nightdreaming!'

His smile broke out, infectious, then sobered. 'All the same, I don't usually send beautiful girls flying into ditches. I must make amends. Can I give you a lift anywhere?'

Linzi hesitated, and he said quickly: 'Where are you bound for?'

'Hillcrest House, but——'

'Hillcrest? Then you must be the girl who—And no one came to meet you?' The young man sounded angry as he picked up her case and opened the car door. 'You mean to say you came by bus, and walked, with this?'

Linzi found her handbag and brushed the hedgerow dust from it. 'Someone was supposed to meet me, but they didn't turn up—the bus driver said it was only half a mile.'

'Half a mile! He forgot about the extra half-mile drive from the gates.' With pleasant attentiveness, the young man settled her in the car and got in himself. 'Vardan really is the limit!'

Linzi relaxed back. 'You know Mr Vardan and Hillcrest?'

'I know the house well—I'm staying with my aunt in the lodge at present. She used to work at the house until she retired a couple of years ago. I'm Andrew Tarrance, by the way. Temporary layabout until I finish my current commission.'

'Oh.' Linzi paused, turning to look at his shadowy profile. 'I'm Linzi Shadwyn—do you always layabout while you finish commissions?'

He responded to her teasing note with a grin. 'I'm busy correlating the results of a year's research into soil conservation, and being well within my limit of completing the typing out of the report I'm being lazy—by order.'

8

'Whose order?' Linzi asked idly.

'Auntie's. She's an old darling—my father's oldest sister—and she's never completely happy unless she has someone to cosset. So she decided I was in need of lots of good fresh Yorkshire air and enormous quantities of good Yorkshire home cooking.'

He lapsed into silence while he negotiated another sharp, steep bend, then went on: 'She was longing to look after young Gilda, but Vardan wanted someone young.'

There was a slight hardening in his voice when he spoke of Linzi's employer and she glanced at him, aware of a natural curiosity. She was certain he disliked Mark Vardan, but equally certain he was unlikely to respond to any feelers she might put out regarding the source of that dislike. She said casually, 'Your aunt sounds a darling.'

'She is. I say,' the lightness was back in his tone, 'why not come and meet her? We're almost there. Then I'll run you up to the house.'

'It's very kind of you, but perhaps I should——'

'It won't take a minute,' Andrew said firmly. 'If you'd gone on walking it would have taken you another half hour.'

Her protests were overruled and a moment later the car slowed to enter a wide gateway. An old-fashioned lamp cast a pool of ghostly radiance between high stone pillars and gleamed on the glossy leaves of the rhododendron bushes bordering the drive. Suddenly Linzi was glad she'd met this friendly stranger instead of trekking this lonely, foreboding drive alone. Then she saw the little grey stone lodge tucked away on the right, a soft warm glow peeping through one window, and Andrew pulled in alongside the low, dry-stone wall that edged a pocket-handkerchief-sized garden in front of the cottage. He was hardly out of the car before the lodge door opened and a tiny, plump woman appeared. Her surprise at seeing her nephew's companion was soon over and Linzi, amid the introductions and Andrew's explanations, was ushered into the cosy, beamed kitchen.

'Call me Nanny Tarrance—everybody does,' said Andrew's aunt, whose blue eyes were shrewd as well as kind. 'I've told him before about that contraption of his. These lanes were never meant for cars, but you can't tell the young ones these days. In my young days we walked and were better for it. Aye, and I could still walk him off his feet, any day.'

Andrew was laughing, and Nanny Tarrance turned indignantly. 'Go on,' she raised a threatening hand, 'many's the time I've skelped you, my lad, and I'm not so infirm yet, so watch out. Now take Miss Shadwyn's coat or she won't feel the good of it when she goes out again, and I'll put the kettle on.'

Linzi's protests were unheeded, and she could not help smiling at the way the tiny, indomitable lady affectionately bullied her tall, broad-shouldered nephew. She slipped off her camel travelling coat and handed it to him, aware of the light of admiration in his eyes which he was making no attempt to hide, and then Nanny Tarrance gave a shocked exclamation.

The fall in the ditch had left its traces, and Linzi looked ruefully at the tear in her stocking and the smudges on her once immaculate beige skirt. But Nanny was staring at the scratches under the filmy nylon and the spreading nettle-stings on Linzi's hands.

Andrew was ordered outside with a torch to bring a dock leaf—'There's a clump just ouside the back gate'—and Linzi was shepherded to the tiny bathroom to repair the damage. By the time this was done Nanny had set the table, for the cup of tea which was to include apple pie, delicious York ham, little home-baked cheesecakes, and a dark rich fruitcake —made to Nanny's own special recipe. A full-scale country supper, in fact!

'I told you,' said Andrew, drawing out a chair for Linzi, 'Nanny is a great believer in stoking the inner man.'

'And making amends for your sins, my lad.' Nanny smiled and sat down to preside over the teapot. She passed a cup to Linzi, then said without any trace of curiosity: 'So you're going to look after the little lass up at the house.'

Linzi nodded. 'For a month, to begin with, until I prove I can cope.'

'You will.' For a moment Nanny studied her with those disconcertingly shrewd blue eyes, then she tilted her head inquiringly. 'But you're sure you're not afraid of finding the countryside a bit too quiet.'

'Not at all.' Linzi suppressed a start of surprise at the casual switch to herself. 'I was born in the country, although we moved into a big town when I was still a child, and we always spent our holidays in the country.'

'Aye, but the winter's on its way. It shows a different face out here on the moors.'

'I'm sure it does.' Linzi smiled. 'But I'm not afraid of being bored.'

'I shall see that she doesn't have a chance to be bored—

in her spare time, that is,' Andrew said quickly, with a warm glance across the table. 'When are you free?'

'She doesn't know yet,' said his aunt, giving him an exasperated look. 'Give the lass time to get here. Now, another cup, dear ...?'

The meal passed pleasantly and the conversation made no return to Linzi's job or the unknown house of her destination which lay so near to this cosy, friendly cottage. Linzi found she was enjoying herself, all the more because the little interlude had been so unexpected, but she was conscious of an underlying puzzlement. She had fully expected curiosity and a certain amount of discussion, within the limits of reasonable discretion, because it was obvious that Nanny Tarrance must know Hillcrest House and the people who lived in it. The impression began to form that Nanny did not need to ask questions, that there was a great deal she knew, that she was not prepared to divulge yet ...

The little mantel clock chiming ten brought Linzi a sharp reminder of how time was passing. Over an hour had flown by, and a sudden sense of reluctance to leave this warmth for the darkness of the night rushed over her. She shook it off as she prepared to depart and thanked the kindly country-woman for her hospitality.

'You must come again, you will always be welcome, my dear,' Nanny said warmly.

'We mean it, you know,' said Andrew, bringing her coat. 'It isn't one of those casual invitations that aren't worth the breath they're spoken in.'

Linzi didn't need this assurance. Already there was a possessive air in the way he was holding her coat, and the light of interest in his eyes that sought her reciprocal response. She turned to slip her arms into the garment, and stilled as a peremptory knocking came at the door.

There was sudden silence as Nanny moved quickly, and the cool inward rush of the night air into the little hall. There was Nanny's voice and a deeper voice, and then Linzi's name.

'Yes, she's here—won't you come in, Mr Vardan? She's just——'

'No, thank you, Mrs Tarrance. If you'll inform Miss Shadwyn I'm waiting.'

The deep voice was brusque and chilling, and Linzi, after the first moments of comprehension, experienced a rush of guilt. After all, she must have missed her new employer, somehow, and now he sounded furious. She hurried from

11

the fireside, but Andrew reached the hall before her.

'We're on our way now—I'm just about to run Miss Shadwyn up to the house.'

'That won't be necessary. I have my car outside.' The deep voice stilled into the silence that came as Linzi passed into the little hallway and under the gaze of the man who stood there.

Linzi looked up at him and her tentative smile faltered and died. All her preconceived notions dissolved and she was not aware that she was near to staring. She had imagined a romantic conception of a musician; a slight, dark, intense figure, with the volatile mien of suppressed nervous vitality, with expressive hands and restless gestures ... deep-lidded eyes, haggard even ...

Mark Vardan was as different from this as to make her notions ridiculous. He was taller than Andrew and broad of shoulders. His eyes were too cold a grey ever to suggest a burning intensity of emotion, his chin square enough to suggest the aggressiveness of the fighter rather than the musician, and in the dim light of Nanny's little hall his mouth looked straight and taut enough to banish any whimsical fancies about artistic soulfulness. It was compressed now as he looked down at her, and he nodded slightly as she stammered:

'Hello, Mr Vardan. I—I'll just get my things. They—they're still in Andrew's car.'

Andrew seemed about to protest, and Nanny said quickly: 'Don't just stand there, lad. Go and get them.'

She followed him outside, very conscious of Mark Vardan's presence as she brushed past him, and shivered a little at the keen thrust of the wind. Hardly giving her time to make final goodnight leavetakings, Mark Vardan escorted her briskly to the big, dark-coloured car beside Andrew's old Austin and closed the door on her before he took the case from the younger man. He got in and slammed his door.

'Why didn't you wait for me at the station?'

'But I did!' Startled by the abruptness of his question, she turned her head towards him. 'I waited nearly twenty minutes, then I decided you'd mistaken my time of arrival or something and I set off by what they told me was the last bus out this way. It was getting late.'

'I'm not in the habit of making mistakes about the times of appointments,' he said coldly, sending the car smoothly into motion.

The rebuff stung, vanquishing any guilty doubts about her

12

delay at Nanny's cottage. She said stubbornly, 'Well, I did wait quite a time. What else could I do but take the chance of the only other transport?'

'Telephoned Hillcrest House,' he said crisply. 'You would have been told the car was on its way to meet you, and you would have been saved a half-mile walk with your luggage, while *I* would have saved a wasted hour and a certain amount of worry as to your whereabouts.'

She took a deep breath, aware of the barrier of antagonism already forming between herself and a man she'd known for less than a few minutes. She said stiffly, 'I was unlucky enough to stumble into a ditch as I came along the lane. Mr Tarrance was coming along just as it happened. He invited me to the lodge and offered me a lift, which I accepted. That's why I'm so late, Mr Vardan.'

'And I was flagged down by a motorist who'd had a break-down. Which is why I failed to be punctual. I don't make promises without the intention of keeping them, Miss Shad-wyn.'

Her mouth tightened. She knew he was angry and that she was stringing out the slight misunderstanding instead of making a tactful effort at ending it, but there was something about his attitude that provoked her. She stared angrily ahead. 'I wasn't to know that. You could have had a break-down, for all I knew, and *I* undertook to be at Hillcrest House today, and today is almost over. I too like to keep my promises, Mr Vardan.'

'I appreciate that,' he said, after a perceptible pause, 'but I'd have appreciated it a great deal more if you'd postponed your socializing till another day. I don't suppose it occurred to you that we delayed dinner tonight until your arrival.'

Linzi groaned softly under her breath. What a start to a new job! She wondered how to undo the damage, and as she sought for suitable words she saw the dark façade of the house looming against the night sky. The clouds had parted and a full moon gleamed silver over a vast old mansion of stone with great diamond paned windows and a massive doorway flanked by solid Doric columns. It was, in actuality, an extremely fine portico, but by now Linzi was too weary and dispirited to appreciate that, or take note of the fine old carved panelling in the high, spacious hall in which she found herself a few moments later. She had only a confused impression of a polished oak staircase leading up into shadows and a minstrels' gallery hanging heavily carved overhead before Mark Vardan was at her side, setting down her case and exclaiming impatiently: 'Where's——? Oh, there you are, Mrs Brinsmead. Will you show Miss Shadwyn to her room and see that she has everything she wants.'

Without waiting for any response, he took Linzi's case and went briskly ahead up the staircase, leaving her with the thin, pale-faced woman who had come silently from a green baize door at the far end of the hall. She came forward, not smiling, and there was veiled curiosity in her eyes as she assessed the girl in the smudged beige suit who stood rather uncertainly in the centre of the expanse of mellowed old parquet.

'Will you come this way?' Mrs Brinsmead made a slight gesture, and with a sigh Linzi began to mount the stairs. The house wasn't cold, yet she felt cold, the kind of chill that springs from an unwelcoming atmosphere. Her heart grew heavy as she followed the housekeeper along the broad gallery and down a panelled corridor, at the end of which was a high window and a long settle on which reposed her case.

It's too soon to judge, she told herself, after a journey that had lasted most of the day and ended inauspiciously; it would all seem different tomorrow, she assured herself as she entered the room Mrs Brinsmead was indicating.

Immediately it seemed proof of the small mental assurance. The bedroom was bright and spacious, light with modern sycamore furniture and clear cheerful tones of lemon and pale spring green in curtains and bed covering. The carpet was green and white, the walls lemon, and, prepared for heavy old oak and dark sturdy folkweaves, Linzi was pleasantly surprised, but the cheerful welcome of a leaping coal fire in the grate surprised her even more. An exclamation broke from her and she turned to the housekeeper, only to see her raise a warning finger to her lips.

In a low voice Mrs Brinsmead said, 'It's Miss Gilda ... she's in the next room and it would be better if we didn't wake her.'

'Oh, of course not.' Linzi subsided and nodded.

'She's been extremely difficult today,' the housekeeper went on. 'With knowing that you were coming she got herself worked up into an over-excited state, and it isn't good for her. Now,' she glanced across the room, 'that door leads into Miss Gilda's room, and this one to a bathroom, which also connects with her room. If there's anything you want you can tell me and I'll see to it. Come straight down to the dining-room when you're ready—Mr Vardan said to delay the meal

14

for you, but I'm afraid it'll be spoiled. We didn't expect you to be as late as this.'

There was a disapproving note in the housekeeper's voice, and Linzi gave a small inward sigh of dismay. 'I'm sorry,' she said quickly. 'I missed Mr Vardan and got a lift down the lane. And I've had an enormous supper—I couldn't possibly eat anything else tonight.'

'Yes, I thought you'd be at the lodge,' said Mrs Brinsmead. 'I guessed you'd probably ask the way there and I suggested to Mr Vardan when he came back that he should ask Mrs Tarrance if you'd appeared there. I was right.'

There was nothing particularly friendly about the tone in which these statements were made, rather were they matter-of-fact with a trace of annoyed resignation underlining them. 'I'm terribly sorry,' said Linzi for the second time. 'But it all just happened. It—you've been very kind. This is a beautiful room. Thank you for making it so welcoming.'

She smiled, but the woman's thin features did not relax. She merely nodded, then went from the room with that curiously smooth, silent movement which Linzi was to come to recognise as characteristic of everything she did.

Alone, Linzi gave a troubled sigh. She had certainly started with a black mark, but was it really her fault? For a moment or so she looked round her new surroundings, then quickly washed and freshened herself before she started to unpack. There was ample space for her things, and when she had finished she glanced round the warm and friendly bedroom, aware that she was still listening unconsciously for any sound from the adjoining room.

But there was none. For what sound she could hear—the occasional sputter of fire and the light flurries of wind against the window—she might have been the only living being in the great old house. Linzi went to the window, drawing aside the curtain and peering out at the darkness. It was as silent and alien as she expected, and she turned back to the brightness of the room. What was her small charge like? Of an excitable nature, if the housekeeper was to be believed, and 'difficult'. The housekeeper had sounded so coldly matter-of-fact, almost uncaring … Linzi frowned. Snap judgements could be a mistake, but she could not help thinking that there wasn't much affection forthcoming from that direction, and children needed affection as much as they needed food. In Gilda's case, even more of it. She was motherless, and her father …

15

Linzi sat down on the bed, her frown betraying a hint of troublement. She must not start imagining all kinds of things at this premature stage, but she must face up to starting off on the wrong foot and do something about it. Mark Vardan had been brusque and curt, and he had made no effort to show understanding, but he had set off to meet her, he had instructed the housekeeper to delay the evening meal, and nothing had been spared to make a welcoming room for the new arrival, all of which indicated that things might have been very different if everything had gone to plan. Abruptly Linzi stood up; pride and annoyance could easily mask good manners.

Without stopping to analyse the impulse to make an apology, she changed quickly into a soft, pastel-blue jersey dress that echoed the rich grey-blue flecks of eyes much more beautiful than she realised and made her smooth, ash-blonde hair look almost silver where it fell sleekly over the deep roll collar. She added discreet touches of light make-up and glanced at her watch. It was exactly ten-thirty. Perhaps she should wait until morning ...

Uncertainly, she went out and stood at the head of the staircase. The great hall beneath was still lit but deserted, and a sense of unease crept over Linzi. There was no concrete reason for it that she could pin down, except that the house was so totally different from her imagined pictures of it. It was so big, remote, and its atmosphere did not seem right for a crippled child to spend her days in. There was an aura of isolation and affinity with past rather than future. Linzi had never considered herself over-imaginative, but now she was not so sure. Already the feeling of stepping back in time was strong as she went slowly down the first flight of stairs.

The illusion was heightened by the great portraits lining the walls, and one in particular that faced her at the half turn of the staircase drew her gaze and made her pause.

It was of a girl, near her own age, in the misty flowing voile of the late Empire period. Long ribbons floated from the high bodice and bows of velvet bound the silky gold hair in its elaborate coiffure. She was delicate and pretty, this girl in misty lilac, with her softly parted rose lips, her slender, still childish hands fluttering towards the small fluffy Pomeranian dog gambolling near her little satin-shod feet. But her eyes were sad, filled with longing, and they seemed to seek Linzi's, as though pleading for understanding through the bygone ages.

16

'Has she got you as well?'

Linzi gasped with shock and spun round. Mark Vardan was standing at the foot of the stairs, irony lurking in the shadows round his mobile mouth.

She stammered, 'Me? I—I don't know what you mean. I just stopped to look at her.'

He gave her a strange look, an encompassing appraisal that suddenly made her aware of herself as she might appear in his eyes. It made her tense inwardly, then the remoteness was back in his expression and he moved forward composedly. 'Is there anything wrong, Miss Shadwyn?'

She hesitated, saw his brows go up impatiently, and impulsively she began to descend towards him.

'Mr Vardan . . . I'm sorry. I've been thinking, and——'

'Sorry?' he interrupted. 'What for? Have you changed your mind already?'

She halted, puzzled. 'Changed my mind? What should I change my mind about? I wanted to apologise for my share of the misunderstanding. About the inconvenience of the meal being spoilt, and——' She gestured, forgetting the carefulness of formal speech, and rushed on: 'Well, I know I shouldn't have stayed so long at the lodge, only she—Mrs Tarrance—was so kind, letting me tidy up and insisting I had a cup of tea, and it turned into supper, and—well, it would have been rude in the face of her kindness to a complete stranger, and the time went so quickly. It just didn't occur to me that you'd got held up and . . .' she stopped, giving a small wry shrug. 'I'm sorry to make such an unfortunate start.'

For a long moment he did not respond, then he shook his head. 'Forget it. Maybe I was a bit curt earlier on, but I was worried. I thought you weren't going to turn up.'

She stared. 'You thought I'd changed my mind, and without letting you know? But I wouldn't dream of doing such a thing!'

'You'd be surprised at the things people do dream of doing,' he said dryly. He glanced at his watch. 'Would you like a drink, Miss Shadwyn? There are several things we should get straight and we may as well settle them now. But if you're tired . . .'

'No, not in the least.' Linzi was anxious to learn more of the responsibility she would have to shoulder and to correct the impressions of doubt he seemed to have gained about her.

The room into which he escorted her had obviously been the library in the more leisurely bygone days of the old house,

17

and it was obviously Mark Vardan's own domain now. It was lofty, panelled from floor to ceiling where the walls were not booklined, and the ambience was essentially masculine. There were piles of bound music scores amid other piles of sheet music on the lower shelves in one alcove, a big tape deck looked faintly incongruous beneath a fine old tapestry whose mellowed tints depicted a grave-faced child seated at a spinet, and a magnificent Steinway grand dominated the room.

Linzi sat down in the chair to which he waved her and felt the warmth from the log fire play pleasantly against her knees. There was a carving, much worn from centuries of polishing, set in the centre of the big curve under the mantelshelf. It looked like an old coat of arms with a Latin inscription, but the lettering was barely decipherable, and Linzi leaned forward to study it, not from idle curiosity but because it reminded her of her father's great interest.

'The date's 1604 if you're trying to make it out,' said Mark Vardan, coming to the fireside and proffering her drink. 'Are you interested in old houses and their histories?'

'Fairly, but my father has an absorbing interest in heraldry —it's his favourite topic.' She smiled her thanks as she accepted the wine. 'He might have been able to identify this, but I'm afraid I can't.'

'It's the coat of arms of the Hylcreces. They were a distant offshoot of an older family, staunch Yorkists whose direct line ended at Bosworth. The Hylcreces claimed the estates and prospered, for nearly two hundred years, until the tide of fortune turned against them in——' He checked and dropped into the chair opposite. 'But you don't want to hear the history of old fortunes and misdeeds long forgotten.'

'Oh, but I'm interested.' She was feeling more at ease now. 'It must be fascinating to trace one's family back so far.'

'They're not my family. Most of the original estate was dispersed a very long time ago. The house came into my grandfather's possession in an extremely unromantic way,' he said dryly. 'The old gentleman made his fortune in commerce and bought the place for the proverbial song. I must grant that he restored it with a loving respect for its original detail. The "Hillcrest" is, of course, the eventual derivative of the original "Hylcrece",' he added.

She nodded. 'So the girl in the portrait isn't your ancestor?' she said after a moment of reflection.

Mark Vardan looked slightly surprised, then he laughed. 'Oh, Gilda's Lilac Girl. No, she was the last of the Hylcreces.'

18

Abruptly his smile faded and he set down his glass. 'I hope you'll be able to make my daughter forget all this nonsense. She's far too preoccupied with this Lilac Girl business, and I want it stopped.'

'I don't understand.' Linzi leaned forward. 'She doesn't— there isn't a ghost, or anything like that?'

'No,' he waved one hand, 'at least not that I know of. But there must be some old story connected with the girl in the painting and it's been forgotten. When my grandfather took over the house he found that particular portrait and three others of the same subject hidden away in one of the top storerooms. They were covered with grime, and according to my mother—who was only a child at the time—there was a chest of clothing of the period and various little personal things, some dolls and a silver hairbrush and so on, the kind of things a young girl would treasure, but my mother swore that the whole atmosphere spoke of a banishment and unhappiness. My grandfather was rather taken with the portrait on the stairs. He had it cleaned and restored, and then another rather strange thing came to light. When he was deciding where to hang it, someone suggested the spot where it is now, and so he had the then existing picture taken down. It was a great massive old painting, much larger, but when it was taken down there was the lighter patch behind it, exactly the same size as the Lilac Girl's portrait, and so it seemed natural to assume that originally she had hung there but been taken down and banished, for some reason or other.'

'It sounds fascinating. Don't you know any more about her?' Linzi asked.

'Not you as well!' he exclaimed impatiently. 'Gilda stares at that portrait as though it bewitches her and is for ever asking me who this girl was and what happened to her. When I can't answer she goes off into a dreamy state and begins to make up her own stories about that confounded girl in a lilac dress.'

'But I can understand that,' Linzi said slowly. 'There's something about that picture, about the girl in it. I felt it the moment I saw it. Oh,' she smiled ruefully, 'you'll say *I'm* fanciful, but it's in the girl's eyes. She seems to be pleading for understanding, or—or help.'

Mark Vardan sighed, then shrugged. 'That's the artist's skill. But I'd prefer that Gilda turned her vivid imagination to the more practical aspects of her schooling.'

'Yes, but ...' Linzi hesitated, wondering if she dared say

19

what she thought. She looked at him levelly. 'Mr Vardan, I know it isn't my business, but isn't it understandable? That Gilda should be so imaginative. After all, this house is very old, it's very isolated from what I can gather, and if there are no other children nearby . . . In view of her—her disability, she must be lonely, and therefore she's going to people her days with pretend people. It's perfectly natural.'

He leaned back, and now there was a light of amusement in his eyes. 'Well, go on. Say it.'

'Say what?'

'Say that I've no right to bring a little crippled girl to a great tomb of a place like this, and that I want my brains examining.'

She looked at the cynical curl of his mouth and experienced a rush of puzzlement. There was something here that did not permit easy understanding, and the memory of fragments of gossip repeated by Ian came back to her mind. She took a deep breath. 'Yes, obviously someone has said that to you, so I'll stick my neck out and ask you again. Why did you bring your daughter to so lonely an old place?'

'Because my daughter wished it.'

A strange note of intensity in his tone made Linzi look sharply at him. His eyes had gone dark, their arrogant amusement lost in the remoteness which sorrow or pain can leave. Suddenly he stood up and took Linzi's glass from her, and there was suppressed violence in his movements. He turned away. 'Gilda insisted. She begged me to bring her back here. Do you think *I'd* have chosen to bring her here?'

'I—I don't know.' Taken aback, Linzi moved uneasily. 'If she——'

'I loathe this place,' he said vehemently, 'and I'd be happy never to see it again. But because of what happened to Gilda, and because I love her more dearly than even my music, I acceded to her wish. And so we are here, and here we stay if it will make Gilda any happier.'

He swung round and there was such bitterness in his shadowed face that Linzi almost gasped.

'Well,' he said grimly, 'does that answer your question, Miss Shadwyn?'

CHAPTER TWO

LINZI awakened very early the following morning. For a little while she lay still, tense with suppressed anticipation of the new day, and let the unfamiliar shapes of the room identify themselves in the grey dimness.

It felt cold and not so welcoming now, and although it was out of her range of vision she sensed the greyness of a fire died out, the sad but unavoidable contrast to the warm friendly glow playing on the ceiling as she had drifted into sleep. There was no sound anywhere within the house and she wondered if she should get up now or wait a little while. It might be inconvenient if she went in search of people and things before they swung into the day's routine. Maybe they got up later, or maybe the walls were too thick to hear ... it was a problem she hadn't given a thought to, the difference of living in with the job, not presenting oneself at a set time for set duties ... Mark Vardan hadn't even mentioned a hint of a routine, a timetable or anything ... she must remember not to think of him as Mark Vardan, but it was difficult to forget the Mark Vardan, celebrity, and remember the Mr Vardan ...

Linzi opened her eyes again. The image of Mark Vardan's haunted features was suddenly disturbingly vivid. Why did he hate this house? Why that strange bitterness betrayed last night, and to a stranger? It was puzzling, glimpsed so unexpectedly through the cold arrogance she had faced at that first meeting, and after his almost curt attitude to her interest in the Lilac Girl. She frowned. Why did he disapprove of his daughter's preoccupation with the painting? A romantic interest on the part of a child seemed innocuous enough. And Mark Vardan himself was a musician of great skill and talent, so he must possess both imagination and sensitivity, a modicum of which his child was bound to have inherited. Unless ... Linzi frowned. Perhaps Gilda was like her mother, who had died in the car smash which crippled the child and hushed the tongues of the gossips ...

Abruptly Linzi flung back the bedclothes. The whispers concerning Mark Vardan and his beautiful young wife were no concern of hers. She was concerned only with the care of a little girl, for whom all the amends in the world were too late to make recompense for tragedy.

It was still only seven-thirty when Linzi had bathed and dressed. In the bathroom she had stood for a few moments near the other door which led to Gilda's room. There was only silence and stillness from the other side of that closed door, and Linzi turned away; the child might be lying wakeful, hating her helplessness as she wondered about the stranger who had come to help care for her, but Linzi could not risk breaking in on a sleeping child and shocking her into wakefulness.

She turned back her bed, tidied her night things, and went slowly out into the corridor. The painted eyes of the Lilac Girl seemed to follow her soft light steps down the heavily carpeted stairs and understand her start of surprise as she heard the music.

The haunting strains were muted but clear, almost familiar but elusive of recognition. Linzi took a step forward, trying to name the music which came from the room into which Mark Vardan had taken her the previous evening, and then spun round with shock as a voice said sharply: 'Don't go in there, Miss Shadwyn.'

Mrs Brinsmead stood at the green baize door, a tray in her hands. She said coldly, 'You must never interrupt Mr Vardan when he is working.'

'I wasn't going to.' Linzi recovered and ventured a smile. 'I wasn't sure what time I was expected down, or anything.'

'Mr Vardan always works for an hour before breakfast, which is at eight,' the housekeeper said in formal tones. 'I was about to call you and Miss Gilda.'

'Oh ...' Linzi looked at the tray. 'I didn't expect to be called with a cup of tea. Could I have mine with her now, and perhaps help with her?'

The housekeeper inclined her head and went briskly upstairs, saying over her shoulder: 'Have you had any experience nursing children?'

'No, but I can learn,' Linzi responded. 'I mean, she isn't ill in the sense of the word, is she?'

'No, but she has to be helped with washing and dressing,' Mrs Brinsmead answered, halting outside the door next to Linzi's room. 'Someone has to lift her in and out of her chair —Mr Vardan usually does that—and fetch things for her.'

'Yes, I realise that, and she has therapy as well, doesn't she?'

'Mr Vardan takes her to orthopaedic for that and her check-ups. That won't concern you. But take my word,' warned

22

Mrs Brinsmead, for the first time showing signs of unbending, 'don't expect it to be easy. She can be very difficult and very possessive. She led the last one a right dance.'

Linzi raised non-committal brows, and the housekeeper opened the door, calling: 'Time to wake up, Miss Gilda. I've brought the new——'

'I've been awake for *hours*! I thought you were never coming!'

The light flooded the room and Linzi saw a small oval face turned eagerly towards the door. Dark eyes startlingly like Mark Vardan's blinked against the brightness, then widened with unabashed curiosity as Linzi came into the room. Mrs Brinsmead swished open the curtains and closed the window, then turned. 'Miss Shadwyn is going to have her cup of tea with you. Well, say good morning, or have you lost your tongue?'

'No, I'm just waiting till you help me up. Is there any post, Brinny?'

'He's not been yet.' The housekeeper deftly hoisted the child into a sitting position, propped a pillow behind her, then flicked on the switch of an electric fire. There was a small sliding flap in the bedside cabinet, and she drew this out, put Gilda's mug of tea on it, and withdrew to the door, her mouth slightly pursed. 'I'll leave you to it.'

There was a silence after she withdrew. Gilda was the first to break it. She said calmly: 'We can talk now that she's gone. Do you want to say how-do-you-do and all the rest?'

'Not really—I know you're Gilda and you know I'm Linzi Shadwyn.' Linzi smiled, partly in greeting and partly to mask her reaction to the remarkable self-possession of the child framed against the oyster satin quilting of the curved bedhead.

She was dark and elfin, with a firm, pointed little chin that broke the otherwise perfect oval of her face. Her colouring was clear and vivid, betraying no trace of 'invalid' pallor, her dark hair fell thick and vibrant from a centre parting, curving like a smooth frame about her well-shaped head and waving slightly where it tumbled over her shoulders, and her serious little mouth held further indication of the spirit and determination in the wide, intelligent eyes. They were studying Linzi quite frankly, and suddenly they sparkled, as though their owner had reached her verdict—a favourable one. Gilda smiled. 'I never heard you in the night, not once.'

'Were you awake in the night?' Linzi sat down and reached for her tea.

23

'Twice. At midnight and at five o'clock this morning.'

'I was sound asleep at those times.'

'Daddy says that people who can get to sleep in a strange bed are lucky. When he used to be away for concerts he never used to get a good night's sleep.' Gilda paused and watched Linzi over the rim of her beaker. 'I never sleep very well because I don't get any exercise to tire me out.'

Linzi nodded. 'That's quite a problem. We'll have to see what we can do about it. Do you get out into the fresh air every day?'

'If I feel like it. But it's boring without Daddy and I don't like to drag him away from his work too often.' Gilda finished her tea and leaned back in the pillows. 'His work's terribly important, you know.'

'Yes, I know. I used to go to concerts with a music-loving friend. He was a great admirer of your father. But I didn't find out that you were his daughter until I'd actually arranged to come here,' Linzi said frankly.

'No, Daddy always tries to keep his two lives separate—now,' Gilda said casually. 'He thinks it's better that way.' She looked away, settled her gaze on an enormous teddy bear reclining amid apricot satin cushions on a small Sheraton settee. She said, 'Do you like my room?'

About to make the instant affirmative, Linzi checked, sensing that the casual question wasn't quite the pleasantry it seemed. She looked round the large, luxuriously furnished room, studying the pretty dressing table with its pastel pink and blue flounces and miniature floral porcelain lamps with finely pleated silk shades, the richness of snowy white carpet and heavy satin drapes, the three big dolls reposing on the Sheraton settee's twin under the other tall window, and the exquisite little French secretaire placed to catch exactly the fall of light from dainty candelabra with matching pleated shades. There was a wealth of fine period pieces in this room alone, enough to delight the eye and heart of any connoisseur, but ... Linzi looked back at the waiting child.

'It's very beautiful—I'd be afraid to touch anything, let alone play with it.'

'My Aunt Sharon arranged it all,' Gilda said flatly. 'I wanted it done all in white, with Swedish furniture and scarlet and blue, and I didn't want all those frilly net curtains. I wanted to be able to see out and put crumbs for the birds and try to get them to feed on the windowsill. But Aunt Sharon said what I wanted wouldn't tone with the room,

24

and this would be more restful. And Daddy, after saying I could have the room done however I wanted it, said he didn't know anything about it and I'd better be guided by her. And I hate dolls,' she added vehemently. 'They sit there looking vacant, as useless as me!'

'A lot of little girls would love to own just one of those dolls,' Linzi said mildly, getting up to pick up one of the despised toys and smooth down the beautiful silk dress.

'They could have them, but the people that gave them to me would be hurt if I gave them away, so I have to keep them on show. I *am* ten, you know.'

'Yes, and obviously you grew out of dolls a long time ago.' Linzi replaced the doll and sat on the edge of the bed. 'But have you thought, Gilda, that people probably racked their brains to think of something to amuse you? They probably thought you might like to experiment making fashionable clothes for those dolls.'

'Yes, I know. But I don't like sewing.' Gilda sighed. 'I don't like doing the few things I can do now.'

Linzi nodded understandingly. 'We'll see if we can think up some new ones, but before we start anything you'll have to tell me about your routine. Do you have your breakfast up here?'

'No,' Gilda gestured towards the dressing gown that lay over a chair. 'Could you pass it to me, please? Daddy usually —Oh, here he is.'

Mark Vardan crossed the room and bent to embrace his daughter before he glanced at Linzi. He took the dressing gown from her and said, 'Go down to breakfast and don't wait for us—we have our own rules, don't we, princess?'

Linzi hesitated, seeing Gilda assume a haughty expression and then giggle as he yanked the bedclothes back and lifted the small, nightgowned figure into his arms. Thin arms folded round his neck with a marked air of possession, and unaware that she gave a sigh Linzi closed the door quietly and made her way downstairs.

She need have no fears about Gilda being unloved after that glimpse of close rapport between father and daughter. There was no doubt about the truth of his statement that he loved his daughter, and therefore no reason to doubt that it was Gilda's wish that they stay here so far away from their London home. But didn't Gilda miss her friends, her school, the fabric of her previous life?

Linzi could not entirely dismiss the puzzling element that

hung over her during her first few days at Hillcrest. On the contrary, it increased as she came to know her small charge better and began to acquaint herself with the house and its environs.

There was much to occupy her at first. By mutual consent there was no mention of lessons that first day. There was much to see, and Linzi was amused during those early hours of her new post to find herself in the role of the one receiving instruction.

Once Gilda was brought downstairs for breakfast she rarely returned to the first floor. At the beginning, she told Linzi, she had slept downstairs in a small room next to the library. But she had disliked the idea of being left downstairs when everyone else retired to their rooms upstairs, and so the arrangement came by which her father carried her up and downstairs each morning and evening.

'Who else lives in the house?' Linzi asked.

'Just us, and Mrs Brinsmead, and Mrs Slaley, the cook. Oh, and Cedric—when he's here,' said Gilda, making a face.

'Who's Cedric?'

'Mrs Brinsmead's son. He's got a stall somewhere in the East End. He comes home when he's broke.' Gilda propelled her chair along the corridor and indicated the door she wished opened. 'Daddy can't stand Cedric. He's simply awful. This is the drawing room, but we never use it. Isn't it vast?'

Vast was an apt description, Linzi agreed, looking round the huge, panelled room with the fading tapestry curtains and heavy mahogany furniture. 'Actually, we only use about five or six rooms,' Gilda went on. 'It's difficult to get help. A woman and her daughter come up from the village to help Mrs Brinsmead, and there's old Jake who lives over the stables and does a bit in the garden, but he's getting past it now. Are you any good at gardening?'

'It depends what you mean by gardening,' said Linzi, glancing out at the rolling acres beyond the lawns and curve of the gravel drive. 'I shouldn't care to start on that.'

'It's pretty wild down there, but I meant the flower borders,' Gilda said. 'When I'm in my small chair—the one Daddy can put in the car when we travel—I can just reach over the side to pick the flowers. So one day Daddy said if I could do that I could pick the weeds as well. Will you help me?'

'Of course,' Linzi smiled as she closed the door behind them and continued the exploration. 'Where now?'

'I'll take you to the kitchen to meet Mrs Slaley—it's about morning-snack time—then I'll show you the shut-off part of the house. It's exciting. All creepy with its dust covers and everything. But Daddy won't let me go there by myself in case I fall out of my chair or something. Silly, isn't it?'

'Not in the least. Your father doesn't want you to get scared when he isn't around to look after you.'

'Yes, I know—I wonder what Mrs Slaley's baking today. She always lets me have a trier.'

'I think Mrs Slaley spoils you,' Linzi whispered a little while later, after the plump, friendly cook had welcomed them to sample creamy nut dainties and currant cookies in the big, homely kitchen.

There was something warm and friendly about country kitchens, Linzi reflected, sipping coffee while Gilda had milk. There was the same cosy, safe feeling here as in Nanny Tarrance's small, spotless kitchen. Safe ... why had that particular word suggested itself? Linzi frowned, then looked up sharply as the door swung open.

It was Mark Vardan, and Gilda grinned at him.

'Yes, we're fine,' she said in response to his greeting. 'Have you come for elevenses?'

'Not really. I wondered if Miss Shadwyn would care to join me for coffee, but I see you're looking after her.' He gave Linzi a slight smile as he spoke.

Gilda nodded, biting into her second cookie. She eyed her father with rather precocious irony. 'You know, you needn't keep coming to see how we're getting along. I like Linzi. And I'm behaving myself.'

'I should hope so.' His grave smile flickered, then died. 'So it's Linzi already. Has Miss Shadwyn given permission for that liberty?'

Gilda's dark eyes puckered with mischief. 'It sort of slipped out.' Her sidelong glance flickered to Linzi. 'I didn't mean it to be a liberty, but Linzi's such a nice name to say. At least I think so,' she added.

'No doubt,' Mark Vardan broke in before Gilda could elaborate further her wheedling argument, 'but Miss Shadwyn isn't in the least difficult to pronounce, and quite as pleasant to the ear.' He tweaked a heavy lock of her hair, a small affectionate gesture that fully compensated for any reproof in his earlier tone, and turned to go.

'Daddy!'

He checked at Gilda's exclamation, his brows lifting en-

27

quiringly.

'I want to show Lin—Miss Shadwyn—over the rest of the house. Can I have the key, please?'

Mark Vardan's brows narrowed into a frown. 'Not the disused wing, Gilda.'

'Oh, yes, please! It's the best part of the house.'

He shook his head. 'It won't fascinate Miss Shadwyn the way it fascinates you, my pet. And she certainly won't thank you for getting smothered in dust.'

'Oh, but it isn't very dusty really, Daddy, and she loves old places, and exploring, and mysterious shut-up rooms.' Gilda propelled her chair towards him, as though to stress further the appeal in her small face.

He hesitated, obviously reluctant, but plainly not proof against his daughter's cajolery. 'Very well—but only if Miss Shadwyn assures me she has no objection to being dragged through the moulder and must of a wing that hasn't been used, to my knowledge, for forty years.' He glanced at Linzi with a hint of apology. 'My grandmother occasionally went into it, and she had it kept dusted and in order, but after her death my grandfather had it closed, along with the entire upper floor. After all,' he shrugged, 'it would take an army of staff to keep the entire house in lived-in order.'

'Of course,' Linzi nodded, 'that's understandable. But I'm not afraid of dust if it amuses Gilda to play there—and if you have no objection to her being there,' she added.

'Heavens, no!' he said rather forcefully. 'This is her home. She can go where she likes. After all, she has to make a good deal of her own amusement, even though I personally would find the disused wing depressing as well as dusty. There's——'

'Oh, thank you, Daddy!' Gilda cried, reaching up her arms towards him. 'It won't be depressing. It'll be fun!'

'If you say so.' He bent to accept her exuberant hug, then straightened. 'But there's one condition. You're never to go in the disused parts of this house alone. Understand? You must have Linzi with you.'

'You said it, Daddy!' Gilda cried gleefully. 'Isn't it easy to say?'

Mark Vardan cast a rueful glance at Linzi before he admonished his daughter: 'True, but a feeble excuse. I hope Miss Shadwyn will accept it as such.'

Gilda chuckled, obviously preparing a further teasing onslaught on her father's slip, but he turned away abruptly, facing Linzi.

'You'll remember what I've said?'

'I'll make sure that Gilda doesn't go exploring on her own,' she said rather stiffly, aware of a warmth in her cheeks that had not been there a few moments ago. Her first name *had* come unexpectedly from him; it had also sounded extremely pleasing on his lips.

His dark eyes scanned her oval features for a moment, almost as though they measured the depth of that deepening rose, then abruptly he turned away. 'I must get back to my work. Remember what I said, Gilda.'

He reached the door, only to be halted by another urgent squeal from his daughter: 'The keys, Daddy! For the secret wing.'

'Oh . . .' His hands went to his pockets, then gestured impatiently. 'I don't have them. You'll have to ask Mrs Brinsmead.' His tone held a hint of abstraction now, and before Gilda could produce any more delaying tactics he hurried from the room.

Gilda pulled a face and propelled herself back to the table and her unfinished cookie. A couple of large gulps disposed of her milk, then she crammed the last of the cookie into her mouth. 'Mm, super!' she said indistinctly to Mrs Slaley, and turned to Linzi. 'Come on, let's find Brinny.'

But Mrs Brinsmead was busy, and she seemed reluctant—understandably so to Linzi—to drop everything to search for the keys. With a brisk promise to do so later, and a suggestion that Gilda might spend the morning more profitably out in the sunshine now that she had a nice new companion, the housekeeper returned to her work.

Once possessed of an idea Gilda hated being sidetracked. Grumbling, she permitted herself to be taken out into the garden, where, out of earshot of the house, she forgot her pique long enough to giggle: 'Fancy Brinny calling you the nice new companion. Isn't she awful? I'd be furious if it were me. Did it make you feel like a Victorian governess?'

It needed little strain of the imagination to feel oneself transported back into the age of crinolines and carriages, the mellow glow of oil lamps, and dark leaping shadows beyond the flickering sconces, thought Linzi, instantly mindful of the atmosphere engendered by a house wherein time seemed almost to have stood still for a century. But her tone was prosaic as she observed lightly: 'I don't think Mrs Brinsmead intended any offence, any more than you do, Gilda, when you

29

call her Brinny.'

Gilda considered this, her eyes narrowed against the bright autumn sunshine. 'I suppose not,' she conceded, 'it's just that she's so bossy, not friendly like Nanny. I'm sure she only stays because Daddy pays her a big salary to do the job.' Gilda paused, then wheeled around. 'Let's go this way. There's a path to the rose garden—it's the only one without steps.'

Ways without steps were terribly important to Gilda, as Linzi very soon came to realise during that exploration of the considerably extensive grounds of Hillcrest House. Sometimes Gilda, manoeuvring her chair with a skill that amazed Linzi, would forget exactly where a path would end and come to a halt in a fury of frustration before the obstacle of a series of steps. The house stood on a rise, and its grounds sloped gently around the driveway area at the front, levelling at the western side and then falling away quite steeply at the eastern side. There was a ravine, a little one, down there, Gilda informed Linzi when eventually they reached the long flat sweep of the terrace that overlooked the rose garden, but that part of the grounds was all uncultivated woodlands.

'Daddy says the gardens are the best part of Hillcrest,' Gilda remarked when they came to a halt at the half-moon curve at the centre of the terrace. 'He'd like to restore them to what they were when he stayed here as a little boy. But you can't get enough staff here, it's too remote, and it would take an army to keep the grounds perfect.'

'I think they're very attractive as they are,' Linzi commented, leaning on the broad parapet of stone and looking down at the formally laid out beds below. Even though summer was gone and the leaves were falling thickly the rose garden was still ablaze with scarlets and saffrons, and the sweetness hung on the air.

'The roses will blossom right up till winter,' Gilda said. 'Once, years ago, Daddy gathered red roses in the snow on Christmas morning to put on Mummy's breakfast tray. It was the Christmas before——' Abruptly Gilda stopped, and Linzi had a strange impression that the child regretted the unguarded confidence.

She said gently: 'It must be very beautiful here when the snow falls. Are there lots of robins?'

'Oh, yes! Nanny Tarrance once had one nesting just outside her cottage. She used to——' Gilda sat up excitedly. 'Oh, Linzi, let's go and see her! Could we? There's a path down there that's a short cut. Could we, please?'

30

Already, in the short time she had known her, Linzi was finding it difficult to resist Gilda's pleas. It wasn't entirely sympathy for the child's tragic disablement; she was a bewitching little girl and she made no secret of the fact that she had taken Linzi to her heart from the first moment of meeting. Linzi was discovering that that kind of affection was extremely difficult to resist. So she smiled, and they turned their backs on the rose garden.

She discovered that Gilda had not exaggerated about the path being a short cut down to the lodge and the main gates. The drive swung out in a wide loop which, perforce, vehicles had to follow, but the path under the trees, edged by little overgrown iron hoops at each side, was little more than five minutes' walk. Something to remember in future, Linzi thought, for the occasions when she wanted to go to the village or catch the bus to Whitby.

Nanny Tarrance was at home, and her surprise and delight at the sight of her small visitor were all Gilda could desire. There were smiles all round as between them Linzi and the older woman managed to lift Gilda and her chair up the two steps at the front door.

'Of course that nephew of mine would be missing when he's wanted,' said Nanny Tarrance, breathlessly, when they were settled in the parlour. 'Now, you'll have a wee bite of something?'

Gilda's eyes widened over her demure grin. 'We've had our morning cookies, actually, but . . .'

'Cookies! I've just taken a cheesecake out of the oven,' Nanny said with a scorn of cookies. 'It should be cool enough for eating by the time the kettle boils.'

She bustled away and Gilda made a small delighted hunch of her shoulders and giggled. 'Do you know, I'm always hungry here. I never used to be hungry at the flat.'

She was plainly enjoying herself, and reluctant to go when Linzi checked the time and knew it was time they returned to the house to tidy themselves for lunch. Though whether they would be able to eat any lunch after sampling generous wedges of Nanny's cheesecake Linzi privately doubted. Then Andrew arrived just as they were leaving and that caused another delay.

He was so unassuming in his pleasure at meeting Linzi again that she hadn't the heart to rush straight away, while Gilda, playing at being demure in a way Linzi was beginning to recognise with amusement, had obviously admitted Andrew to her circle of favourite people. 'I remember seeing you when I was terribly young,' she told him.

'I haven't forgotten you, either,' he said gravely, and Nanny Tarrance smiled fondly.

'Children take to him the same way as they take to big daft dogs,' she said in an aside to Linzi. 'Sometimes I wish he'd be a bit more serious about the older lassies. A nice sensible lass like yourself, for instance,' Nanny added slyly. 'But there, he always picks the wrong sort.'

Linzi said nothing, her attention partly on Gilda's merry face as the child responded to Andrew's blarney. She was waiting for a tactful opportunity to draw Gilda away; it was almost lunchtime and Mark Vardan might be waiting impatiently.

'I'd like to see him settling down—he's twenty-six, you know. It's high time he stopped fooling around,' Nanny said bluntly. 'But I might as well talk to the wall, of course. Now, Andrew,' she said in a changed voice, 'don't make them late for getting back. It's——'

'But, Nanny, we're making a date!' cried Gilda, and giggled at the pretended shock in Nanny's expression. 'We're going for a picnic. While the weather's still fine. May we, Linzi? Oh, please say we can!'

The suggestion took Linzi by surprise. Automatically she thought of the difficulties entailed and her own responsibility for Gilda's safe-keeping, Then she thought of Mark Vardan; would he give permission?

Andrew watched her hesitating and seemed to deduce the cause of it. 'I'm sure we can overcome the problems,' he said quietly, 'and I hope I needn't say that I'll take greatest care of both of you.'

'I don't doubt that for a moment,' she said slowly, 'but I'll have to ask Gilda's father.'

'He'll say yes straight away,' Gilda said confidently. She clasped her hands eagerly. 'What a gorgeous idea—I've never been on a picnic. When?'

'How about next Sunday?'

Gilda's smile vanished. 'But that's ages away. It might be cold and raining by then.'

'It won't.'

'How do you know?'

'Because it's going to rain tomorrow, and the next day, and the day after that.'

'Are you a weather forecaster?' Gilda demanded.

'No, I've got to be out all day for the next three days,' Andrew said, assuming a lugubrious expression that made Linzi smile.

'So it'll all be over by Sunday. Okay, that's a date,' said Gilda precociously, and Andrew bowed.

'Now, I'll see you both up to the house,' he said as Linzi moved forward.

But Gilda, who was the most proficient expert at delaying tactics that Linzi had ever come across, wanted to make their plans watertight.

'I'll give you our phone number and you give me yours,' she said solemnly, 'just in case anything happens.'

Nanny gave a despairing shake of her head, but paper had to be found so that the numbers could be exchanged. Gilda took a pen from her blazer pocket and leaned over to rest the paper on the edge of the table. She tore the sheet in half and presented one piece to Andrew, then folded the other piece and stowed it away in her pocket. Only then did she consent to depart.

With Andrew's strength to help they made the uphill return journey in a record fifteen minutes, but even so it was long after one when they got back to the house.

Mark Vardan was standing by the dining-room window, and the set of his mouth betrayed an annoyance that wiped all the laughter evoked by Andrew from the faces of the two latecomers.

'Where the devil have you been?' he demanded. 'Don't you know it's almost half past one?'

Gilda gave a series of tiny rapid nods. 'Yes, but you see we went to see Nanny Tarrance and then Andrew came and he wants to take us on a picnic on Sunday, and he says——'

The expression on her father's face got through to her at last. She sobered, and propelled herself quickly to her place at the table. 'I'm terribly sorry, Daddy. We didn't mean to keep you waiting.' She shot him an innocent glance from under long dark lashes as he took his place. 'Isn't it strange how time goes so quickly when one is enjoying oneself?'

But he was not mollified by this blatant bit of guile and his glance of displeasure turned to Linzi.

'I should be grateful if in future you would endeavour to see that Gilda is here promptly for meals,' he said coldly. 'Apart from inconveniencing my timetable and ruining food it's hardly fair to an excellent cook whom we were fortunate to get. See that this doesn't happen again.' Without giving

33

the dismayed Linzi a chance either to explain or apologise, he asked his daughter curtly if she wanted soup.

'What kind is it?' she said in a small voice.

'Mushroom.'

'No, thanks, Daddy. I don't like mushroom.'

'Since when?' he said sarcastically.

Gilda merely turned her head away, looking at Linzi's distressed face as Mark lifted the heavy tureen lid so that Linzi could help herself. Presently Gilda said in a muffled tone: 'It wasn't Linzi's fault, Daddy. She did keep reminding me about the time, but I was enjoying myself more than I've done for ages.'

His mouth tightened and he appeared unmoved by the child's plea. 'Miss Shadwyn's job is not to *remind* you about the time, Gilda,' he said curtly, 'it's to see that you keep to the rules of our domestic routine here—heaven knows, there aren't many. Unless she exerts a reasonable discipline and you submit to it I see little point in keeping her here. I may as well heed your Aunt Sharon's advice and pack you off to that special school she took the trouble to sort out for you.'

He stopped speaking and an appalled silence descended. Shock rounded Gilda's eyes and drained the lovely rose from her cheeks. She stared at her father as though he had pronounced a frightful sentence upon her and struggled for words.

'You—you wouldn't, Daddy!' she got out at last.

'Oh, but I would.'

Another awful silence came, broken by the rattle of the serving hatch by the side of the fireplace. Thankful for the diversion, Linzi got up to collect the tray with the main course set on it, only to be forestalled by the silently entering Mrs Brinsmead.

'I usually see to this,' the housekeeper said disapprovingly.

Linzi returned to her chair, and the housekeeper quickly transferred the hot dishes to the table. Her tone obsequious now, she asked if Mr Vardan wanted his coffee there or in the library, and then withdrew silently.

The duckling and crispy roast potatoes and tender sweet peas were delicious, despite having been kept hot beyond the serving time, as was the homemade strawberry icecream which followed. But Gilda ate practically nothing during that silent, miserable meal, and finally Mark Vardan crumpled his napkin and dropped it on his side plate.

He frowned. 'I suppose Nanny Tarrance stuffed you so full

34

of milk and cakes it's not surprising you don't want any lunch.'

This was so near the truth that Linzi sighed. But before Gilda could make any protest he stood up abruptly and excused himself in brusque tones. When he had gone Gilda drew a deep shaken breath and bit her lip as she stared at Linzi.

'Do you think he meant it?' she quavered.

'About sending you to school?' Linzi sighed. 'I haven't been here long enough to judge how seriously your father means anything. Some people say things in anger they don't mean at all,' she said at last. 'But I should say he meant every word of it, Gilda,' she added sadly.

The child's mouth drooped. 'He's always like this when he's working.'

Linzi sighed again. She hadn't got off to a flying start at all, and Gilda looked heartbroken. Resentment of Mark Vardan rose in Linzi's breast. He had demonstrated at that very first meeting how curt and arrogant he could be, despite a subsequent lapse into charm which had completely disarmed her, but now ... He certainly wasn't going to make any allowances for her being new or needing a little time to adjust to the particular circumstances of the case. Did he want her to be an unrelenting disciplinarian with his daughter? Instinct told her that this too could well meet with his disapproval, should he be in an indulgent mood at the pertinent time. It was all very difficult, decided Linzi, trying to subdue her own feeling of hurt and think only of the child. For it was Gilda's happiness that mattered most.

'I hate Aunt Sharon,' the little girl muttered rebelliously.

'But why?' Linzi forgot her musings. For there was more in Gilda's utterance than the usual wild childish vehemence common to most similar statements. The unknown Aunt Sharon had plainly gone to a great deal of trouble in arranging the furnishing of Gilda's room, and surely the idea of sending her to a school where she would be among children of her own age and where her handicap would not single her out was not one to induce the passionate hatred and the fear now plain in Gilda's wide eyes.

'Because she wants me out of the way,' said Gilda.

Linzi gasped, unbelievingly. 'You can't mean *that*?'

'It's true, but you don't have to believe me if you don't want to,' Gilda said coldly.

'It isn't that,' Linzi's eyes were gentle. 'I don't know your

35

Aunt Sharon, so how can I judge if it's true? Or if you're misjudging her? She's probably trying to do what she thinks best for you.'

Gilda's mouth tightened. 'She's trying to do what's best for herself, you mean.'

The strange remark both puzzled and shocked Linzi. It seemed an odd, if not vituperative observation to come from a child's lips. What had given rise to it? Or what fantasy had Gilda woven about her aunt, until she could scarcely separate truth from fancy? Was Aunt Sharon sister to Mark Vardan; or sister to Gilda's mother? Or was she simply a family friend, a courtesy aunt? Linzi wondered.

But her questions had to remain unanswered. With a petulant thrust Gilda backed from the table and sniffed, 'You'll see one day. But I don't want to talk about her—it makes me unhappy.'

Whether it was due to her grievances concerning the unknown Aunt Sharon or to her father's implied threat, Linzi could not tell, but it cast a shadow over Gilda for the rest of that day. She remained sad and withdrawn, and acquiesced without protest when Linzi broached the matter of lessons. The previous governess had thoughtfully left a book of notes which were of great help to Linzi in quickly assessing Gilda's present scholastic whereabouts. Some of the cryptic little notes made Linzi smile to herself as they confirmed something she already suspected; like most children, Gilda was capable of shining if she felt like it, but if she didn't feel like it ...

However, Linzi was a born teacher with the gift of imparting knowledge and at the same time inspiring the respect of her pupil. The afternoon passed quickly and by four o'clock Gilda had forgotten her petulance, even though she was still subdued. She had also forgotten about the key to the disused wing and regained a ghost of her former eagerness when the housekeeper, arriving to say that afternoon tea was ready, laid a large, old-looking iron key on the schoolroom table.

'I think that's the key you wanted, Miss Gilda,' she said shortly.

Gilda picked up the key, examining it eagerly, then her small face sobered. 'We won't be able to go in today now. There won't be time.'

'There's another day coming,' retorted the housekeeper. 'Now don't keep your father waiting again,' she added, with a sharp glance at Linzi.

36

'Do you think he'll still be angry?' Gilda whispered after Mrs Brinsmead had gone.

'I hope not.' Linzi sighed, knowing how much Gilda looked forward to the early evening spell between tea and dinner which Mark usually devoted to his daughter. 'Come on, or we'll be in trouble again.'

She was a little surprised at her tension, and her sense of thankfulness when they joined Mark in the library and discovered he seemed to have got over his annoyance. He inquired affably how lessons had progressed, and responded equally affably to his daughter's inquiries as to how *his* work had progressed.

The sight of the bulky music score on which he was working fascinated Linzi, and she would have loved to add her own questions about the concerto he was composing for piano and orchestra—still more to have stayed to listen to the recording which Gilda was about to play back on the tape deck. But she would not—could not—intrude, and this was the end of her duty time, anyway. She was free now for the evening, even though she was unlikely to take advantage of this so often during the long dark evenings of the winter which would soon be here.

But that was one of the disadvantages of taking a resident post in an isolated country house, a disadvantage she'd considered very carefully before making her decision, Linzi told herself when she let herself out of the side door for a short stroll before she changed for the evening meal. She had allowed instinct to guide her, even though she knew the risk of finding herself in an uncongenial household was a very real one, and despite a somewhat unsatisfactory start she had no real fears on that score. Already she loved Gilda, and knew she was winning the little girl's trust and affection; and for Mark Vardan one must make allowances, she thought firmly. It could not have been easy for him to sacrifice so much of his musical life, his career even, for the sake of Gilda's emotional security.

The westering sun cast long sepia shadows across the drive as Linzi retraced her steps and its deep golden glow reflected in a myriad rich splinters of brilliance from the diamond mullioned windows of Hillcrest. A beautiful old house, she thought inconsequently. *Why did Mark Vardan hate it so much?*

She did not know why the name of Sharon should spring instantly into her mind, or why the questions should tumble

37

in its wake. Was she old or young? Why was Gilda so afraid of her? Certainly she wielded a great deal of influence as far as Mark Vardan was concerned. He would not have allowed her a free hand in the décor of Gilda's room, nor in the discussions which had so plainly taken place regarding the child's future.

Linzi let herself into the quiet house and stood for a moment, feeling its silent, intangible atmosphere reach and wrap round her, almost as though it drew her into the destiny waiting within its walls. But she could not define her strange, disturbed mood as being anything to do with the house or the sad-eyed girl in lilac who pleaded mutely from the great portrait on the stairs.

She could think only of Mark Vardan—and a woman called Sharon ...

CHAPTER THREE

IT seemed that Andrew's surmise was to prove right. The rain did start the following day, a persistent, monotonous downpour from skies leaden with grey mist. The air wasn't cold, almost the reverse; there was a warm, limpid stillness that induced a tendency to depression unless one made determined efforts to combat its effect.

Gilda, however, was unmoved by the sight of the streaming exterior. She seemed to have recovered from her deep unease and dismissed the rain with a matter-of-fact 'We want it all to get down before Sunday,' and begged Linzi to arrange the day's programme of study so that the afternoon would be free for the exploration of the disused wing.

Linzi, prepared for demands to rush straight there the moment breakfast was over, was touched by this slightly guileful request despite herself and agreed. But she could not help reflecting that it might have been better to reverse the order of the day. Gilda's mind was plainly not on maths before the mid-morning milk break, nor was it inclined to wrestle with her French translation, although Linzi had already discovered that she had a flair for languages.

Both teacher and pupil sighed when it was time to close lesson books and go to lunch. By then Gilda was bursting with excitement and even Linzi had to admit to a degree of tension. Why she should experience this odd sense of expectancy, merely at the prospect of looking around dusty old rooms which had been shut up for the best part of half a century, she did not know, but experience it she did. Even Mark Vardan noticed and commented.

'It's because Linzi's like me in some ways,' Gilda informed him before Linzi could speak for herself. 'There's something we have to find out. I can't explain it, Daddy. It's just that there's something making me want to find out.'

'Find what out, for heaven's sake?' he asked with a hint of impatience.

'I don't know!'

She shook her head, her small features a mirrored miniature of his own impatient expression. She looked at Linzi, as though for support, and heaved a large sigh. 'I can't explain it, Daddy. It's like—it's like when you have a piece of music haunting you. It floats around in your mind and you have to pin it down. Only sometimes you can't pin it down, not the way you want to, and you have to chase it for a long time before——' She stopped despairingly. 'Don't you understand?'

His expression had closed during the impassioned little outburst. 'Yes, I understand, Gilda. But I don't approve of these strange compulsions in a child.' His gaze switched to the silent Linzi. 'A natural curiosity about life, even the past, I can go along with, but not this. It's too near an unhealthy obsession.'

Gilda pealed into laughter. 'You do sound serious—just like my last governess. She used to say——'

'Never mind what Miss Timms used to say,' Mark Vardan interrupted impatiently. 'It's this Lilac Girl business, isn't it?'

He turned away, his eyes troubled, as Gilda's small features became an instant betrayal. His mouth tightened. 'She has nothing to do with us, Gilda. If she had anything to do with our past or our family I might begin to understand. But she hasn't. So why . . .' He left the sentence unfinished and let his hands fall to his sides.

Linzi knew a sudden desire to reassure him, to tell him that his concern about his daughter's obsession, as he termed it, was understandable, but he need have no fears. Gilda had lost so much; wasn't it natural that she should resort to a child's world of fantasy? And didn't all children love exploring and secrecy? Gilda had simply woven a mystery about the sad-eyed girl in the great portrait on the stairway, and her subconscious told her that in the hidden portions of the old house she might come nearer to a solution that would solve the mystery she had created.

But something in his expression told her that this was not a propitious moment to offer her theory.

He said, 'Remember what I told you; be careful.'

For a little while after he had gone Gilda remained subdued. Then her suppressed excitement began to bubble up again and the dramatic air of childlike secrecy infected Linzi despite her efforts to remember Mark Vardan's words and not encourage his daughter in childish fantasy. When she walked down the long library corridor, her hand resting protectively on the back of Gilda's chair as the child propelled herself towards the big panelled door at the far end, her heart was beating unusually fast.

Gilda had the key and manoeuvred herself sideways so that she could reach the lock, but she could not turn the key and with a cry of impatience she swung round to Linzi.

'I can't. It's stiff!'

'Shall I try?'

'Yes ...' Gilda was still wrestling with it, reluctant to admit failure, and Linzi waited until she gave up and edged back a little.

The strangest feeling came over Linzi as she touched the key, still warm from Gilda's small fingers. *Don't be silly!* she told herself. *It's simply part of the house that's been shut up.* But the feeling that she was on the verge of some discovery would not be dispelled, and when the lock gave suddenly she exclaimed aloud.

A gasp came from Gilda as the heavy door swung inward. It creaked, and the dry closed-up smell of age and silence stole out from the dimness beyond.

Linzi hesitated.

'Are you scared?' whispered Gilda.

'No—not very. Are you?'

'No—just it's a bit creepy,' came the staunch little negative.

Linzi clamped down on the fanciful nudges of imagination. There was no reason at all for this strange prompting of intuition that alternately urged and warned. Hadn't Mark Vardan said that the Lilac Girl had no connection with them? Hadn't it all happened and been forgotten a long time ago?

But Mark hadn't said *that*!

What had happened and been forgotten a long time ago?

'Have you got the torch?'

Gilda's whisper made her start violently. Determinedly she closed her mind to those echoes from the past and said firmly: 'I don't know what we're whispering for. Yes, I've got it here, and I want you to wait until I go down this passage and let some light in before you come through—there must be some windows,' she added as she stepped forward.

'Some of them are shuttered—the side ones,' Gilda called after her from the lightness of the library passage.

Linzi moved carefully, shining the torch ahead of her. There was carpet underfoot, covered with dark red drugget, and heavy panelling lining the walls to ceiling height, and another door at the end of the passage. Almost prepared for resistance, she tried the knob and felt it give easily, surprisingly easily. Light rushed in from a long narrow hall, and she turned back to call Gilda.

The child was already coming quickly, her eyes bright with excitement. 'Look—you can see the driveway and a part of the terrace from here. Doesn't it look different?'

She rubbed at the grey-bloomed pane of the first window she came to, then moved on impatiently to the second of the three tall windows that marched the length of the hall. She craned up, rubbing another patch and peering through before the unfamiliar view palled almost instantly and she swung round.

'Where shall we go first?'

Linzi shook her head. There were two doors facing them, and beyond the opening of the corridor from the main part of the house was another door and another passage that led, presumably to the rear of the wing. 'It's all yours, Gilda, my pet,' she said with a gesture.

'In here first,' said Gilda ...

Linzi felt as though she were walking back into time as they explored those long silent rooms. Nothing had been changed, excepting the gradual addition of the muted veil of age that faded colours and filmed the surfaces not protected by the ghostly palls of dust-covers.

There were tapestries of soft greens and ambers, vines of fruit, flowers and leaves intertwined in stately friezes high above eye level, and great mirrors reflecting Linzi's wide, wondering eyes at every turn. Regency ladies, in misty voiles and beribboned silks, looked down from the walls. Pompous gentlemen, some in perrukes, others in the scarlets of regimental glory, stared down the years with haughty eyes, and the timorous faces of children peeped from formal poses

41

against red velvets or the restraint of family groups.

A heavy silken rope with a huge tassel hung by a green marble fireplace in one room. Gilda, one hand to her lips, tugged it and then shivered expectantly.

Nothing happened, and the echoes of her nervous giggle quickly stilled her mirth. A spinet with delicate eighteenth-century pictures on its painted lid entranced her, and its soft tinkling notes were surprisingly sweet, but it was in a smaller room, almost the last one they came to, that a strange intentness stilled her eager voice.

She stayed motionless in the centre, her wide eyes slowly surveying every detail of the dainty feminine sitting room. The wallpaper was still clear and unblemished, lilac and ivory satin-stripe with tiny gold sprigs embossed in it, and the cushions of the window seat, once a deep violet, had muted to the same evocative tint of lilac. The woodwork was white, the carpet unmistakably Aubusson, and the furniture beneath its dust-covers neat and uncumbersome in outline. Above the fireplace was a portrait in an ivory and gilt oval frame; of a girl in a lilac dress.

For long moments Gilda stared up at it, then a soft sigh escaped her. 'This is *her* room,' she said.

'*Was*, perhaps,' said a dry voice from the doorway.

Linzi spun round, her hand flying to her throat and her heart turning over with shock. The cool, considering gaze of Mark Verdan fell to the fluttering fingers at her throat and returned to her startled face.

'Did I alarm you?' A trace of amusement showed in his lifted brows. He came forward into the room. 'I'm sorry, I didn't think.'

'It *is* her room,' repeated Gilda, recovering more quickly than Linzi. 'Can't you feel that she was here? I can.'

'A lot of other young women—and older ones for that matter—must have looked upon this as "their" special sanctum,' he returned equably. 'This house has spanned more than a few generations in its time.'

Gilda nodded, her volatile interest leaping impatiently to something else. 'Daddy, can we take the covers off? I want to come here every day. I could have my lessons here. Oh, yes! Isn't that a super idea, Linzi?'

Mark frowned. He shook his head. 'It's not practicable, my pet.'

'But why not, Daddy?'

'For one thing, Mrs Brinsmead has enough to cope with. I

42

hate to think of even suggesting to her that we open out this wing. It would take weeks of work to put it right.'

'No!' His daughter betrayed horror by shaking her head quickly. 'I don't want anyone else here, not even to know. And not Mrs Brinsmead. We can do it ourselves easily.'

His mouth compressed. 'You mean I can. Or Linzi. Isn't that it?'

Gilda's small face shadowed. 'It doesn't need anything, only the covers taking off.'

'I could do that quite easily,' Linzi said, wondering as she spoke if her offer was intrusive.

'I don't want anything altered. I don't want it even touched,' Gilda said stubbornly. 'Anyway, somebody's started to take the carpet covers up.'

'Yes—I did.' He walked across the room and looked down at the exquisite colours. 'It was the day Sharon and I came through here, when I decided to bring you up here.' He tugged at his lower lip. 'I must make arrangements about this,' he added, more to himself than Gilda.

But the blunt clarity of recollection had come into her eyes, and comprehension. 'That was when she was talking about it! It was this! She said it would look heavenly in her lounge but she would never be able to afford to buy one like it.' Gilda propelled herself towards her father. 'And you said——'

'That'll do, Gilda.' He turned, and there was anger suppressed in the movement. 'It's time to go back.'

Linzi had not noticed the dusk stealing into the room until he spoke. She moved obediently towards the door, drawing it open as she reflected that it was nothing to do with her if Mark Vardan decided to present a priceless Aubusson carpet to a woman called Sharon, even though the idea was so obviously resented by his daughter.

He was shepherding Gilda back to the main part of the house, and vaguely Linzi heard him ask Gilda something about a pen. The child launched into one of her long, involved explanations, and it was not until she was alone with Linzi and preparing for bed that the guilty little admission came.

'I think I've lost it, and I can't think where.' Her small chin looked more pointed than ever with earnestness. 'Can you remember, Linzi?'

Linzi thought, and shook her head. 'Did you leave it in the schoolroom?'

'No. You gave me a new one—a red ball-point. I—I must

43

have dropped it outside. I know I borrowed it and clipped it in my blazer pocket, but——'

'Just a minute!' Linzi exclaimed. 'Did you have it down at the lodge when——'

She got no further as Gilda's face brightened.

'Yes—when I wrote Andrew's phone number down. I remember now: I put it on the piano lid and forgot to pick it up. Oh, how am I going to get it back? I told Daddy I was sure I had it among—oh, listen—he's coming now! And I——'

'Don't worry,' Linzi said quickly. 'I'll slip down to the lodge straight away and——'

'You won't tell him I——'

'No.' Linzi turned as the door opened and Mark entered. He always came up to lift Gilda into bed and stay with her for a little while until she settled down and he kissed her goodnight.

A little shyly, Linzi smiled at him and made her own goodnight to Gilda before she went quickly from the room.

Mindful of her promise, she went straight to her own bedroom and collected a jacket. Uncertain of the pathway in the dark, she decided to walk down the main drive to the lodge, even though it was much the longest way. Besides, she told herself, it was a fine night, fresh and cool after the rain, and the walk would do her good.

Andrew was not at home, but Nanny Tarrance was delighted to see Linzi. Yes, the pen was there, quite safe. She'd thought it was one of Andrew's, until this morning, and he'd told her he would go up to the house with it as soon as he got home.

Linzi thanked her, looking at the gold-capped pen, which seemed an expensive one, before she dropped it into her pocket. But it wasn't easy to take her leave of Nanny, and very difficult to refuse the inevitable offer of a cup of coffee. An hour slipped by very quickly, at the end of which Nanny Tarrance had encouraged quite a lot of confidences from Linzi about her home and family, and imparted quite a lot about her own nephews and nieces, of whom she seemed to have quite a number. Sadly, Nanny had never had any family of her own. Her fiancé had been killed in action at Dunkirk, and after the war she had gone back into service, receiving the courtesy title of 'Mrs', until her retirement. She remembered old Mr Vardan very well and recounted several anecdotes, but there her reminiscences concerning the Vardans ceased,

44

and once again Linzi experienced the impression that Nanny Tarrance knew when to hold her counsel.

Andrew did not return, patently to his aunt's disappointment, and Linzi left shortly after nine-thirty to make her way back to the house.

The darkness was intense after the warm brightness of the lodge, and she set off with unwonted briskness up the tree-lined drive, reflecting that she must get used to carrying a pocket torch if she was going to do much walking at night during the long dark winter months that lay ahead. By the time she was half-way up the quite steep drive her eyes had accustomed themselves to the darkness and it was still inkily black. She was almost to the top, where the incline levelled out and the drive forked, to the old coach-house and stables at one side and through the shrubbery to the forecourt at the front of the house, when she heard a sound. Her steps faltered, then quickened as the first tremor of unease shook her. She could see nothing, only the glimmer of the portico lantern through the trees, and she exclaimed aloud breathlessly at her own over-febrile imagination. The trees thinned, she could see the great dark bulk of the house fifty, perhaps sixty yards away, and then she heard the grit of a man's footfall.

She froze, and the man stepped out of the trees in front of her.

He stood there, and Linzi gave one frightened cry. She launched herself into flight, into a wide half-circle to avoid him, and tore towards the friendly glow of the light.

The man put out a hand towards her, and said something that Linzi did not even hear. His steps followed her, but long before he had taken a dozen paces she was flying across the forecourt, to thrust at the heavy door and pray that it wasn't locked for the night.

It gave instantly to her touch, and she almost fell inside, right into the arms of a startled Mark Vardan.

'Linzi!' He staggered slightly, then grasped her firmly. 'Was that you who screamed?'

'There's someone out there! A man!' she gasped breathlessly. 'He stepped out of the trees and——'

'Steady! It's all right.' Mark held her firmly, his voice and presence reassuring. 'You're quite safe.'

For an instant he waited, giving her time to regain her composure, then held her away. Over the bridge of his outstretched arms he regarded her quizzically. 'Sure you *did* see

45

somebody? The trees make oddly shaped shadows at night, especially when the wind stirs the branches.'

'No, I didn't imagine it. He called to me.'

Mark's slight smile faded. 'Stay here. I'll go and take a look.'

'Save yourself the bother,' said a voice behind her. 'It was only me.'

Linzi stiffened perceptibly. She felt the cool draught from the open door and Mark's hands tighten for a moment before they fell away from her shoulders. Over her head he said curtly: 'So it's you. I didn't know you were here.'

'Nobody did.' The newcomer lounged nonchalantly into the hall. 'I only got here half an hour ago—and you wouldn't have thanked me for barging in to announce myself while you were working, now would you, Mr Vardan?'

Mark's lips compressed. 'This is Mrs Brinsmead's son, Cedric,' he said to Linzi.

'And you must be little Gilda's new teacher-pal,' Cedric grinned at her before Mark had time to complete the introduction. He gave her a mocking little bow. 'Sorry I scared you, darling. I just wandered out for a smoke and wondered who was coming up the drive.'

He was a slight, dapper youth, in a black taffeta shirt, silver-grey pants, and a dark grey leather jacket. His blond hair was almost the colour of bleached straw and his pale blue eyes held an insolent quality as they surveyed Linzi from top to toe.

Mark said, 'She was hardly likely to expect you looming out of the shrubbery.'

He looked annoyed now, as though only Linzi's presence was preventing him from saying a great deal more. Suddenly she felt rather foolish and somehow to blame for the frown of irritation narrowing his brow.

Cedric, however, was unabashed. His bold stare continued to survey her and he grinned confidently: 'Tell you what ..., How about a little drink? You've discovered the Abbot's Arms—not a bad little pub?' At her uncomprehending stare he grinned again. 'Time you did, then—the only bit of night-life round these parts. Come on, darling. Just to show there's no hard feelings.'

Conscious of Mark's frown, she managed an awkward smile. 'Of course there isn't, but I can't tonight. Thanks all the same.'

He shrugged. 'Perhaps another time?'

'Perhaps.' She looked from him to Mark Vardan and bit

46

her lip. She had no desire to sample what he called the only bit of local night life in Cedric Brinsmead's company, but she was too gentle by nature to rebuff anyone, even one so brash as he, and as she edged back she avoided her employer's dark frown. 'Excuse me—goodnight,' she murmured, and made her escape from the end of what now seemed a ridiculous little incident. Already it was difficult to credit that she'd been scared out of her wits by the pert Cedric in his leather and taffeta gear; or that she'd almost crashed head-long into her employer's arms. He must be thinking she was an idiot, to scream like that . . .

She was in her room, taking off her jacket, when her fingers encountered the forgotten pen in one pocket. An exclamation of annoyance escaped her as she looked at the taper of gold and black. Leave it until tomorrow and let Gilda return it herself? Or return it herself now before it had the chance to go astray again?

With the thoughts her steps had turned towards the door. She hesitated, reluctant to give in to the impulse to hurry downstairs again, and then with a strange little surge of excitement cast off the frail bond of restraint.

Her hand had touched the switch, bringing darkness at its bidding, when she heard the music. She stopped, her surge of excitement checked as the tumultuous chords from Mark Vardan's keyboard swelled through the night. Slowly she closed the door, almost reluctantly, and still the music echoed and swirled within the room. Without putting on the light she crossed the dim room and stood by the casement she had forgotten to close before she went down to the lodge.

She opened it to its widest and leaned on the sill. Cool rainwashed air stole round her, caressing her face, and out of the night came a different music, a soft, sad melody that evoked a vision of Mark Vardan's strong hands dark against the white keys, sensitive even in their strength as they picked out the melancholy, lingering notes. She looked down at the long panel of amber that lay across the lawn immediately below. Mark must have the french windows opened wide for the music to come so clearly. Usually it was muted, audible only in the close vicinity of the library; the walls and panelling of the old house were heavy and solid. She had not realised that her room was immediately above . . . The music stopped abruptly in mid-phrase, and so did her musing thoughts, until the unseen pianist resumed his melody, only to falter at exactly the same place.

47

For a long while she stood there, unconsciously willing him to overcome the difficulty he was facing. Beneath the dominant theme there was a note of passion that seemed to strain to escape the minor key, and gradually she picked out the two opposing motives with which he was experimenting, then suddenly there was a wild cadenza, a series of violent chords, and silence. The echoes quivered in the night and Linzi realised she was holding her breath and staring down through the darkness. The amber panel of light vanished and a sharp click told her he had pulled the windows shut. The silence became intense, and the cool darkness shivery. Linzi closed the window and groped in search of the light switch.

Her eyes were thoughtful and her parted mouth betraying a trace of uncertainty as she put the pen on her bedside cabinet. Gilda could return that herself tomorrow morning.

Cedric stooged around for a couple of days, to Mark's scarcely concealed irritation, and Linzi guessed that he only suffered the youth's presence in deference to Mrs Brinsmead, without whose service Hillcrest House could not function as a comfortable place of residence. Fortunately he appeared to divide his time between the local night-life and the large colour TV in Mrs Brinsmead's sitting room, although the fringe area reception did not entirely satisfy him and twice he volunteered the information that he knew of a gadget that might help matters.

'How much?' said Mark Vardan, maintaining a pretence of interest.

'About fifty quid.'

'Not worth it for three months.' Mark's mouth went down at the corners. 'The new mast will be transmitting then.'

Cedric shrugged, not a whit abashed, and scuffed his toe over a fading patch in one of the hall rugs. 'I know a bloke in the trade if ever you want a bit of carpet on the cheap. You name it, he'll get it. All those fancy oriental ones as well.'

'I'll bear that in mind,' said Mark in the kind of tone which Linzi already recognised as the one which meant the complete opposite.

Cedric grinned. 'We aim to please. Got tonight off, darling?'

'She hasn't,' Mark said, before Linzi could reply.

'On Saturday! Coo, you need a union, lovey. That's slave-driving.' Cedric shook his head. 'Just make sure you have things arranged better next time I come.'

He departed on the Sunday morning, after spending an hour tinkering with the silencer on his motor-cycle—'Making it a trifle more inefficient than it already is,' Mark observed acidly—and over the roar of exhaust and minor explosions shouted a farewell that made Gilda's small face stiffen with annoyance.

'Did you hear what he called me?' she demanded. 'He called me "princess". Only Daddy is allowed to call me that,' she added imperiously.

'I don't suppose he knows that. He means it in the same way,' Linzi said, feeling more kindly disposed to Cedric now that he had gone.

'I object,' said Gilda with a toss of her head. 'Do you know what he said the first time he came here?'

'No,' responded Linzi indulgently, her gaze following Mark's tall figure as he walked back into the house. 'What did he say?'

'He said: "I think those little pins of yours are just lazy, Gilly girl. You ought to try making them work again." As if I didn't!' Gilda exploded indignantly. 'How dared he say that to me? After all the doctors I've seen!'

'How many doctors have you seen?'

'Well . . . two. Our own and Mr Verradene, the specialist—you always call surgeons 'Mr', and he's an orthopaedic surgeon,' Gilda said earnestly. 'Do you know, he said my case worried him tremendously because his treatment hasn't done me any good, and it should have done. He says there's still a reflex there, and the treatment *should* have worked. He thinks something must be hidden, something the X-rays don't show. He and Daddy talked about surgery, but Mr Verradene decided to wait a while. He hoped the treatment and nature would take over. I'd been in hospital for three months, you see, just to get my leg done properly.'

Linzi made no response beyond a sympathetic nod of her head. This was the first time Gilda had talked about herself in this way, and instinct told her not to press for further confidences.

After a moment Gilda looked up. 'It was broken in four places. They didn't realise then I still couldn't walk, even when it set properly. They were more worried about my head and if there'd be any scars on my face. But there wasn't—only this. You can hardly see it now.' She turned her head to

49

one side and parted the dark hair. 'It's there, just a thin white line.'

Linzi bent over her, her own shadow blotting out the sunlight. She peered where the little girl indicated, but could see only the tiniest mark on the white scalp. 'It's faded away now, darling, and I can't see a single, tiniest blemish on your brow anywhere.'

Gilda nodded solemnly, accepting the assurance as truth. 'Do you know that they let Daddy stay at the hospital for two days and nights. He was so worried about me. He was in Paris and he cancelled his concert to fly back straight away. He was supposed to be going to Australia the next month, but he didn't go. Oh, it was awful!'

The child fell silent, the shadows of memory darkening on her sombre little face. Linzi looked across the sunlit garden and in her heart she sighed for the tragedy of the crippled child. Was it never going to end? Was poor Gilda doomed to a wheelchair for the rest of her life? Robbed of the joy of freedom to run and skip and dance, and robbed by the same fate of her mother. She never talked of her mother, and Linzi could not help wondering how much she still grieved in secret for her. Had the rumours been true? That Mark Vardan and his wife had kept their marriage together solely for the sake of the child? That Lucille Vardan had taken a lover, a married man, and Mark Vardan had found out and threatened to make his knowledge public? The man in question had been a well-known political figure, and his ambition had given in to the barely veiled threat of blackmail. Mark Vardan's gamble had paid off; the affair had ended and the wagging tongues had quietened. There had been a reconciliation, more of a façade worn in public, Ian had termed it, then there had been the accident in which Lucille lost her life, and Gilda ...

Linzi heard a tiny stifled sound and looked down. A small glistening pearl was trickling down Gilda's cheek and her mouth was set tightly, trying not to give way to tears. Linzi stooped and put her arm round her, and instantly Gilda reached up to cling to her with fierce arms.

'You believe me, don't you?' she choked. 'I can't help it. I didn't do it on purpose. I'd never hurt Daddy. It was the only way, and—oh, Linzi, you won't go away, will you? Ever. You're the best friend I ever had. I——'

'Hush! Of course I won't go away as long as you need me.' Linzi hugged her, trying to comfort her, and for the moment the content of the broken utterances did not hold any particular significance. It was not until later, when she thankfully reminded Gilda that it was time to get ready for the eagerly looked-forward-to picnic with Andrew, that Gilda's impassioned plea evoked a hint of puzzlement. What had she meant by saying she didn't do it on purpose? Do what on purpose?

And which was the only way?

It was all very puzzling, and it caused Linzi to wonder if she were imagining a certain tension underlying the child's outward gaiety during that afternoon with Andrew. Had it always been present? Not perceived until now by Linzi's previously less discerning eye?

Almost as though she realised something of the trend of Linzi's thoughts Gilda teased and giggled and flirted in her precocious, small-girl way with Andrew, a way fully reciprocated by an amused Andrew, until Linzi, studying the sparkling eyes and flushed cheeks of her excited charge, began to wonder if her imagination was misleading her after all.

Perhaps she had read too much into Gilda's emotional outburst that morning. In the circumstances it was understandable; she had come to this job prepared for all kinds of difficulties, ready with endless patience and understanding, far more than she had needed so far, because it was a situation that appeared to demand a very special kind of treatment. So perhaps it was natural that she might imagine something that didn't even exist, because of that special feeling of responsibility. And yet . . .

She sighed ruefully. The object of her concern was gleefully plying Andrew with tongue-twisters of her own devising and almost choking with mirth at his lapses into gibberish as he tried to match her challenge. The forest glade to which he had brought them was green and sheltered, the sun poured down its golden dapples through the leaves, casting their patterns on the thick blue rug on which Gilda lay and illuminating her vivacious little face. The thin legs were tucked under the full pleated cream skirt as she leaned her weight back on one hand and pointed derisively at Andrew with the other. Looking at her, it was difficult to credit that those pale little limbs glimpsed under the cream pleats were so useless, that she could be so utterly carefree.

'Caught you again!' she cried delightedly, and Andrew, unable to speak for laughing, collapsed back on the grass.

Gilda subsided triumphantly. 'Oh, it's turned out a super-

51

delicious day after all,' she sighed happily.

'After all?' Andrew pretended to frown as he divided a broad blade of grass into thin strands. 'Did you expect rain in spite of my weather forecast?'

'No.' Gilda turned a wide gaze to Linzi. 'I made a bad start this morning. I forgot to be sensible, didn't I, Linzi?'

'Did you?' Linzi returned gravely.

Gilda nodded vigorously. 'But I haven't been silly like that for ages, honestly.'

Her meaning was crystal clear as her steady gaze stayed solemnly on Linzi's face; she wanted Linzi to forget that disturbing little incident.

Instead, Linzi's doubts began to revive all over again. But she merely nodded and smiled, and knew she was not mistaking the relief in those dark eyes. She relaxed back on Andrew's tweed jacket and tugged idly at a small clump of fern, feathering the fronds through her fingers. 'I wonder if Cedric got home without breaking down,' she remarked inconsequently to divert Gilda.

'Who's Cedric?' demanded Andrew, then exclaimed: 'Oh, I remember. Isn't he your housekeeper's son?'

'Mm, and he's awful!' Gilda pulled a face. 'He creeps around the place and wants to know everything. Do you know, he nearly frightened Linzi out of her wits the other night on the drive, and he——'

'He did, did he?' Andrew glanced at Linzi. 'I must teach him a lesson next time he lands here.'

'And we couldn't go in the secret wing because he was hanging about,' Gilda went on, 'and he said he'd always wondered what it was like in there and could he come and explore it with us. So I pretended that we didn't know because we'd lost the key, and then he said we'd better not tell his mother or she'd be furious because she'd given us the only key. So we've hidden it, and nobody's going to have it except us.'

'And what is this secret wing?' Andrew asked idly.

'It's where——' Gilda stopped and looked at Linzi. 'Shall we tell Uncle Andrew?'

'If you'd like to—I think we can trust him to keep a secret.'

'Well, it's where the Lilac Girl lived, a long, long time ago. Her portrait hangs on the staircase, and she was very beautiful, and very rich, but terribly unhappy. You see ...' Gilda's face became rapt as her vivid imagination began to invent freely, weaving a romantic tale of a rich little Cinderella who loved a poor man and was forced into the arms of an ageing

Croesus who kept her prisoner in his great mansion while he haunted the gaming rooms and flirted with a *demi-mondaine* while the——'

'And what do you know of *demi-mondaines* at your tender age?' Andrew interrupted.

'I read adult books—sometimes I get fed-up with childish stories,' Gilda said artlessly. 'I read a simply super book about the Prince Regent while I was in hospital. All about the Brighton Pavilion and Beau Brummell, and what happened——'

'You'd better spare Linzi the recital of debauchery,' Andrew broke in, laughing. 'Anyway, I don't believe a word of it. I bet if the truth was known your Lilac Girl married the curate, had ten children and adopted five stray cats, knitted warm and serviceable shawls for the deserving poor, and ruled her husband with a rod of iron.'

'She didn't! I know she didn't. Oh, if only I knew her name.'

'Ermyntrude, perhaps? Or Matilda,' suggested the irrepressible Andrew. 'Or Gertie.'

'No, it was something beautiful yet simple. Like ...' Gilda shook her head. 'I can't think of the right name for her, but I know she was desperately unhappy and something dreadful happened to her, something tragic, and I mean to find out, somehow ... because ...'

Her voice trailed off and wistfulness descended again, taking her far away into her remote world of dreams.

Andrew's expression had lost its amusement. Glancing at him, Linzi's own face sobered and a strange little shiver passed over her. It was as though a cool little breeze had wafted into the glade, bringing on its wings a faint scent of lilac, even though the sun was casting the deep metallic gold of autumn everywhere and the lilac had long since drifted into its drowse of dormancy from which it would not awake until the spring ...

Linzi shook her head to dispel the eerie little notion. Andrew had lain back, and she reached forward to prod him, smiling as she glanced to Gilda. 'Come on, I think we'd——'

Her smile and words were vanquished as she saw the child's expression.

Gilda was staring past her, sitting as though transfixed, and her eyes were wide with terror. One hand went to her mouth, then slowly extended, to point a trembling finger at a spot beyond Linzi's shoulder. Her lips moved stiffly.

53

'Look!' she whispered fearfully. 'It—it's the Lilac Girl!'
'What!'

Unbelievingly Linzi turned her head. She hadn't heard aright. Gilda was dreaming. Then her own breath caught in her throat and her spine ran cold.

Under the shadows of the old oaks lining the road stood a girl, a girl in a misty lilac dress.

Linzi's hand went to her mouth. The girl in the misted lilac was watching them, a ray of sun lighting the pale silky hair that fell to her shoulders. She seemed to want to speak, and suddenly she took a step forward.

Linzi began to tremble, and behind her Gilda screamed.

CHAPTER FOUR

For a moment there was one of those strange stillnesses in which an eternity of time seemed to be held. Then Linzi and Andrew moved as one, she to kneel protectively beside Gilda; he to stride towards the girl in lilac.

'Is—*is* she real?' Gilda whispered.

'Very real,' Linzi laughed shakily. 'Listen, she's talking to Andrew.'

'He's bringing her across.' Gilda still clung to Linzi's hand. 'But she did look like our Lilac Girl, didn't she?'

'She still does.' Aware that her limbs still had a slightly shaky feel, Linzi stood up, looking towards the girl who was walking across the sward at Andrew's side.

The resemblance to the girl in the portrait was uncanny. There was the same pale soft hair, the same slight figure and small delicate hands, and those parted rose lips. But the twentieth-century touches were very evident. The eyes weren't sad, only a little concerned as they looked at Gilda, and the silky hair bore the unmistakable stamp of an ultra-modern and equally ultra-expensive stylist. The hands were tipped with a silvery lilac lacquer, the shoes were Italian, and the misty dress was beautifully cut in softest finest wool spun.

The newcomer held out one hand, making a rueful gesture.

'I'm sorry I startled you. I guess I must have looked a bit spooky just standing there, but you looked so cosy I hated to barge in.'

Linzi laughed shakily. The girl's American accent was the final reassurance of reality. 'No,' she said, 'we weren't expecting anyone, and for a moment we thought you were someone else.'

'Yes—you thought I was a ghost. I'm sorry,' the newcomer stooped to Gilda, whose small face hadn't quite regained its colour, 'but I am real—touch me!'

Uncertainly, Gilda accepted the proffered hand and let hers linger a moment within its warm, living touch. 'I'm Gilda Vardan—what's your name?'

'Alayne.'

'How do you do.' Gilda held on to formality. 'This is Linzi —Miss Shadwyn—and this is Mr Andrew Tarrance.'

A hint of mischief curved the Lilac Girl's lips as she solemnly shook hands. 'Now that I'm forgiven, what's all this about a ghost?'

'Oh, nothing. I was just being a bit silly.' Gilda was obviously going to be cautious. 'Unless you're talking like an American ghost, Alayne.'

'I am American—I live in Boston and I'm over here on vacation with my aunt—but I'm not your ghost.' The mischief died from the newcomer's eyes and suddenly she knelt down on the edge of the rug. 'I'm intrigued, though, because I kinda feel something exciting—I don't know exactly what, but something.' She paused, looking up at the silent Andrew as though making up her mind about something and then coming to a decision. 'Promise you won't laugh—I know some of you Britishers think we're crazy when we come over here to look up our long-lost relations, but I'm looking for a particular house. I don't even know what it looks like, even if it still exists, but I know it was around here some time. You see, my great-great-,' she took a deep breath, 'great-grand-father was born in this part of the world somewhere around the year 1828. He came to Boston as a young man of twenty, was penniless when he landed, then carved himself a special niche in an import business and founded our company. But he used to say that there was something he had to make right in the Old Country, something he'd promised his mother when he was a tiny kid and she was dying. But by the time he could make the journey back he was a man near his fifties. It was too late, and the family story goes that he came back home a bitter man with a hatred of Britishers that he tried to hand down to his sons and grandsons.'

Alayne paused and shook her head. 'Please don't think that lasted! My brother's just got engaged to his secretary— an English girl from Beckenham. She came out to work in

Boston early this year and he fell for her the moment she walked into his office.'

Andrew made a politely conventional response when she stopped speaking, and for the moment none of them noticed the intent expression on Gilda's face. Then Alayne gave a rueful exclamation, and a slight shiver.

'Gee, it's turning cool—and I guess I'd better get back to the car. My aunt will be sending out search parties. She didn't want to come out of our way—she lives very much in the present—but I did wonder ...'

'Are you looking for Hillcrest House?' asked Gilda.

Alayne spun round. 'Did you say *Hylcrece*?'

'Yes. It's Hillcrest now. I live there.'

'You live there?' Alayne's eyes widened incredulously. 'You mean it's all true? There really was—is a Hylcrece House? Oh, I can't believe it!' She whirled to look at Andrew. 'Do you know, we've been driving round between here and York for *two* hours looking for Hilby. We've been misdirected twice and lost three times and stuck in a bend of one of your crazy little lanes. Aunt Louella said she didn't believe the village ever existed, or the house, or our ancestors.' She began to laugh. 'And I get out of the car to walk back and look at a tiny signpost leaning in a hedge back there, because it might just say Hilby, and I see you folks picnicking and wonder if you're visitors yourselves or locals who might know, and I hit right bang on target. I don't believe it!'

'It's true.' Gilda upturned her face solemnly. 'It had to happen. You're the Lilac Girl—I know!'

'I'm *who*, darling?'

Gilda looked into the charming face of Alayne, who had dropped to her knees again on the rug. 'You're exactly like her. Her portrait hangs on the stairs. She wears a lilac dress and her hair is the same as yours. But her eyes are sad. I'm glad you've come. I think she wanted you to.'

Above the child's head Alayne met Linzi's gaze and some of the excitement ebbed from her face. She bit her lip and concern troubled her eyes.

They seemed to ask for explanation and Linzi took a deep breath. 'It's true,' she said slowly, 'there is a portrait of a girl in Empire dress. She's so like you that you could be sisters, if you were dressed the same and had a similar hairstyle.'

Alayne glanced at Andrew, as though for confirmation.

He shook his head. 'I haven't seen the portrait. I've only been in the house on two occasions, and to be honest, I never took much notice of the paintings.'

'I noticed this one the first night I came,' said Linzi. 'All I can say is that it's uncanny.'

'Will you come home with us?' said Gilda.

'To the house? Try and stop me!' cried Alayne delightedly. 'I keep thinking I should pinch myself to——'

'Alayne? Where've—Alayne! So this is where you got to!'

They all turned towards the owner of the querulous voice. A matronly lady in blue was stumbling across the rough verge of the road, her expression quite cross. She reached the comparative smoothness of the grass and gave a gesture of exasperation. 'I thought you'd got lost!'

'This is Aunt Louella,' Alayne smiled. 'She's having a terrible vacation making me keep to the schedule—but I've got a cast-iron excuse this time.'

Her excitement bubbling again visibly, she introduced her new friends and told Aunt Louella the tremendous news. With scarcely concealed impatience Aunt Louella heard her out, but betrayed more interest in the name of Mark Vardan.

'He's marvellous,' she enthused. 'I saw him conduct in Boston three years ago. But, honey, you can't stay now. We just haven't the time. We have to be in Edinburgh by six.'

'Six? You'll never make it,' said Andrew. 'It's four now.'

'About a hundred and eighty miles? We should manage it if we step on it.'

'Not from here,' he assured them. 'It'll take you at least twenty minutes to get to the main road and another twenty to reach the motorway. Then you can think about making it in a couple of hours. Say seven and you'll be nearer the mark.'

Aunt Louella groaned. 'I told you, honey. All these winding little lanes. Come on, let's go.'

Alayne hung back, desperation in her eyes. 'I can't leave now. I must see the place. To be so near ... Listen, can we phone Lewis? He'll understand.'

'No, honey, we can't. We'll throw out the whole schedule. Besides, where would we stay?'

'You could come back here after Edinburgh,' said Gilda in a calm little voice. 'I'll tell my father and he'll invite you to stay with us. Then you won't have to rush away.'

She sounded so adult and practical that Linzi could not restrain a tender smile. She looked up pleadingly at the indomitable Aunt Louella, and the older woman's features puckered with indecision.

'How can we come back? All those reservations and——'

57

'I'll come back.' Alayne's eyes darkened with determination. 'We'll follow through as planned, until Stratford. Then I'll see you off on the Paris plane and I'll come back here alone. No, don't argue. My mind's made up.' She searched quickly in her handbag and tore a page from her diary. She scribbled on it and handed the leaf to Gilda. 'That's our address and number in Edinburgh, for four days. Then Inverness. Promise you'll call me?'

'I promise,' said Gilda.

'See you in about three weeks. I can hardly wait!' She kissed Gilda, then turned to Aunt Louella, who was hovering with ill-concealed impatience. 'I'm ready now.'

Linzi and Andrew walked with them to the road. There, Alayne turned for a final wave to Gilda before she took her farewells. 'See you soon.' They watched her run on ahead of the older woman to the big white convertible parked a little farther along the narrow road. The powerful engine roared into life as Aunt Louella climbed in, and a few moments later only the faint haze of exhaust hung on the still air.

Linzi turned, and a touch on her arm halted her.

'Just a moment. I may not have a chance later on ...' Andrew kept his hand lightly on her arm. 'I have to go back tomorrow and it'll probably be about three or four weeks before I steal a few days to come through. But there's a special occasion lining up next month, on the fifteenth, and I'd like to take you. Will you keep that evening free?'

Linzi hesitated, and wondered why she hesitated. She liked Andrew, didn't she? 'All right. I'd love to,' she smiled.

'Good. I'll get the tickets straight away while there's a few going.'

They walked back to where Gilda sat waiting patiently on the grass. She looked up at them, flushed and bright-eyed with happiness, and sighed. 'We didn't dream it, did we, Linzi?'

'No, but it's time we got back. There's a coolness in the air now,' Linzi said briskly, stooping to pick things up and stow them in the big holdall.

Andrew was shaking the rug and folding it before handing it to Linzi to carry while he swung Gilda up into his arms.

It was not until much later that evening, long after Gilda had gone to bed, that the astonishing realization suddenly clicked into Linzi's brain as she made her own preparations to retire.

The series of vivid still-life pictures passed rapidly before her mental eye, ending in that moment when Andrew stood folding the rug.

But Gilda should have been sitting on the rug.

Linzi caught at the edge of the dressing table and stared unseeingly at her own reflection. Try to remember. Gilda *had* been sitting on the thick warm rug all the time they had been having the picnic. No one had lifted her off. Had she still been sitting on it when Alayne arrived? Linzi closed her eyes. Suddenly it was vital that she remember every moment of those fifteen or so minutes after that shock of seeing Alayne in her lilac dress, standing like a misty little ghost under the oaks. For Gilda couldn't possibly have lifted herself off the spread of the rug, at least two feet of distance.

Or could she . . .?

The thought was never far away during the following week. But the more Linzi tried to pin down her memories of the exact sequence of that eventful afternoon the more nebulous they became. There had to be an explanation, and it was probably quite simple; the rug had become rucked up or turned back when Alayne knelt on it, and Andrew must have pulled it from under Gilda's slight weight before he shook it and folded it. I must have imagined it, Linzi thought. And yet . . . the impression of Gilda moving stayed so strong she wondered if she should mention it to Mark Vardan. But what purpose would that achieve? Raise a glimmer of hope that some spark of life had returned to Gilda's thin little limbs? A false, cruel hope? He would probably think she'd dreamt it all; in retrospect the whole afternoon was rapidly taking on a curiously dreamlike quality, as Gilda herself had remarked.

Mark had been cool and non-committal when the story of Alayne was recounted. He had given his consent to the invitation being issued, and Gilda had written the letter, which she had posted to the Inverness address where it would await Alayne's arrival there—'Just in case it misses her at Edinburgh,' Gilda said—and suddenly everything seemed to go flat. Mark said, 'You'll probably find she isn't in the least like the girl in the portrait when you see her standing under it,' and Gilda retorted, 'She is. You wait and see.'

He shrugged and glanced at Linzi, as though for confirmation of his own surmise, and she gave an awkward gesture.

'There is a strong resemblance, Mr Vardan. We——' she

stopped and bit her lip, for she had promised Gilda she would not tell him that they both thought they were seeing a ghost. 'I got quite a shock,' she said slowly, 'until we heard her speak.'

'The ghost of our Lilac Girl?' Mark laughed sardonically, as Gilda had prophesied. 'You're nearly as bad as my daughter. I hope I'm back from London in time to meet this vision.'

'You're going away!'

'I must, darling.' He regarded his daughter patiently. 'Only for a few days, and I'll probably be bringing Aunt Sharon back with me. She wants to see you.'

There was a silence. Gilda's stony expression said exactly what she thought of that idea, even though she obviously knew she dared not try her father to the extent of putting her opinion ino words, and Mark Vardan's mouth tightened.

His expression and the silence made Linzi feel embarrassed, but while she sought for something to break the sense of awkwardness Mark moved to the fireside and bent to switch on a second bar of the electric fire.

'If we're going to have guests, and one of them American, we'll have to get some heat into this place,' he remarked. 'If I thought . . .'

'If you thought what, Daddy?'

The momentary haze of reflection which had clouded his face vanished. 'Nothing,' he said, and went from the room.

There was a postcard of Edinburgh Castle from Alayne the next morning. Gilda read it aloud, then propped it on a side table and asked: 'Is your letter a nice one?'

'It's from Andrew. He's got the tickets for the gala opening of Red Manor. It's a new night spot about ten miles away.'

Gilda's eyes sparkled. 'Is he taking you?'

Linzi nodded.

'There was a bit in last Saturday's *Gazette*. Didn't you see it?' Gilda did not wait for Linzi's negative response. 'It's going to be a super affair—they're going to televise it. What are you going to wear?'

'I don't know.' Linzi had not realised it was such a spectacular occasion when Andrew briefly mentioned the date; now, as she mentally reviewed her wardrobe she realised she hadn't planned for social high jinks being part of her new life. The wry little smile vanished from her mouth as she remembered something else. 'I didn't bring anything very glamorous with me—I may not be here in November. I'm still on trial for a month, remember?' she reminded Gilda.

Gilda's smile also vanished. Her mouth pursed as she considered the implications, then she relaxed. 'Oh, that's all right. It's all settled. Didn't Daddy tell you?'

'Tell me what?'

'That we want you to stay.' Gilda inclined her head with emphasis. 'I suppose I shouldn't tell you, because it seems, you know ...?' her eloquent eyes expressed the unspoken aspect of etiquette and she waited for Linzi's nod of understanding before she went on confidingly: 'We were talking about you last Friday, and Daddy said he was so thankful you'd fitted in so well here and you seemed so sensible. He said now that the problem was settled he could relax and get on with his work. So you see, the month on trial doesn't count now. That was just in case you—in case we found——'

'I know.' Linzi broke in to release Gilda from her predicament of tact, but her faint smile was rueful. Somehow the thought of Mark Vardan categorising her as sensible brought no pleasure at all, rather a sense of disappointment that was almost hurt ... Hurt? What a ridiculous thought! She forced a smile. 'How could your father know that I wouldn't prove hopeless at teaching you? All the same, when the four weeks are up next weekend I think I'd better ask——'

She got no further.

'You *are* going to stay?' Gilda cried. 'You're not going to leave now? Not when Aunt Sharon's coming?'

'Of course I'm not going to leave, on my own account,' Linzi said gently. 'But I can't take it for granted until your father tells me himself that he's satisfied with the arrangement and wishes to put it on a more permanent basis.'

'Oh, he *is*! It's all settled.'

Linzi, however, was not so sure, and as the week drew to a close without any sign from Mark Vardan of his intention to confirm the agreement's becoming a more permanent one she decided to broach the matter herself at the first suitable opportunity.

Her chance came unexpectedly quite late on the Saturday evening.

Gilda was safely tucked in bed; Mark Vardan was working; Mrs Brinsmead had retired to her own quarters, and Linzi was left with the rest of an evening which suddenly seemed to stretch out into a lonely infinity. She felt no inclination to venture out into the lonely darkness, nor to start on her weekend letter home, so she indulged this rare latitude by settling down in the big sitting room with a couple of glossy

American magazines she had discovered in the fireside rack.

The silence stole about her, hemmed in by solid old walls and heavy panelling through which little sound could penetrate; she might have been the only living occupant in the great house, and an awareness of this solitude rushed upon her as she turned the last page and closed the magazine. Suddenly she needed sound and movement. She got up and switched on the big television set Mark had had installed mainly for Gilda's amusement.

The sense of loneliness fled, leaving normality again, and she switched off the centre light, leaving only the tall standard lamp glowing beside the set before she returned to the shadows and curled up within the comfortable chintzy depths of the settee to watch the film.

Perhaps because it starred one of her favourite actors she did not realise it was rather a long film or that the room was turning decidedly chilly. The coal fire was laid in the grate but had not been lit that day, and somewhere in the room there should be the portable electric fire, but she was not yet at a sufficiently shivery stage to warrant uncurling herself from her cosy position. Wilingly she let the film engross her, and the final climax was very near when the door opened. Light flooded the room, giving her such a shock she sat bolt upright and exclaimed aloud.

Mark Vardan stood in the doorway, staring at her startled face.

He came forward. 'I'm sorry—did I frighten you? I didn't know you were in here.'

'No—I didn't hear the door open. I——' She was uncurling long slender limbs from beneath her as she spoke, but he checked her with a gesture.

'No, don't move, please. I won't disturb you any more.'

He moved across the room, behind her, and she heard the soft opening of a drawer and the slight rustling sounds of papers, as though he searched for something. Then his light tread vibrated in the thickness of the carpet and he came back within her range of vision. At the door he halted.

'Aren't you frozen? This room's like an ice-box. Why didn't you light the fire?'

Before she could protest he strode to the fireside, to reach for the box of matches on the mantelshelf and kneel on the cream fleecy rug.

'No!' She forgot the shivers that now made her their target. 'Don't bother—please!'

She started to her feet, having a vision of Mrs Brinsmead's expression when she discovered a grate to clean out next morning. 'The film's practically over and I'll be going to bed in a few minutes. It isn't worth it,' she insisted.

He seemed about to ignore her protest, then he straightened and glanced round the room. 'Isn't there a portable fire in here? There should be.'

Linzi shook her head uncertainly, and he gave an impatient gesture.

'There was one in here. Where the devil——! I'm positive I told that woman to get the heating organised and see that all the rooms we use have an electric fire in them. Why do I have to see to everything myself? I——' He stopped abruptly, as though becoming aware of the other sounds in the room, and looked from the television screen to Linzi. 'I'm sorry. My ranting is spoiling your viewing.'

She shook her head, and he rested one arm along the mantelshelf, turning his own attention to the silvery screen.

As she had said, the film was almost over and it was ending now in the way most of the older movies usually did. As the kiss faded and the credits began to roll Mark moved to switch off the set.

'The good old clinch,' he said ironically. 'Come and have a drink—it'll warm you more than that did.'

She was very conscious of chill now and she stood up obediently. The involuntary shiver she gave did not escape him and he exclaimed sharply: 'Don't let me find you sitting in here again without a fire. Warmth is one comfort on which I'm not prepared to economise for myself, and I certainly don't expect you to do so.'

He touched her shoulder, motioning her across the hall towards the library, and explained that he had already arranged for the engineers to overhaul Hillcrest House's somewhat ancient central heating system. 'Not that I'm unduly optimistic,' he added as he ushered her into the library. 'I'm afraid they'll say it's ready for the scrap heap.'

Linzi gave a sympathetic murmur, realising the enormous outlay and upheaval the installation of a new heating system would entail.

'However, if we're to winter here something will have to be done.' He moved to the drinks tray. 'Sherry, whisky, dry or sweet Martini? Afraid there isn't a very wide choice. Oh, how about Bacardi and ginger? That should dispel the shivers!'

'Sherry, please.' She played safe, uncertain of his over-generosity in dispensing more potent mixtures, and saw the corners of his mouth lift slightly.

He brought her the glass and took the chair opposite, stretching out his legs towards the glowing log fire and giving a sigh of satisfaction.

The warmth and the cosy room made Linzi incline to-wards a small sigh of satisfaction herself. However, she re-mained sitting up straight and regarded him rather shyly.

'I was wondering, Mr Vardan . . .'

'So formal?' His brown eyes quirked, but he waited for her to go on.

'The month is nearly up. My trial month.'

'Is it? Already!'

She nodded.

'And how do you feel about it? Think you can face the winter in our wilds?'

She looked down into her glass. 'I don't think it's how I feel about it. You are the employer, Mr Vardan.'

He pursed his mouth. 'Very well, Miss Shadwyn, since it has to be settled officially . . . I have no doubts about your popularity with my daughter, or her welfare in your care, but . . .' He hesitated. 'I feel bound to remind you again what it means. Come November and the darkness starts to fall in the afternoon—it makes the days short and the evenings very long. There are no amusements beyond what the village has to offer, and no cinemas or night spots within reach of the last bus once the summer service is chopped at the end of this month. It doesn't worry me, I can work anywhere, given reasonable peace, and it doesn't appear to worry Gilda in the least. I think she does genuinely prefer country life, apart from considering the appalling restrictions she has to face wherever she happens to be. But I wonder if you're self-sufficient enough.'

'There's no way I can prove that, except by staying and try-ing, is there?' she said quietly.

He looked down at the fire. 'Gilda's coming to depend on you more each day. She'll depend on you a great deal more when she's forced to stay indoors by bad weather. If you've any doubts, I'd rather you said so and went now than wait until it's too late to find someone else.'

'I'm sure.'

He was silent, his eyes reflective. Then he said slowly: 'I know Nanny Tarrance would willingly take over, but much as I love her I'm not in favour. For one thing, it isn't fair to drag her out of her well-earned retirement, for another, I want someone young, who can enter into a little fun with a child but remain reasonably sensible.'

Sensible! Linzi sighed and put down her glass. 'I won't let Gilda down, I promise,' she said steadily.

She felt his regard on her face, as though he weighed the worth of her words, then rather abruptly he stood up and moved across the room.

He said slowly: 'If this doesn't work out I shall have no alternative but to fall in with Sharon's idea and send Gilda to this school. I'm still not quite sure that it wouldn't be the better solution, but I know Gilda hates the idea, and she's suffered so much I haven't the heart to force the issue.'

'Don't you think it may not be the idea of the school she hates so much, but the thought of being separated from you?' Linzi asked slowly.

'Yes ...' a sigh escaped him. 'But I can't stay here permanently. For a while, certainly, until Gilda comes to terms with her loss and her disability, but not indefinitely. Besides, I'd hoped that she and Sharon would form a closer bond because I——'

Abruptly he checked, as though he regretted saying too much. He came back to the fireside and said in a different tone: 'There's only one other point: Christmas.'

'Yes.' Linzi waited.

'Will your family expect you to join them at home?'

'I hadn't thought that far ahead,' she admitted. 'I suppose they will.'

'Would you be prepared to forgo your personal reunions this year?'

'If you'd like me to stay with Gilda—of course,' she said without hesitation. 'My people will understand. But will you want me? I mean, you'll be having your own family and friends.'

'I have no family,' he said brusquely. 'Not in the way you speak of a family. It's possible that some of my friends may decide that they'll recapture the long lost spirit of Christmas round my fireside, but I'm sure Gilda will be very disappointed if you don't stay here over the holidays.' He paused, not looking at her. 'However, that is a decision you must make yourself, and if your own people will be too disappointed at not seeing you naturally we'll understand.'

'No, I think in the circumstances they would be dis-

65

appointed if I chose to leave Gilda,' she said quietly. 'We're all adults at home. My sister-in-law's baby won't be born until February and my other brother is planning to spend Christmas with his girl's family, so there won't be a family reunion at all this year. In fact,' she added, 'I shouldn't be surprised if Father doesn't do what he's been suggesting for for years now: take Mother to spend Christmas at one of these four-day Christmas parties some of the country hotels run and save her the annual cooking marathon.'

'Well, if you're sure about that ...' He looked at the empty glass he held. 'Another?' He gestured towards the drinks tray.

'No, thank you.' She stood up, a little shy under his gaze. Then she burst out impulsively: 'Please don't worry—I'll do everything I can to make it a happy Christmas for her. Perhaps we could organise a shopping trip for her, and a party ... I'll think of something to make it a little more special for her.'

'I'm sure you will—thank you. I'd be very grateful, but it won't be easy. She's always loved Christmas and I'm afraid this one is going to be bleak.' As he spoke he reached for an embossed folder which was tucked behind a bronze statuette of an anchor on the end of the mantelshelf. 'This arrived last week—they've invited me to be a guest of honour.' His mouth curved sardonically as he passed the folder to her. 'I shouldn't have thought I was quite in this line ... Would you care to accompany me?' he asked casually.

The folder announced the gala opening of the Red Manor, and Linzi's gasp of pleasure at the unexpected invitation turned to an intense disappointment of which she was ashamed. Wistfully she handed it back and managed a smile. 'Thank you, but I'm sorry—I've already arranged to go.'

'I expect your ticket could be disposed of,' he cut in, 'if that's——'

'No, I'm going with Andrew Tarrance. He's just written to say he's got the tickets.'

'Of course.' Mark turned away and replaced the folder. 'I should have realised.'

'I'm sorry, Mr Vardan,' she bit her lip, sensing his displeasure, 'but I never thought ...'

'How could you?' he said coolly. 'There's no need to apologise. I thought it might provide an opportunity for you to meet some of the locals, that's all.'

'Thank you,' was all she could say, and avert her head to

hide a disappointment that was quite disproportionate. After all, her conscience reminded her, Andrew had gone to a lot of trouble to get the tickets, the supply of which seemed to be limited, so wasn't all this concern over a second invitation rather out of place? Despite this reasoning, however, the sense of loss refused to be stifled by loyalty and was only mitigated by the thought that Mark Vardan would be there that evening, anyway ...

The following day he suddenly decided to take Gilda out for a drive. Gilda was aglow with the idea, but immediately assumed that Linzi would be joining them. She was distinctly put out when her father said firmly:

'I think not. Linzi may have other plans for today.'

'She hasn't.'

Mark looked coolly at his daughter. 'Isn't Linzi to have *any* free time? You must learn not to impose on her good nature. For my sins I will amuse you today and Linzi shall have a well-deserved break.'

Gilda knew that tone of voice; so, by now, did Linzi. But she wondered if she imagined a certain sardonic glint in her employer's eyes, almost as though he were challenging her to find her own amusement on a long, sleepy country Sunday.

She was too proud to admit that the day might prove long and lonely, and the house inordinately quiet without the sounds of Gilda's chatter and the glimpses of a tall dark man about the place. She wrote her letter home and walked along to the lane end where there was a pillar box set in the wall. For a while she pondered on her next move, to walk on down into the village or return to the house to complete one or two personal jobs in her room and then go for a long walk after lunch. She decided on the latter, and was glad of that decision, for halfway through lunch Cedric arrived, bumptious as ever and boasting about the M.G. he had just acquired.

'Only had one owner, two years old. Isn't she a smasher?'

Linzi agreed politely; it was a sleek, stylishly lined car, but she had private doubts as to Cedric's competence to handle its power.

He grinned in his familiar way. 'You need a good goer for sporting birds. What about it, darling?'

'What about what?' Linzi asked lightly.

'You and me! You've got the day free, haven't you?' Without giving her a chance to refute this statement he went on: 'We'll have a run to Scarborough and try and find some life. This place ... dunno how you stand it, lovey.' He put on an

67

exaggerated shudder of boredom and eyed her expectantly.

'I'm sorry,' she said gently. 'I've already made my plans for the day.'

'Cancel them.' He lounged round the kitchen, thumbs in pockets, and put his face close to Mrs Slaley's plump cheek. 'She'd be daft not to, wouldn't she?'

'She'd be daft if she fell for your blarney.' Mrs Slaley, who had little love for Cedric, hastened to Linzi's rescue. 'Why should she fall over herself for you? You land down here without a word of warning and expect a girl to drop everything and run to your bidding.'

'That's the way it should be. Bet if you were a few years younger you wouldn't see me stuck, Mrs S.'

'By, but I would!' Mrs Slaley polished the copper base of the pan she was drying and frowned at the gleaming surface. 'I'd see you stuck by that big head of yours, my lad.'

'You'd better not let my mum hear you being cruel to me. She thinks a lot of me.'

'Bring her along and I'll say it again. Now if you want any dinner sit down there and shut up,' the cook ordered crossly. 'Holding us up when we want to get cleared away. Other folks want their Sunday afternoon off as well, in case you didn't know.'

'You could have dished up for me while you were nattering,' he yanked a chair to the big table and looked round for Linzi.

But Linzi had gone, seizing her cup of coffee and the chance to slip away while the wrangle between Cedric and Mrs Slaley went on. She brushed past Mrs Brinsmead in the corridor, noticing that Cedric's mother was looking as dour as usual, and hurried up to her room. There she finished her coffee in peace, then donned walking shoes and a windproof anorak. A few minutes later she let herself quietly out of the conservatory door, unseen by anyone.

For the first time since she had come to Hilby she walked as far as the end of the valley and began the steep climb up the hill, to where the winding grey road left the patchwork of field and copse behind and edged right up along the brow of the moor. On the summit she stopped for a little while, looking back on the great bowl of the valley dropping beneath and picking out landmarks she recognised.

There was the solid grey shape of the church at the far side of the village, and the blue slate roof of the little school that was now closed because there were only seven children

68

of primary age left in the tiny scattered community and the bus now collected them each day to take them to Holmefield, the next village; and there was Hillcrest House, banked by woodland on three sides and from this distance showing the full architectural sweep of its layout. As she watched a moving streak of scarlet caught her eye. The M.G. was carrying its new owner abroad in search of a little life.

Linzi turned and moved on, deciding to continue her walk across the moor, and soon her cheeks were tingling with the high strong wind that swept unimpeded across the heights. The bracken was red and gold now, and the dead heather a rich peaty brown. It seemed to billow as far as the eye could see, misting at the horizon into a wavering skyline of violet-tinged clouds, and she did not encounter a single living soul during those five miles, except for the hardy moorland sheep who grazed the narrow verges of the road. She could well imagine the bleakness of winter here and understand Mark's doubts about a town girl's capacity for self-sufficiency. When the mists descended and the snows came the isolation would be complete.

Her lonely day had almost ended before Mark brought his daughter home. He watched with an air of cynicism as Gilda began a gleeful account of their day—'We went to York and had a super lunch and then we went to the Minster and along the Shambles—it's just like Dickens' Old Curiosity Shop—and then we drove to Scarborough, and on the way there we stopped at a little tea shop in a village where they make gateaux with *five* layers and I had two pieces, and then we went to the pictures and saw *Snow White and the Seven Dwarfs*, and Daddy kidded me all the way home that I was scared of the wicked queen 'cause we had to go downstairs because of my chair and she seemed to loom right up over us. Oh!' Gilda paused to draw a deep breath, 'we've had a super day! What did you do, Linzi?'

Linzi smiled a little wryly, and Mark Vardan's mouth curved slightly.

'Yes, what did you do with your day off, Miss Shadwyn?'

'Nothing as exciting as yours.' She met his gaze steadily and tried to pretend that the challenge in his eyes didn't needle her in the least. 'But then I wasn't looking for excitement, Mr Vardan. I thought I had made that clear to you,' she added quietly.

She had the satisfaction of seeing the flick of his brows acknowledge her shaft, and yet even as she spoke she recognised a certain obliqueness in her statement. For wasn't there a nebulous air of excitement increasingly present in her life, one she had not yet thought to define?

With a sudden start she realised that whatever it was had succeeded in filling the desolate gap Ian's departure had left in her life, and this flash of self-knowledge stiffened her determination not to allow Mark Vardan's disconcerting changes of mood to get under her skin. As long as he was convinced of her seriousness regarding her responsibility towards his daughter that was all that mattered.

'Actually, I've had a very enjoyable day,' she said with just a shade too much emphasis, and held his gaze defiantly.

He gave an almost imperceptible nod of his head. 'So you didn't miss us,' he said smoothly.

For a long moment she weighed this decidedly weighted question before she turned to the watchful, interested Gilda. 'I missed Gilda every bit as much as she missed me,' she said softly, then, before he could make any further retaliation, she stooped quickly and kissed Gilda's cheek. 'Goodnight, pet,' she whispered, and went quickly upstairs to her room.

She felt quite satisfied with her dealing with Mark Vardan's provocative attitude, but her peace of mind as she made ready for bed that night might have been considerably shaken had she pondered a little deeper on the reason for that strange air of excitement—and why she was possessed by such a determination to stay at Hillcrest House...?

CHAPTER FIVE

THE heating engineers arrived on the Monday morning.

Much to Gilda's glee, they needed to start in the schoolroom, and when Linzi patiently transferred her charge and textbooks into the sitting room it seemed that they wanted to be in there also.

Tools, bits of piping, and a thin, laconic youth without any apparent special function seemed to be everywhere, and there was a continual trek back and forwards to Mrs Slaley's kitchen for the making of mugs of tea. By lunchtime there was total disorganisation of the usual quiet domestic routine of the house.

After lunch Mark retired to his own domain, without comment although his expression was eloquent, and Cedric, who had stooged around all morning offering unwanted advice, received a telephone call which sent him hurrying forth to his car within twenty minutes.

It was obvious that lessons had little chance of uninterrupted peace, and still less of Gilda's concentration, until Gilda herself provided an inspiration—one, alas, that held a distinct element of blackmail.

'I think I could work better in the secret wing—we wouldn't hear that hammering there,' she said artlessly, 'and we could play Jane Austen as well.'

'Play Jane Austen?' Linzi frowned with puzzlement. 'What do you mean by that?'

'Well, you know the little sitting room, the Lilac Girl's sitting room? If we made it all tidy—I could dust and set out the ornaments if you helped me—we could pretend we lived then. Perhaps the Lilac Girl knew Elizabeth Bennet, and perhaps Mr Darcy came to call and she played the spinet while——'

Linzi was shaking her head gently. 'Not all the way from Hertfordshire, darling.'

'But they didn't stay there! They went to live happily ever after at Pemberley and Mr Bingley bought an estate in a neighbouring county to Derbyshire so that Jane and Elizabeth were able to visit each other quite easily. Yorkshire is a neighbouring county to Derbyshire at one bit of its border,' Gilda said triumphantly. 'So it is possible.'

'Yorkshire is also the largest county of all,' Linzi reminded her, 'and they couldn't cover great distances quickly in those days. Besides,' she hesitated, perception making her realise how much Gilda's handicap would cause a greater than usual dependence on the world within books for her imaginative outlets, 'we have to remember that stories are only——'

'I know what you're going to say,' Gilda broke in impatiently. 'The Lilac Girl was real and the others are out of fiction. But we can still pretend.' She paused, her eyes sparkling. 'I'm going to tell you a secret. I'm going to write a play! I'm going to start where her story ended and we're all going to play parts in it, and—and——'

'Have you started to write it?' asked Linzi, when Gilda paused to seek further inspiration.

'No, but I've thought it all out.' Gilda's brow furrowed with concentration. 'You can play Elizabeth and I'll play the Lilac Girl, but she's been thrown from her pony and has to rest on a chaise-longue all day. She loves Andrew, but she's

71

afraid her older sister will steal his affections, and she invites Elizabeth and Darcy to come and stay with her until she's better, because while they're here her sister will have to help to entertain them and not be able to go out driving with Andrew in his carriage. And then her sister tells her she's foolish to love Andrew because he won't want anything to do with a girl who has to rest on a chaise-longue all day.' Gilda paused somewhat breathlessly and waited anxiously for Linzi's comment on this first draft of the proposed dramatic effort.

Linzi nodded solemnly. 'You seem to have the initial ingredients. Who is going to play the sister?'

Gilda frowned. 'I don't know. I was going to call her Sharon, but it isn't a Jane Austenish name, is it?'

'Not exactly.' Linzi shook her head. 'I don't think you should call her Sharon, not when ...' She fell silent, the thought occurring that Gilda's Aunt Sharon must be young and attractive, when it was so patent that she was the inspiration for the child's 'other woman' in her flight of imagination. The thought disturbed, and she said rather briskly: 'You won't have enough people to play all these parts, Gilda.'

'I know,' the child sighed. 'But it would be fun, wouldn't it? I wonder if we could persuade Daddy to play Darcy ...'

A series of doors slamming before a sudden rush of wind through the house, followed by a crash and an embarrassingly clear oath from an irritated male unseen saved Linzi—or Gilda—further contemplation of this last possibility, somewhat to Linzi's relief, and caused her to agree to the child's suggestion without any more protest.

'We'll collect our books and make a start straight away,' she said quickly.

'On the play?' said Gilda innocently.

'On history,' Linzi responded with a return of her cool.

The impromptu arrangement worked out surprisingly well. No one disturbed them, and as Gilda had foretold, the noises of men at work did not penetrate the silent rooms of the secret wing. Lessons filled the morning, and after lunch the afternoons were given over to Gilda's project. Within a few days the Lilac Girl's sitting room took on quite a lived-in air and Linzi found her own imagination became infected by Gilda's enthusiasm.

Each time they came through from the main part of the house they brought supplies of dusters, polish and cleaning gear filched surreptitiously from Mrs Brinsmead's store cupboard, and gradually furniture and paintwork shed the film of ancient grime, revealing a patina of soft and mellow beauty. One alcove was enclosed by double panelled doors at its lower level and intriguingly shaped glass-panel doors above. Behind the dome-shaped glass were tapestry curtains, their pleated folds stiff with age, concealing the boxes stacked on the cupboard shelves. In the boxes was a treasure trove of ornaments and trinkets, packed heaven only knew how long ago.

Gilda polished and dusted industriously, propelling herself deftly from place to place, her face enrapt as she considered where each piece should be placed and frequently changing her mind half a dozen times before coming to a decision.

Linzi hung miniatures and small pictures, often finding the shaded outlines on the wallpaper where they might originally have hung all those years ago, and fixed the delicately chased silver sconces above the satinwood secretaire which was Gilda's favourite piece.

'I'm sure it was here,' the child said, wistfully opening the drawers one by one, all of which were so disappointingly empty. 'I'm sure she sat here to write her letters. Perhaps she kept a diary.'

'Perhaps.' Linzi touched the golden-smooth grain of the secretaire, and looked at the finely pierced gilt rail at the back. 'If you're going to use this, darling, you must take great care of it—I'm sure it's a very valuable piece.'

Gilda nodded, but it was plain that she had scarcely heard the gentle warning. 'Do you think she had a lover?'

'No—I think Andrew was right and she probably married the curate.' Linzi decided it was time to heed Mark Vardan's words and keep Gilda from becoming too introspective. 'I think I'll bring the steps in here tomorrow afternoon and clean the windows.'

'Oh ... you'll need the tall steps—you won't fall off?' Gilda ventured doubtfully.

'Of course not,' Linzi promised, laughing.

She managed not to, and the result was well worth her hard work when the late afternoon sun streamed down through the tall windows and cast its golden haze over the room.

It held an undeniable air of enchantment now, and it was all too easy to succumb to the illusion of stepping back nearly two centuries in time. All the covers were put away, the soft, clear tints of the Aubusson glowed in the centre of the room, the wide old-fashioned floorboards shone at the surround, and everything looked right; only the big china light switch by the door and the opaque glass bowl suspended by three chains from the ceiling rose told of the sole item of modernisation—a modernisation itself already more than half a century old.

'I'm going to have this for my personal sitting room,' Gilda announced suddenly. 'I shall have my lessons here, and you and Daddy can have tea here with me.'

'You'd better see what he has to say about that,' Linzi warned. 'And remember, soon it will be too cold to sit here without a fire.'

'We can light one. This should come out.'

'Careful!' With visions of soot billowing forth, Linzi hurried to the fireside where Gilda was leaning forward, trying to pull out a firescreen which had been wedged tightly under the ornamental iron canopy above the grate.

'I can't move it.' Gilda clung to the arm of her chair with one hand while she tried to get a grip on the edge of the screen. 'Can you?'

'No. Leave it until——' Linzi gave a cry as the chair swung round with the force of Gilda's struggle and Gilda toppled forward. The child saved herself in time, wriggling back, and held up a sooty hand. She pulled a rueful face. 'Have you got a tissue, please?'

Linzi's expression was thoughtful as she took a tissue from her pocket and watched Gilda rub at her grimy fingers. The small incident had happened so quickly, but she was certain she had seen Gilda's foot dart forward off the step of the chair to brace herself against falling. A sudden flash of hope so incredible she hardly dared admit it made her catch her breath. She took the grubby tissue and looked hard into Gilda's faintly inquiring eyes.

'How much can you move your legs?' she demanded abruptly.

'I can't.' Gilda's wide, innocent gaze took on the shadow of sadness. 'Only this way.' She locked her hands under one knee and hoisted the useless limb up until it crossed over the other one. As though to underline this she repeated the action to uncross her legs, then rested her hands on the two pale thin knees now side by side where they protruded from under the grey pleated skirt. 'It's in my back, you see. It's something, they don't know what, but all the life went out of my legs. They won't work any more. I—I wish they would, so that——'

74

The child's mouth worked and she looked blindly away.

Contrition tore at Linzi's heart. She bent and put her arm round Gilda's shoulders. 'Don't, darling,' she whispered. 'I'm sorry I've upset you, but you have to keep on hoping, you know. Perhaps that "something" just needs a long rest to heal itself. You must try to believe that.'

Gilda sniffed and nodded. 'The lady that gave me physiotherapy at the hospital said that as well. That's why I have to keep doing those exercises that Daddy helps me to do every morning and night. But I don't want him upset—please don't tell him, Linzi,' she begged, her voice strengthening with urgency.

'Tell him what?' Linzi looked puzzled.

'That—that——' Gilda shook her head. 'What you've just said to me. It only hurts him to raise his hopes for nothing.'

'I wasn't going to,' Linzi said gently.

'Promise.'

'I promise.' More to humour the child than anything, Linzi made the solemn undertaking, although she could not help feeling puzzled over Gilda's insistence that her father would be hurt by any discussion of her disability. For she would have judged Mark Vardan to be a man more likely to be hurt and angered by an apathetic acceptance of it.

At dinner that evening Gilda appeared to have recovered her bright spirits as she told her father of progress in 'her' new sanctum. 'But we'll need a fire soon,' she informed him. 'Do you think Jake would carry a supply of coal in for us—we daren't ask Mrs Brinsmead. You know what she is, Daddy.'

Mark closed his eyes despairingly. 'What next, child! Darling, that fire hasn't been lit for years—I don't know how long. If the chimney isn't blocked with birds' nests it'll need sweeping. No, forget it, Gilda.'

'Couldn't I have an electric fire, then?' she persisted. 'One of those flickering log kind? I'd rather have a real fire, but if there *are* any birds' nests ... Oh, it would be awful to smoke them out,' she added, horror clouding her tender-hearted expression.

'We're the most likely to be smoked out.' He shook his head. 'The wiring wouldn't carry it—it must be threadbare by now. You don't seem to realise that nothing's been done to that part of the house since my grandfather had electricity installed fifty years ago—this was the first house in the village to have it. But I'm not going to start renewing the electrical installation in there, so forget it,' he repeated, his glance straying to Linzi, as though he held her responsible for encouraging his daughter's latest whim.

To Linzi's dismay Gilda's mouth trembled. The tears weren't far away, and Mark Vardan's own mouth betrayed impatience in the hardening of its outline as an uncomfortable silence descended over the room. For once he did not help himself to a second cup of coffee, nor did he wait until Linzi had finished hers before saying abruptly: 'Come on, Gilda, time for bed.'

Through the open doorway Linzi saw him wheel the chair to the foot of the stairs and carefully lift his daughter out of it. The child's long hair spread its dark cloud over his shoulder as he gathered her close and began the ascent to his hour-long task. Unaware that she sighed, Linzi got up to close the door, then went to finish her coffee. Mark Vardan's partly smoked cigar still smouldered in the ashtray, and she leaned forward to pick it up, her gaze thoughtful as she carefully stubbed out the thin brown cylinder.

Was he beginning to weary of his self-imposed task? It took quite a considerable time to go through the routine each evening; Gilda had to be bathed, got into her night things, her limbs given the work-out they would not do themselves, and there was the inevitable spinning out of the things she did for herself, teeth-brushing, hair-brushing, and attention to manicure, before she was ready for the final settling down into bed.

Linzi had been prepared from the beginning to take over some of the responsibility, but Mark Vardan had given no indication of wishing to opt out, and certainly Gilda showed no inclination of allowing him to do so. She made no secret of her possessiveness towards her adored father. How would things work out when Mark, for the first time since Gilda came out of hospital, was away from home?

The question gave rise to several more which Linzi was still pondering when she went up to say goodnight to Gilda before retiring to her own room. There were all the practicalities like carrying the child downstairs each morning, lifting her in or out of her chair, into her bath ... Mrs Brinsmead and I will have to co-operate and organise everything while he's away, Linzi thought.

Compassion welled into her heart again as she contemplated the child's helplessness and dependence on others for so many of the routine actions of everyday living. She stood still in front of the dressing table and her slender fingers ceased the pinning up of her soft silvery fair hair. The sleek strands fell to her shoulders, falling into its natural curve about her ears, and for a moment she stared unseeingly at her reflection. If only they could do something for Gilda! Surely the present-day wonders of medical science could restore use and mobility to the child's limbs. Had they just given up hope? Had they told Mark Vardan there was no hope? Was this why he had virtually given up his career, because he knew that the cautious, non-committal reports of the physician and surgeon cloaked the dreadful truth?

The comb dropped with a faint clatter on the glass top as Linzi spun round. She had a sudden, overwhelming urge to talk to Mark Vardan, and without pausing to question it she slipped back into the blue shantung blouse discarded five minutes previously and hurried downstairs.

He seemed surprised and not entirely welcoming when he responded to the tap on the library door, but something in her expression got through to him, for he stood back, motioning her to enter.

At first she wasn't sure how to begin, until he said sharply: 'Gilda ... ?' and she shook her head.

'No—she was almost asleep and settled quite happily when I went up. It's just—if I could talk to you, Mr Vardan. It *is* about Gilda, though. You see ...'

Once begun it was far easier to confide in her normally remote employer than she had imagined; in fact, it became difficult to stop, and she did not realise how much of herself emotionally she was betraying as she recounted the moments when Alayne first appeared, the incredible illusion that Gilda had moved, and the second occasion in the secret wing when she believed that the child had made an attempt to save herself from overbalancing out of her chair.

He listened intently, making no interruptions, but a slight frown gathered between his dark brows. She saw it, and faltered, uncertainty returning.

'Please don't think I'm interfering. It's—it's just that I can't bear to think of Gilda ... for the rest of her life ...' Linzi swallowed convulsively. 'I felt I had to tell you, even though I promised——' Too late she remembered the confidence betrayed and the small gallant insister on that promise.

But he had not missed the unwary lapse. His eyes narrowed. 'You promised what?'

She sighed. It was useless to try evasion with a man like

77

Mark Vardan. 'Nothing vital. Gilda told me one day that it upset you to be reminded of it any more than necessary.'

'I'm reminded of it countless times each day, every time I see her. But it's another reason entirely that upsets me.' He turned away, but not before she glimpsed the naked pain deepening the lines about his mouth. In a different tone he went on: 'They haven't given up Gilda's case, don't fear that, but for the present they've done everything humanly possible, and believe me, I've not given up hope.'

There was a silence. Then the small sounds of the room stole to Linzi's ears; the sudden flare of a flame in the fire, the steady tick of the clock, the sigh of the moorland wind outside, muffled by the heavy dull crimson drapes across the window.

Mark Vardan moved abruptly. 'I'm grateful for your concern, and I see no reason not to admit that I'll go away with a much easier conscience knowing that you're with my daughter.'

The unexpected admission brought a lump into Linzi's throat. She murmured, 'Thank you ...' and he raised one hand in a gesture of repudiation.

'I've arranged for old Jake to come up to the house each morning at eight-thirty. If you and Mrs Brinsmead can manage to have Gilda washed and dressed by then he'll carry her downstairs, and return each evening about nine to take her up again. I shall only be away three or four days, and of course you must telephone me immediately if anything goes wrong.'

'Yes ...' She hesitated. The interview—if one could call it that—seemed to be at an end, and yet she lingered, aware of a strange reluctance to leave.

His movement had taken him back to the beautiful gleaming Steinway, and he glanced over his shoulder once before seating himself at the keyboard. Her hand touched the door as his dropped to the piano keys, and she froze, afraid now to make the disturbing movements of withdrawal, as the first fierce runs and chords of the Revolutionary Etude spurted under his flying fingers. All the fervour and conflict of the piece swirled within the room, and through it she suddenly perceived the strange sense of release to be found through music. As the dying notes ebbed away into the final ghosts of themselves Mark Vardan said abruptly.

'Do you believe in the power of music?'

'I'm not sure what you mean by power.' Her fingers had

numbed round the door knob, so tightly had she been gripping it. 'Do you mean release?' she asked hesitantly.

He shook his head. 'One can find release—or escapism—
in many other more mundane activities. I mean the power of
music to convey, to inspire, to expose the innermost soul—
and sometimes reveal the unwanted truth concealed there.'

She could only grope at his meaning, subconsciously realising that his kind of insight was a gift given only to a few,
along with the ability to show it to those with sufficient perception to understand. She took a step forward. 'I only know
that music can cast a potent spell.'

'Stay there,' he said.

She stiffened, and he turned his head.

'Now forget me. I'm merely an instrument. And forget
yourself. Afterwards, I want you to tell me what this music
says to you.'

He began softly, a minor motif in single notes, then a subtle
elaboration gradually developing into a dominant theme.
Within moments Linzi recognised it as the melody to which
she had listened so often in the stillness of her room. There
was the second theme within the grander melody, the opposing force in ever stronger conflict, the sense of a passion
seeking to subjugate the tender lyrical strain in the treble,
and then there was the hesitancy, as though the darker force
retreated and left the unanswered question. Linzi found she
was holding her breath, waiting for the moment when he
would falter and seek to release the frustration of the unfinished composition in a flurry of angry chords. But this
time he didn't. The sweet melody swelled, rippled triumphantly, and settled into a soft, whispering peace.

Without knowing how she got there, Linzi found she had
moved to the piano. She looked down at those strong supple
hands, the shadows of dark hair just visible where the white
cuffs met the wrists, and then raised her glance to the enigmatic eyes surveying her.

'Well?'

The fear that he would laugh if she spoke her impressions
kept her silent. She knew now the source of the two opposing
themes with which he was playing, the two greatest forces of
humanity; she knew also the shock of a discovery never made
in any concert hall with Ian: that Mark Vardan possessed
the power to open the door to her soul.

She saw the quiver of a smile fleetingly touch the corners
of his mouth, then his hand closed round her wrist and drew

her to his side, and down to the long stool. His clasp stayed warm, keeping her a willing prisoner while his right hand picked out the two themes.

'Love,' he said softly, '—and hate.'

'I thought you'd laugh if I said those,' she whispered.

'Why should I laugh?'

There was a quizzical tenderness in the profile so near her own. It was enough to make her forget reserve and confide suddenly: 'Because I don't know enough of music to venture an opinion to an expert. I used to go to concerts with—with a friend when I was living in London. But I know now that music never really got through to me. I think I was just influenced by the fashion of concert-going, joining in the discussions over coffee afterwards and trying to sound clever and knowledgeable.'

He did laugh then, releasing his grasp and beginning to play. 'What you say is true of a lot of concert-goers, but few of them have the honesty to admit it.' He was playing lightly now, more relaxed, and a shiver of delight ran down Linzi's spine as the romanticism of *Clair de Lune* caught at her senses. Once his sleeves brushed her arm, and once the pressure of his shoulder as he moved communicated an awareness of him that should have spelled out the dangerous rapture in which she enmeshed.

When he took his hands from the gleaming march of black and white he turned and looked into her spellbound face. She knew what was to happen, but was helpless to resist when he put one hand under her chin and tipped up her face. His thumb feathered the corner of her mouth for a moment before he drew her mouth to his own.

Afterwards, she was sure that he intended only the lightest of kisses, a flirtatious coda to the mood engendered by his music, but when the sweet pressure of his lips lightened and she made to draw back he stared wordlessly at her for an instant, then caught her fiercely in arms that denied escape. He murmured something, then his mouth parted hers, straining her head back so that she had to catch at his shoulder to ease the pressure on her back.

When he released her she was shaking. No man had ever kissed her with such bruising intensity, yet even as she stared at him with darkened eyes the wild flame of response was leaping in her veins. Had he chosen to continue making love to her she knew she would have scarcely been able to resist.

80

The room swam back into focus, his dark head silhouetted against the amber brilliance of wall brackets alight.

'Linzi . . .' He frowned into her bemused face.

She shook her head numbly, still unable to credit the effect he had wrought in her within the space of minutes.

'You look shocked.' His mouth had gone hard.

'No, I——' She bit her lip, trying to control her startled senses and the beginning of a fear flexing its chill fingers. He looked angry. As though he . . . as though it were *her* fault! Her mouth groped for words to break a suddenly intolerable situation, and then abruptly he twisted free of the piano stool and stood up.

'No—don't say it. I suppose I should apologise.' Bitterness masked the averted profile. 'That's what you're waiting for, isn't it?'

She clasped her hands tightly. Her head lifted proudly. 'An unwilling apology for a kiss, Mr Vardan? Who would expect that, these days?' she whispered unsteadily.

'No?' The movement of his head was cynical. 'I don't believe you're that kind of accommodating employee, my dear Linzi. But I do believe you're naïve enough to think that I care for little except my child and my music. In one sense you'd be right, but in another—no!' He loomed above her and the muscles clenched along his jawline. 'Have you any notion of how I feel? Living the life of a recluse? For that's what it amounts to,' he said harshly. 'So don't make that mistake. By nature I'm no recluse. Nor a celibate.'

She drew a deep breath, unable to mask the disturbance his bitter injunction had caused. 'I never gave that possibility a thought, Mr Vardan.'

'I don't suppose you did.' His shoulders moved, the weariness in their gesture seeming to drain the harshness from his voice. He turned away, crossing beyond the range of her vision. She heard the chink of glasses upturned on a tray and twisted her body as she rose from the stool.

'What will you have? A safe little sherry?' His tone was regaining its more usual timbre.

'Nothing—I'd better go.'

'Not until I've made amends with a drink—and you've answered one question.'

He was barring her way, making it difficult for her to refuse. She took the glass, trying to evade even the momentary contact of fingers the tiny action might entail, and missed the ironic curve of his mouth as he noticed the giveaway

81

evasion.

'What is the question?' She kept her head high, looking fixedly at the bronze archer beyond his shoulder.

'Was it me or my music that drew you tonight?'

Her lips compressed. 'I don't think there's any point in my answering that question—which should never have been asked,' she added in a low voice.

Abruptly she turned away and set her untouched drink down on the tray. Without looking at him she walked towards the door. She had almost reached it when he said sharply:

'One moment, Linzi . . .'

Her finger tightened convulsively round the doorknob, and she felt the faint vibrations of his footfalls across the heavy carpet. Then his hands grasped her shoulders. Against the lean hard strength of him she braced herself, afraid of his nearness and determined not to turn to face him. But he made no further move, and only his breath stirred a tendril of hair over her ear as he said softly:

'You're an extremely attractive girl, Linzi, too attractive for your own good. Tonight you've made me realise just how much I've missed in life during these past months. Unfortunately, I also realise how easily an intolerable situation can arise in circumstances like these. I have no wish to embarrass you—I don't need to tell you that Gilda adores you already and I know she'd never forgive me if I had anything to do with her losing you. So,' imperceptibly the warm hands tightened on her shoulders and drew her back against him, 'unless you're prepared for a certain natural reaction, it may be wiser to stay away from me.'

'I quite understand! No further warning is necessary.' With a sob she tore herself out of his grasp. 'But it's a pity one was needed at all!'

She fled to the privacy of her room, where she stared into space with anguished eyes, now almost unable to credit that the feverish little scene had actually happened. But it had . . . the still quivering tenderness of her mouth from the force of his kiss told her that . . . and he had warned her to stay away from him!

Linzi groaned softly and pressed trembling hands to her face. The hot colour welled up as the memory of his words burned into her brain. *Naïve . . . accommodating . . .* Did he think she had come to him with the intention of being provocative? Had it amused him to demonstrate the easy power he possessed to play on feminine emotions? Before he realised

82

she was infinitely more useful in her present capacity as companion to his child?

So much for her foolish heart. How quickly she had fallen under his spell—only to discover her own weakness, and that enchantment was just the same old sensuous attraction of the flesh.

'*But not for me,*' she whispered soundlessly. '*I've fallen in love with him!*'

CHAPTER SIX

A SENSE of flatness descended over the house after Mark's departure for London the following Tuesday. Linzi tried hard to convince herself that she was thankful for a respite when she need no longer keep a guard over her every nuance and expression while in his presence, but after a few hours she was forced to admit failure; she *wasn't* thankful that he was gone; on the contrary, every sense cried its longing just to see the tall figure cross the hall, hear the crisp sounds of his steps on the parquet, feel the particular intangible atmosphere of just knowing he was at home ...

Gilda too was quiet and subdued. Even a card from Alayne the next morning failed to lift the sober little expression for very long.

'She's at Inverness. She's hoping to see the monster, but Aunt Louella says they'll be disappointed.'

'Aunt Louella would.'

'Yes.' Gilda heaved a sigh. 'I think she's bossy—exactly like my Aunt Sharon.' She studied the postcard again, then passed it to Linzi, giving another sigh. 'I do miss Daddy—I wish it was next Friday now.'

'But he should be back at the weekend—he said about four days,' Linzi exclaimed.

'I know.' Gilda propelled herself towards the window. 'But Aunt Sharon will be gone by next Friday and we'll have Daddy to ourselves again.'

'She'll only stay a few days?'

Gilda nodded. 'Thank goodness. She doesn't like Yorkshire. All those miles of moor, and the mists, and no shops. She just likes London and going to France or Italy.'

Mentally Linzi echoed the child's 'thank goodness' with untoward fervour, and as the week wore on she found herself becoming more and more tense. It was with a feeling of shock that she analysed the cause, to discover that she was dreading the advent of Sharon almost as much as Gilda.

Although she knew she shouldn't she could not help asking:

'What's Aunt Sharon like, darling?'

Gilda sniffed. 'Sweet on one side of her face and mean on the other.'

'Oh, no, I'm sure she isn't. You mustn't say things like that.' Linzi had to make the reproof, even though her heart wasn't in it, and added helplessly, 'Sometimes one can't take to a person at all, but it doesn't mean that person is entirely at fault.'

'You asked me,' Gilda said sulkily, 'and I told you the truth. But wait and see for yourself if you don't believe me.'

Linzi stifled dismay, mixed with anger at herself for ever bringing up the subject, and shook her head. 'Of course I believe you, and I should have made it more clear—I meant to ask what Aunt Sharon looks like, not what kind of a person she is.'

Gilda's small shoulders flicked upwards. 'I suppose she's all right to look at—she used to be a model before she started her own boutique. She's taller than you, and she's got red hair—I don't like red hair.' Gilda thrust out a petulant lower lip. 'The housemistress at school had red hair and she was horrid. She's older than you, I think,' she added.

The knowledge that this last referred to Aunt Sharon and not to the unpopular housemistress at Gilda's last school did nothing to ease Linzi's foreboding, nor did any of it prepare her for the reality when the crunch of tyres on gravel heralded the return of Mark Vardan at four o'clock on the Saturday afternoon.

Linzi's pulse raced as she glimpsed the dark head and the strong square chin through the reflected glaze on the windscreen. Then the leaping pulse flattened with wariness as the passenger door swung open.

Gilda's basic facts had been accurate enough. The girl getting out was tall, about five foot nine. She had red hair, and she looked about twenty-five. But Gilda had not specified the particular kind of auburn that rippled with gold glints, nor that the five foot nine carried a superb figure—'The kind of curves that fit a man's hands,' Ian had once remarked of a new feminine acquaintance—and that the twenty-five years had endued the sophistication and the assurance that only a

84

measure of maturity could bring. Sharon was fortunate enough to have the best of both worlds—a still youthful beauty with a superb poise to go with it—and she knew it.

She was wearing a cream trouser suit with the newest slim line, her shoes were black patent Georgian with huge silver buckles, and she had completed the outfit with a brilliant emerald silk shirt knotted casually to reveal an intriguing glimpse of cleavage and a slender tanned midriff.

'That proves it!' whispered Gilda fiercely. 'She's not a real redhead—they can't tan! They just freckle. I know because a girl at school used to——'

There was no time for more. Sharon had waited for Mark to walk round the front of the car and was strolling with him into the house. And Gilda was hopelessly wrong.

Sharon was a 'real' redhead, and such tan as her shapely body might have acquired had not been allowed to spoil her flawless creamy complexion. She came into the hall, exclaimed huskily: 'Hello, darling poppet,' stooped to embrace Gilda, and then straightened to glance at Linzi for the first time.

Unfriendly eyes assessed Linzi's simple dress of blue jersey wool, little calf-courts and softly swept back hair before the pink lips smiled without warmth.

'You must be Linzi.'

No proffered hand as Mark straightened from kissing his daughter to make the introductions, only a brief acknowledgement and then the turn of an exquisite profile and the deflection of a slim shoulder which plainly relegated Linzi to the rank of a paid subordinate.

Dinner that evening was an uncomfortable affair. Gilda wore the earnest mask of best behaviour, which adequately disguised her normal winsome piquancy but failed to hide from Linzi her dislike of the newcomer. It did not deceive Mark, either, and several times he directed a warning glance at his daughter, glances which Gilda returned with a trace of sulkiness in her dark eyes. Linzi was painfully conscious of Mark's cool, reserved manner towards herself and she was thankful when the meal was over and Sharon's 'Well, I expect Miss Shadwyn will be glad to have a little time to herself while I'm here,' made it quite obvious that Linzi was not to be included in the cosy aftermath with drinks in the library.

It was natural; Sharon was the child's aunt, and obviously close to Mark, and there was no real place at the family hearth for the governess once the day's lessons were done.

But when Mark said: 'Yes, I'm afraid Gilda takes unfair advantage of Miss Shadwyn's good nature,' she felt a stab of hurt far more acute than any which resulted from Sharon's supercilious attitude.

She murmured a stiff, formal goodnight and withdrew, determined to show him that she hadn't the remotest desire to trespass on a family occasion. The following morning when she went into Gilda's room Sharon was already there, sitting on the bed and sharing early morning tea with Gilda. Almost immediately Mark arrived, and once again Linzi withdrew, feeling definitely superfluous.

The morning was fine though cold, and after breakfast Sharon suggested a drive. To forestall any embarrassment from the assumption Gilda was obviously about to voice concerning Linzi's accompanying them Linzi said quietly: 'Yes, it's a beautiful day for a drive. Will you need me today, Mr Vardan?'

Her tone and her expression clearly denoted her preference to be free for the day, and after a slight hesitation he said quickly: 'No, of course you're free to spend the day as you wish.'

'Thank you—I hope you have a nice day, Gilda.'

She sensed him glancing after her as she mounted the stairs, then Sharon's husky voice broke the silence, asking gaily: 'Well, where shall we go, darling? Shall we go to the coast or into the country, poppet?'

'We're already in the country, Aunt Sharon,' came Gilda's cold little voice. 'We'll go wherever you would like to go.'

Linzi bit her lip and closed the door of her room quickly. She had no wish to eavesdrop and knew she should not take sides, but it was difficult not to feel sympathy for Gilda. Already she was beginning to realise why the child disliked Sharon so much.

Sharon was indisputably attractive, but her personality was of the kind that invariably antagonised her own sex. She was a man's girl, and she knew it; she also knew that men knew it, the awareness of her feminine power was in every glance she directed at Mark. Gilda's clear child's perception, while not consciously defining this, had instantly seen through the artificial air of bonhomie assumed specially for her benefit.

Linzi selected her warm dress and slipped out of her skirt and blouse. Mark Vardan was unlikely to perceive the undercurrents, and less likely to understand his daughter's attitude. He simply knew that she hadn't taken to a closer acquaintanceship with Sharon, and, manlike, was irritated at what he plainly assumed to be childish temperament.

Linzi sighed, and suddenly a remark of his flashed into her mind; a remark that he had left unfinished, and now took on a sharply painful significance missed at the time. *'I'd hoped she and Sharon would form a closer bond, because I ...'*

A tremor passed over Linzi's mouth and a soft little moan escaped her. At the time she had not given a second thought to that remark, beyond the fleeting assumption that perhaps he cherished hopes of resuming his musical life soon and could delegate some of the responsibility to the young woman who seemed eager to accept it.

But at that time I didn't know ... Linzi closed her eyes despairingly. *At that time I hadn't known Mark Vardan's kiss ...*

She turned abruptly from the mirror and the betraying emotion reflected there, and shrugged into her jacket, for once uncaring that her mouth was innocent of lipstick and her eyes untouched by make-up. It was all quite clear now; the source of Gilda's dislike, and her fear.

Mark Vardan was contemplating marriage. To Sharon.

They had gone when she went downstairs.

She let herself out of the side door and walked slowly down the drive, her plans for the day as yet unformed. She felt lonely and dispirited, and suddenly conscious of the silence about her. The only sounds came from her own footsteps crushing the ripples of red-gold leaves that had swirled into two streams at the edges of the drive. Even the birds seemed temporarily to have deserted their woodland playground.

The lodge had a closed, empty look about it, although the thin curl of smoke drifted gently from the chimney. Nanny Tarrance would be at church, in her best navy-blue coat and velour hat with the cluster of petersham ribbon tipping the brim at one side. The outfit that had one airing per week for church, and one per month for the W.I. meeting, Andrew had once teased her laughingly, trying to persuade her to break out into something a little more exciting.

'A daring beige—or whatever you call that pale mud hue. Or a dashing grey. Shock the vicarage with pink!'

Nanny had merely smiled fondly at him. 'I was brought up to wear navy for Sundays, my lad—serge and velour in win-

87

ter; linen and straw for summer—and I'm getting a bit too old to start shocking anyone. Besides,' her good, country-woman's face had sobered, 'God is not going to notice what colour my coat is. Only the colour of my soul concerns Him.'

The teasing had died from Andrew's face at the simply spoken words and he had put his arms round Nanny and gently kissed her cheek.

The remembrance of the little incident brought a tightness to Linzi's throat and a sudden longing for Andrew's sturdy, comforting presence. If only he were at home! But he wasn't, and his last brief letter had given no definite information of when he would be coming again, apart from the planned date for Red Manor, and that was still three weeks away.

She walked on down the road, meeting no one until she passed Hill Brow Farm, where the gruff-voiced farmer bade her good morning as she passed the gate. Almost everyone had a greeting for a stranger, it was one of the heartwarming things about this part of the country, she reflected, and people had time to talk instead of rushing headlong into the day like they did in the cities. And yet country people accomplished a tremendous amount of activity during their working day, despite that deceptive deliberation with which they approached life.

Her blue eyes were musing as she reached the village and saw the morning bus standing by the green. The little shop was open and she went in to buy a paper, was tempted by a bar of chocolate, and on sudden impulse boarded the bus. She would go to Scarborough, wander around, find somewhere to have lunch ...

The journey took almost an hour. There were few passengers apart from herself, and most of the journeyings were between the villages that dotted the long winding road to the coast. Noon found her at a vantage point high above Royal Albert Drive from where she could see the whole lovely sweep of the north bay.

The tide was out and the crisp, newly-washed beach was almost deserted. Gone were the children and the sandcastles, icecream and buckets and spades, flying beachballs and scampering dogs; the season was over till another summer brought the cars, the coaches, the tumbling children, hot tired mums, and dads not quite deaf for once to the unending: 'Daddy—I want,' that would be repeated endlessly all along those now empty golden sands.

Linzi made her way down the long slope and almost immediately found a companion, a large yellow labrador who welcomed her boisterously and plainly expected an instant acceptance of his invitation to play. She had forgotten what fun a large, friendly dog could be, and for a while she forgot her loneliness in the exhilaration of helping him to work off his excess energy. She threw sticks, trailed a long stalk of sea-weed for him to pursue, until she was too breathless to continue, at which he stood and barked, then turned skittishly and raced into the sea. She watched him while she got her breath back, then gave a laughing cry of protest when he emerged and shook himself vigorously all over her and several metres of surrounding beach.

She was brushing droplets off her jacket and laughing when a boy's voice shouted: 'Leo!' and the golden head jerked round.

'Come here!' called the imperative young voice, and with a 'Sorry, I've got to go' look in his brown eyes, Leo departed obediently to the summons of his young master.

'Did he soak you?' asked the boy as he drew near. 'He won't stay out of the water, and he always does that!'

'No,' she shook her head and smiled. 'He's a pet.'

The boy gave her a whimsical little grin, then loped off along the beach with Leo prancing boisterously ahead. The young voice and the deep-throated barks grew distant, and the sense of exhilaration gradually ebbed. Slowly Linzi climbed the ramp to the promenade and retraced her steps along the sea-front. It was nearly one, she was vaguely aware of approaching hunger, yet reluctant to eat alone. The day stretched before her, long hours to be filled, and totally without promise.

She stared unseeingly at the fathomless blue and sighed for her disconsolate heart; she had come to this new job with such brave new hope. In it, and caring for Gilda, she was going to forget the ill-starred affair with Ian; instead, the void in her heart had remained unfilled for so short a time she could scarcely credit the fact that Ian no longer mattered to her peace of mind. Unaware that she had even stopped, she rested her arms on the promenade rail and gave herself up to introspection.

The fact that she had ceased to care for Ian surely meant that she had never really loved him; attracted, yes; infatuated, perhaps; but in love, no. Then wasn't it possible that this feeling she had for Mark Vardan was also just attraction, just brief infatuation, sparked by a few moments of enchantment and a kiss he'd doubtless forgotten long since?

It had to be so. She had to believe that this emotion would prove as intransient as the first, for her peace of mind and her happiness. Because there was no future in loving Mark Vardan. She had to steel herself against his magnetism, she told herself desperately; had to be sensible and recognise——

'Linzi ...?'

The name was so far away it scarcely penetrated. She frowned, gripped the iron rail as though to wake herself from her daydream, and turned as the car braked to a skidding halt about twenty paces further on.

'Linzi——! Wait!'

She turned, startled, and the car door slammed shut. Unbelievingly she saw Andrew running towards her, his face alight with surprise and delight.

'It *is* you!' he cried.

She exclaimed, and pleasure flowed into her heart. He looked down at her, momentarily silenced by the unexpected meeting, then laughed. 'You were the last person I expected to bump into—are you alone?'

She nodded.

'Come on, then, I'm killing time too. Had your lunch? Or are you going back?'

Disappointment sobered his face as this possibility occurred to him, and she said quickly: 'No—I've just got here. I decided to spend the day exploring Scarborough.'

'Good—in you get.' He opened the car door. 'Funny thing, I was thinking about you this morning.'

'I've been thinking about you, too,' she exclaimed, still warm with delight at this meeting. 'But I never dreamed you'd be here.'

'Ah, that's only one of my special talents—turning up when least expected,' he grinned before he closed the door and went round to the driver's side.

'Are you home for the weekend?' she asked as he pulled away from the kerb.

'No, I've been giving a lift to one of my students. His wife's just had a baby—she's staying with his parents here—and of course they can't afford to run a car, let alone a home of their own. Personally, I think it's crazy,' Andrew said with some vehemence. 'He has another eighteen months to do. How can he complete his studies and cope with the responsibilities of a wife and a baby? Luckily his parents and the girl took to one another, so she's living with them for the time being. But it means that he sees her only at weekends. He's lucky in that he's been getting a lift each Friday night this last month, but yesterday he did a relief job at an exhibition over in Bradford, bringing in a welcome fiver, which meant he missed his Friday lift. So, as I had nothing special lined up for today, I volunteered to bring him over, and as the sun was shining I took an impulse to have a look at the sea before surprising my aunt,' he concluded.

'And surprising me,' she said, settling back happily to enjoy the drive along the Marine Parade. 'When are you taking him back?'

'Tomorrow morning—at the unearthly hour of seven a.m. —I've no lectures tomorrow morning, but I've an appointment at nine-thirty, so I have to make a fairly early start. Until then—I'm yours, my lovely lady!'

Along by the old harbour he slowed. 'Where would you like to eat?'

'I'm the stranger here, so I'll leave the decisions to you,' she said lightly, then bit her lip as she remembered her mood when she left Hillcrest House. Inwardly she groaned. She had been totally uncaring about grooming. What on earth did she look like? 'But nowhere pretentious, please,' she added hastily.

'Pretentious?' he echoed. 'What do you mean? Are you afraid of being seen with me?' he asked whimsically.

'Oh, no! You idiot! You see, I just decided at the last minute to come out for the day and I didn't bother to change or anything. I was just going to have a sandwich and a cup of coffee at a snack bar.'

There was no immediate response, and she turned to see why. There was a trace of a smile hovering round his good-humoured mouth and the narrowing of amusement at the corner of his eye. He stopped the car and slewed round to face her.

'You look as lovely as ever to me. Oh, Linzi,' he shook his head mockingly, 'you're not fishing for compliments, are you? Because you're the last girl who needs to do that.'

She went scarlet. 'Oh no! I never thought ... It's true, Andrew. I never dreamed I'd meet you. I didn't even know I was coming here until I saw the bus in the village and suddenly made my mind up to spend the day here.'

His amusement had faded. Suddenly he put his hands on

91

her shoulders and shook her gently. 'Honey, I'm only teasing. Honest.'

She returned his gaze soberly, seeing the glints still dancing in his blue eyes, and then something else occurred to dilute the initial pleasure of the encounter.

She said slowly: 'Yes, I know, but Andrew ... I don't want to take anything for granted. Are you sure you're not putting off any other plans for today, just because of me?'

His hands slid away from her shoulders and he was silent so long she became certain that he was trying to frame words to tell her that indeed his careless invitation had been on impulse, that he did have prior arrangements. Then his mouth curved. He said softly:

'It's true. Auntie was right. You *are* different. Sweet, sincere, unselfish.'

Before she could divine his intent he leaned forward and cupped his hands gently round her face. He kissed her full on the lips, then three times, briefly but deliberately, murmuring, 'Sweet' ... 'sincere' ... 'unselfish' ... between each kiss.

She was too startled to feel any response beyond the physical warmth of his lips, and when he drew back she experienced the odd, detached sensation of another girl sitting there receiving those unexpected compliments and their silent but none the less forceful emphasis.

'Do you know what Auntie said to me that first evening after you'd gone?' he asked.

Linzi shook her head wordlessly.

'She told me: "That's the girl you should marry, my lad." ' He paused a moment. 'Guess what I said to her?'

Again Linzi could only make the same negative gesture.

'I said: "How could I propose to a girl I'd just sent flying into a ditch?" '

There was a silence. Abruptly he turned and dropped one hand to the wheel and the other to the gear lever. 'We'd better go, or I'll be proposing to you any minute now—and you'll be refusing me,' he added wryly.

Linzi was conscious of an air of restraint lying heavily between them as Andrew left the coast behind and drove inland, heading west along the Pickering road. She scarcely noticed the autumnal, sun-bathed colour of the countryside as the car sped along, nor did it occur to her to query their destination. She could only think of Andrew almost proposing to her, and the strange instinct with which he knew she

92

would not respond. One moment he had been teasing, the next ...

The despair of the morning returned full tilt to depress her spirit and she was close to tears. She had never even imagined that Andrew might feel anything more for her than casual friendship. Certainly he had never betrayed any hint of deeper feeling, but she knew beyond doubt that he was now experiencing a strong awareness of attraction and was uncertain of both his own reaction and hers.

For a moment she recoiled from the thought, suddenly angry that the relationship had so quickly changed. She had depended so much on what she had thought of as an uncomplicated friendship, one which made no demands emotionally. And then her mood took an uncharacteristic swerve and she wished she hadn't given in to the impulse to board that bus. Why hadn't she missed it, the way she usually managed to miss buses when it was vitally important that she get somewhere punctually? Then she would not have met Andrew and this situation would never have happened, and things would have gone on exactly as before. She didn't want Andrew to fall in love with her any more than she wanted to be in love with Mark ...

Even as the thought winged into her mind she knew that to be untrue. Just to think of Mark made her pulses throb and her heart swell. The prospect of never seeing him again, the thought of never having known him, and the knowledge that for one brief space of time he had become aware of her as a woman was enough to convince her that given the choice she would not have chosen to avoid the path that led her into his life.

Suddenly she felt ashamed of her flash of resentment against Andrew. She *had* welcomed his advent with untoward enthusiasm, perhaps enough to make him believe she cherished secret hopes in his direction. She stole a look at him and saw his profile was set and unsmiling, and a soft sigh escaped her. What could she say to restore their former easy camaraderie? Was he too sitting wondering how to break the silence?

The notion gave her courage to venture, with a catch in her voice: 'Andrew ...?'

'Mm?'

'Are you sitting there trying to think of something to say, as well?'

'Oh, Linzi ...' He gave a choked exclamation, half a groan

and a wry laugh. 'Are you?'

'Yes, and I still can't think of anything to say.'

'Don't try—unless you can think of some new and brilliant observation on the weather!' A flutter of black and white above a hedge caught his attention and he exclaimed: 'A magpie—one for sorrow, Linzi . . .'

'And there's his mate—two for joy.'

'Thank heaven!' He increased speed, only to slow a few moments later. 'Look at that hopeful creature with his head over the gate. Let's stop and feed him—I think there's an apple under the dash.'

They had travelled a little distance while he spoke and looked for a convenient spot to pull into at the roadside. Linzi sorted the apple out from the assortment of books, maps, papers, scarf, and other oddments—everything but gloves—which were stuffed into the glove shelf and they got out and walked back to where a big brown horse whinnied impatiently as it waited.

'This one's an old hand at cadging—bet you get far too many sugar lumps for the good of your teeth,' Andrew said sternly, taking a penknife from his pocket and slicing the apple into four pieces.

The horse tossed his head and gave a little anxious prance, as though to say: well, get a move on, I'm peckish, and Andrew turned to Linzi. 'Hold it on the flat of your palm,' he said, giving her the apple.

The soft mouth nuzzled her palm, snorted with satisfaction, with the inevitable result which needed a large clean hankie to dry up, and Linzi backed away, rubbing her sticky hand and laughing.

The small incident restored them to normality and after that it was easier to resume their former amity. They stopped for lunch at an old coaching inn, Andrew exulting because the traditional Sunday fare of roast beef and Yorkshire pudding was on the menu, followed by rich apple pie lathered in thick fresh cream. Afterwards they explored the village, then returned to the car and Andrew drove down over the Wolds, eventually sweeping out to the coast again and making for Flamborough Head.

But high on its heights the wild wind swept down from the north, reminding them that despite the brilliance of the sun and the azure clarity of the sky the year was not so very far from its close. Linzi turned from the magnificent vista, her cheeks and ears tingling from the cold assault of the wind, and was not sorry to return to the warmth of the car. Within another hour the sun was setting and the dark clouds of night were rolling in from the east.

She noticed that Andrew was keeping to the coast road, but it was not until the lights of Scarborough came into view that he said: 'Hungry?'

'Not terribly. Andrew,' she hesitated, 'I know you're about to suggest another meal——'

'You're right,' he interrupted. 'I'm starving after all that fresh air. I thought about ringing the Beverley out at Barrmoor. They say it's very good since they opened the new grillroom.'

'Yes, but will you let me share?'

'Certainly not.' His tone was decisive. 'I'm not in the habit of issuing invitations to girls and then letting them pay.'

'I never thought you were,' she said quietly. 'But today didn't really belong to the category of a—a special invitation. Please don't be offended,' she went on hurriedly, 'but I feel it isn't quite fair to you—it's going to be a very expensive day, especially as it was unexpected. Now be honest, please, and admit it,' she ended appealingly.

'Afraid you might have to wash dishes?' he quipped, flashing her a teasing grin.

'Of course not, and you know it,' she flashed back.

He laughed. 'I believe you would—wash dishes to help a man out of a spot. You're that kind of girl.' For a moment he paused, then added in an altered tone: 'I expect you're working all hours looking after that poor kid. I hope Vardan appreciates you, but I bet he doesn't.'

'You don't like him, do you?' she said, suddenly remembering that first evening of meeting him and the same hard note in his voice as he spoke of Mark Vardan.

'I don't know him well enough to like or dislike him,' Andrew responded curtly, 'but I know enough of him to recognise his type.'

Linzi moved sharply, a retort springing to her lips, then she snapped back into control and looked steadily ahead into the white probes of the headlights. She had no desire to quarrel with Andrew, and instinct told her that discussion of her employer could easily lead to that. Yet she knew she could not leave Andrew's dislike unchallenged.

She asked quietly: 'How can you type a man and pass judgement unless you do know him?'

'Because many things become obvious to the onlooker—at

95

least to another man?'

'Which things?'

'His arrogance, to start with, and the way he assumes that everyone will instantly fall in with his wishes. And his utter selfishness.'

She had never heard such vehemence from the usually easy-going Andrew. She felt a spark of anger. 'You must have solid reasons for such accusations, surely.'

'I have,' he said grimly. 'Two years ago Vardan suddenly decided to close the house and sell it. He dismissed the entire staff and put the selling in the hands of an agent—that was when my aunt retired. She was then the housekeeper. A business——'

'Yes, but he was entitled to do what he liked with his own property,' she interrupted, puzzled now as well as angered by this unexpected attack on her employer. 'Besides, he had other problems, as you must know,' she said quietly.

'I know about the break-up in his marriage. It was common gossip here, but that was no excuse for his behaviour towards a friend of mine. A doctor who was backed by a consortium of business men wanted to buy the house and turn it into a holiday home for handicapped children—children not so fortunately endowed as Gilda. My doctor friend was tremendously bucked when he heard the house was coming on the market, it was exactly the kind of place and surrounding he'd envisaged, and he started negotiations to raise the capital straight away. And then, suddenly, Vardan changed his mind and said he wasn't selling. No explanation, no apology, and he knew of the plans that had been made. I think the least he could have done was to tender a personal word of explanation, under the circumstances. Had the prospective buyer been a property developer it might have been different, but this was a special case,' Andrew concluded heatedly.

That Mark Vardan had once contemplated selling Hill-crest House came as a surprise to Linzi. But the circumstances which Andrew had just recounted were even more surprising. She had to admit that Mark could be autocratic, arrogant, even, but she found it difficult to believe he could be as callously indifferent as Andrew claimed.

'I'm sure there must have been a misunderstanding,' she said at last. 'I don't think Mr Vardan would deliberately inconvenience anyone, or slight them. He——'

'So you're defending him! I might have known.' Andrew's mouth turned down at the corners. 'I'd forgotten the feminine angle. Even my aunt, at her age, refuses to hear a word against him,' he said disgustedly.

'And I agree with her,' Linzi said with spirit. 'I don't think I ever told you, but the evening I arrived, when he didn't meet me, he'd stopped on the road to help a motorist who'd broken down. That was how he missed me. If he ran true to the type you seem to believe him to be he would have driven past and left the motorist to get out of trouble as best as he could.'

'Maybe,' Andrew said grudgingly. 'But then, a few months ago, when he decided to move up here more or less permanently, he seemed to expect that the old staff would instantly be available, just waiting to jump into their former jobs. Well, they weren't. Except for old Jake, who has the other lodge and would resist to the last breath any attempt to uproot him from the Hillcrest garden, all the others had either retired or gone elsewhere. The only one who did volunteer to help out was my aunt. And she was turned down.'

'Yes, but she *is* retired,' Linzi reminded him. 'Be fair, Andrew. No one would expect her to take on a permanent job now. She'd worked hard all her life and deserves some leisure now. And you forget, Gilda has to have a teacher as well as a companion.'

'Gilda should never have been brought here in the first place,' Andrew flashed. 'It's the craziest scheme I ever heard of. To bring a crippled child here, away from her proper home and her friends, and hand her over to the care of a stranger while he gets on with his own interest ... It's exactly what I'd expect of a highly inflated ego like Mark Vardan's.' Andrew paused while he changed gear viciously for the hill, 'Gilda ought to be at school, with children her own age, not leading a life here that's totally unrelated to reality.'

Shock kept Linzi speechless for an instant, then she regained her voice. 'No! You're wrong!' she cried. 'Completely wrong. Gilda wanted to be here. It was because of Gilda that Mark came back. Don't you know that he's given up everything for her? That in truth he hates the place?'

'I'm not surprised at that. It must be the dead end of beyond in comparison to the rarefied circles he's used to moving in. But as for Gilda wanting to be here, that's nonsense. This is one case where a child is *not* the best judge of what is best for its own welfare. In my opinion,' Andrew added curtly,

97

'Vardan is indulging her in order to appease his own conscience.'

Linzi recoiled. 'What do you mean by that?'

'I mean that the whole tragedy might have been averted if he had concerned himself as much with his private life as with his career.'

Suddenly Linzi could not bear to listen any more. In the darkness her hands clenched as she cried: 'I think not! How dare you pass judgement like this on a man you admit you don't know well enough to like or dislike? Simply because of an imagined slight to your aunt and a business deal that fell through for one of your friends. Mark Vardan idolises his child, and did everything to save his marriage, and you've no right to suggest otherwise.'

Her hands unclenched slowly and sank on to her lap. She drew a deep, trembling breath. 'I can't believe that it's you saying these things. I never imagined you could be so uncharitable. I—I thought——' She stopped, making an angry little gesture. 'I just don't understand.'

'That I'm not the soul of good nature everybody thinks I am?' He laughed shortly. 'I am, most of the time, but every so often something or someone rubs me the wrong way and I have to say what I think. And I just can't like Vardan.'

'So I gather.' Her mouth tightened. 'Will you take me back, please? I don't think either of us would enjoy a meal after that.'

She heard him sigh, then swear softly under his breath. The car's speed quickened, and she wondered inconsequentially why men invariably released their anger in speed if they were behind the wheel of a car. Then the thought vanished and she felt her own anger dissipating in misery. Andrew, of all people, being so derogatory. She could scarcely credit it. And why? For reasons that seemed feeble, and an unreasonable quirk of dislike.

The twenty miles back to Hilby seemed to take hours, and she felt near to tears when the familiar stone pillars and the high iron gates loomed in the glare of the headlights. Andrew stopped the car outside the lodge and turned to face her.

'I'm sorry the day ended like this,' he said steadily, 'but I'm not going to apologise for what I said. My opinion of Vardan stands unchanged.'

She made a small movement of her slim shoulders and reached for the door catch. 'Everyone is entitled to form opinions, but I don't want to hear any more of yours.'

'Linzi!' His hand shot out and closed over her wrist. 'You're not walking up there alone.'

She raised fine silky brows. 'Why not?'

'Because I'll see you to the door, after—You *are* coming in for a few minutes, to see my aunt?'

'I don't think so,' Linzi said quietly. 'She's so generous she'll insist that I stay to supper, and after—after what we've said tonight I don't think we'd be very good company for her. Goodnight, Andrew. Thank you for the drive and taking me to lunch.'

She looked pointedly down at the hand still grasping her wrist, and he shook his head, not releasing his grip.

'I've made you angry, haven't I? But I had to say it, had to—to warn you.'

'Warn me?' She stared at him, her face very pale in the dim illumination of the car's roof light. 'I don't understand.'

'Don't you?' His eyes were returning to their blue gentleness and his mouth had a pleading curve. 'I think you do.'

She shook her head. 'Let me go, please.'

'Don't fall in love with Vardan.'

With a tiny exclamation she tore her hand free. 'For heaven's sake ...! I work for him. I have no intention of falling in love with him, or any other man!'

Liar! screamed her heart, but for once she cared nothing for scruples. She turned to thrust her way to escape, and Andrew exclaimed sharply, 'I wish I could believe that, but I can't.' The door swung open and he cried: 'Linzi—please! Won't you hear me out? I have to make you understand.'

The cold night air rushed into the car, chilling her physically as well as in spirit. 'I understand already, Andrew,' she said coldly.

'You don't. Because you *are* in love with him—or very near it. You wouldn't be so angry, so ready to rush to his defence if you weren't. You haven't been with him long enough to forge bonds of loyalty strong enough to warrant such defence, and such emotion.'

'Nor long enough to fall in love with him!'

'No, Linzi. You can fall in love in a moment, at one glance, at the very first meeting. I know.'

Something in his voice caught at her, made her hand go slack on the car door, made her wait with the pain and curiosity of instinct which told her she would not like what she was about to hear yet compelled her to listen.

'You never met Lucille Vardan?'

It was a statement, rather than a question, and she gave a small negative gesture.

'I have,' he said in a curiously faraway voice. 'Three times; five years ago. She was the most beautiful woman I ever saw. She was enchanting. Dark, slender, vivid, like a glorious flower. She loved Mark Vardan, and he broke her heart.'

Linzi felt the numbness constricting her body. She wanted to move, wanted to stop Andrew's voice, but that same numbing fear kept her a prisoner.

'It was one summer. I was staying at the lodge for part of the vacation—I was still at college then. Gilda was a tiny mite, I remember her in a bright yellow sundress, running along the terrace with a scarlet flower in her hand for her mother. And I remember thinking how like Lucille the child was, even at that tender age the winsome personality was very marked.'

Not so like Mark, then ... That legacy of beguiling charm was a gift from Lucille ...

Andrew was still speaking, the air of retrospection softening his expression. 'Aunt Esther was still housekeeper then, a job she'd done since Mark went to prep school. After he left the nursery there were no more children at Hillcrest House until Gilda came, but old Mr Vardan, Mark's grandfather, wouldn't hear of her leaving. But after he died, when Gilda was only a few months old, the house was closed more often than it was open. I suppose if Mark's father hadn't remarried and decided to settle in Canada when Mark was still only in his teens it might have been different, but of course Mark was set on staying here so that he could continue at the Paris Conservatoire, and the old man wanted him to stay. It certainly paid off for Mark, for the old man left him the house and everything else.'

The cynical edge to this last remark renewed her anger. She said tautly: 'That's unfair and unnecessary, Andrew.'

'Maybe it seems unwarranted to you,' he shrugged, 'but not to me in those days. Everything fell into Mark Vardan's hands like ripe fruit from the tree. He didn't have to work his way through college like I did. Nor was he prepared to sacrifice anything—except his wife's happiness.'

'I don't believe you,' Linzi said in a small choked voice.

'You've only heard the other side of the story. I knew Lucille, and even though it was only for a short time it was long enough to make me see the truth behind it all. You never saw the sadness in her eyes that first morning I met her.'

100

He paused, and Linzi felt the cold numbness touch her again.

'I'd taken some groceries up to the house, and my aunt made some coffee. Lucille came into the kitchen and asked if she could share our coffee. She told me that Mark had gone back to London that morning, he was one of the guest conductors at that year's season of Proms, and she was worried about him until she heard that he'd got there safely. I could have talked to her all morning, she was one of those people you feel instantly at ease with, and I sensed she was lonely, but Aunt Esther broke it up as soon as we'd finished the coffee, and then Gilda came running in with a thorn in her finger.

'Two days later Lucille came down to the lodge and said could she ask me a favour. I said of course, and it turned out she wanted to go to Leeds for some things for Gilda. If I could spare the time she would fit in with whichever day suited me. I arranged to take her the next day, but she decided to leave Gilda with my aunt because the child had had tummy-cobbles during the night and she was afraid the day might prove too exhausting. By the end of that day I felt as though I'd known Lucille all my life and I'd have done anything for her. But she talked constantly of Mark, how proud she was of him. But I could tell that something was wrong, that she wasn't happy and was striving desperately not to show it. Make no mistake,' he interjected vehemently, 'she was utterly loyal to him then, whatever they said about her later, *if* it was true. She was devoted to him, and to Gilda. Only once, the night before I finished my short holiday and I took her for a short spin and a drink, did she betray the truth. I can still see her standing under that rustic arbour affair down at the Abbot and hear her soft voice as she said: "Mark's greatest love in life is his music, and I've accepted that." That was the last time I ever saw her.'

Andrew let his breath go in a deep sigh. 'They didn't come the following two summers, and I was in New Zealand by then. When I heard about the crash I couldn't believe it. She was so alive, so vivacious. It wasn't so far from here where it happened. She'd been here with Gilda for a couple of weeks, and they were driving back to London to join Mark. It seems she'd missed her turning, and the weather was foul, and it must have upset her judgement enough to make a mistake. She never regained consciousness.'

There was a silence after he had stopped speaking. Un-

101

bidden came the moral code instilled into Linzi long ago by her mother: *Never judge anyone until you've heard both sides* ... This was the other side. Alongside the thought came the knowledge that Andrew the boy had loved Mark Vardan's wife; and Andrew the man had never forgotten.

He did not move, did not seem even to notice as she got out of the car. Only when she closed the door did he start and his lips mouth a protest.

She shook her head and hurried into the darkness. As she stumbled along she could think only of a friendship which could never be the same again, the friendship on which she had come to depend, and the warning that had come too late.

CHAPTER SEVEN

THE memory of Andrew's disclosures haunted Linzi during the following days. She found herself studying Mark at every opportunity, searching for some sign in his expression, in his mien, that would bear out Andrew's stubborn belief. But she could see nothing to confirm or deny the possibility that the blame for his broken marriage and its ultimate tragedy might lie on the conscience of the man she had come to love.

She was unaware, however, that her surveillance was noted by other eyes and construed in a way which missed the real truth but betrayed another. Sharon's expression became more thoughtful as the small betrayals totalled their score, and her manner towards the younger girl, never very affable, became tinged with a cold dislike holding a certain note of calculation. She also, to Gilda's dismay, showed no sign of departure.

'She's never stayed over a week before,' Gilda whispered despairingly on the Friday evening, during one of the few opportunities she now had of being alone with Linzi.

'It's a long way to come for a weekend,' Linzi pointed out, her conscience forcing her to avoid any temptation to side with the child. 'I don't suppose she'll stay more than a fortnight.'

Gilda's small brow furrowed. 'I don't want her here when Alayne comes. It'll spoil everything!'

This possibility was undeniable. Alayne's letter had come the previous day, telling them that she was now in Stratford,

102

and this weekend she was returning to London with Aunt Louella, who was leaving for Paris on Monday, and on Wednesday she was coming north again, *'Looking forward to her visit and longing to see them all again, with,'* she hoped, *'a big surprise.'*

'What do you think the surprise will be?'

Linzi shook her head. 'I can't imagine.'

'Because she says "she hopes",' Gilda mused. 'Do you think that means she's not sure herself what the surprise will be?'

'It sounds a bit uncertain,' Linzi agreed. 'Perhaps you'd better not get too excited in case it falls through.'

'Do you think it's a present she's ordered and she's afraid it doesn't come in time?'

'I think you're a most mercenary child,' said Mark, coming into the lounge in time to hear the hopeful assumption of his daughter.

'I'm not a mercenary—they're civilian soldiers who fight for the side that pays them most,' retorted Gilda.

'It adds up to a similar sentiment where you're concerned, young lady.'

'Gilda, do I hear you sounding greedy?' Sharon had followed Mark into the room. She crossed to the chair where he was seating himself and perched on the arm, one hand resting on the high back behind his head to support herself. She gave Linzi only a glance, then frowned archly at Gilda. 'I hate greedy little girls.'

'I like getting presents.' Gilda's small chin looked more pointed than usual as she elevated it coolly. 'So if that makes me a greedy girl I shall have to put up with your hating me, won't I?'

'Gilda!'

Mark's sharp rebuke came simultaneously with Linzi's more softly voiced warning. For a second his glance encountered Linzi's and he gave a rueful grimace. 'Apologise to Aunt Sharon,' he told his daughter in no uncertain tones.

The inward struggle between obedience and defiance was plain in Gilda's expression. Then she looked into space and said clearly: 'I thought it was wrong to hate anything or anybody, and right to be honest, but I'm sorry if I sounded rude, Aunt Sharon.'

'I'll forgive you.' Sharon's red lips curved, but the smile didn't quite reach her eyes. 'We all love presents, don't we?'

No one responded to this observation, and a moment or so

later Sharon said: 'I *did* remember to bring you one, but I haven't seen you reading it, Gilda.'

Linzi bit her lip, remembering the two beautifully leather-bound and gilt-tooled classics Sharon had brought for the child and afraid that Gilda was about to forget her manners again. Before the thought had completely formed Gilda was doing exactly that.

'They're very nice books, but I've got them already,' she said flatly. 'I've got all of Jane Austen's except *Northanger Abbey*.'

Mark looked furious. He made a move as though to rise from his chair, and Sharon's hand fell to his shoulder, as though to restrain him.

'No,' she broke in, 'don't scold her, Mark. I had no idea I was duplicating the books. And it *is* disappointing to be given something one has already.'

'She deserves spanking.' His mouth grim, he slowly relaxed back. 'No one could keep track of the vast number of books that child has accumulated these past few months.'

Gilda looked unashamed, and there was another rather strained silence. Linzi glanced down at her magazine and wondered if she should extricate herself with some excuse and retire to her own room. But it was only quarter past eight; not yet even Gilda's bedtime. She sighed, and looked up to find Mark's gaze on her face.

The feeling of warmth that was now becoming familiar came into her cheeks, and desperately she willed the rose to ebb from her skin. Every time he looked at her she was made vulnerable by the memory of the evening in the library, and the fear of betraying herself. Did he remember? Did he fear her ever forgetting his warning? Bitterness tugged at her heart; as though she could forget . . .

She averted her head, and the magazine slid from her lap. She was grateful for the small interruption, and as she stooped to retrieve it Mark transferred his attention to his daughter.

'Talking of Jane Austen, what's happened to the latest venture?'

He appeared to be regaining his good humour, his dark eyes softening with the tender lights that so often came into them as he watched his child.

'What venture, Daddy?' Gilda was wary.

'The play you told me about. The one you and Lin—Miss Shadwyn were concocting. The ancient shades of the Hylcreces walk again! A diversion, after the manner of Jane Austen. By courtesy of our one and only Lilac Lady,' he enlarged in jocular tones.

Gilda merely looked blank, but Sharon tilted fine brows with elaborate puzzlement.

'Darling, what are you talking about?' she asked. 'What play?'

'Don't ask me—I'm the last one to know.' He shrugged. 'But there've been tremendous goings-on in the west wing since you were last here.'

'Since Miss Shadwyn came?' Sharon said coolly, with a sidelong glance at Linzi.

'He means our literary project,' Gilda put in rather quickly.

'And you mean your father, not "he",' Linzi reproved.

'I'm sorry.' The speed with which the apology came, accompanied by a smile flashed from Linzi to Mark, must have seemed pointed to Sharon in comparison to the grudging effort she had received a few minutes previously. 'I didn't mean to be rude.'

'You never do, do you?' Mark said with sarcasm, and Gilda had the grace to bow her head.

'But what's this about the west wing?' Sharon widened her eyes at Mark. 'You're not thinking of opening out the rest of the house, surely?'

'No, Gilda's done a spot of exploring—and Miss Shadwyn a considerable amount of hard work, I suspect.'

'Really?' Sharon's brows narrowed. 'In what way?'

'Making it fit for human habitation.' Mark laughed carelessly.

But there was no answering amusement in Gilda's face. The set of her mouth betrayed anger, and her hands balled into fists a few moments later when Mark, responding to Sharon's questions, said of course they could have a look round the next morning.

'It's still very dusty,' Gilda warned. 'You might get dirty, Aunt Sharon.'

'I shall have to take care not to touch anything, won't I?' was the cool reply.

'I nearly got a bat caught in my hair one day,' Gilda informed her glibly.

'A bat?' Some of Sharon's cool deserted her momentarily. 'I don't believe it!'

Gilda shrugged.

'It was a big cobweb.' Linzi could not allow the blatant fib

105

to pass, no matter how much she sympathised with the child's desire to keep an interfering grown-up out of her secret world. 'But it was easily mistaken for a bat in the dust and the gloom,' she added for Gilda's sake.

Sharon flicked an amused glance at Mark. 'Miss Shadwyn's imagination seems almost as preposterous as Gilda's. I'm afraid there isn't much serious school work being done, from what I can see.'

'But you haven't seen us working this week,' Gilda reminded her in a deceptively gentle little voice. 'You said yourself that we should all relax for a few days while you were here.'

'Did I? I forgot.' Sharon apparently decided not to pursue the argument. 'Well, it isn't so very long until Christmas. About nine weeks or so. Then we shall see ...'

At its face value the trite little observation sounded innocuous enough, but the flash of dismay in Gilda's eyes spoke of the ominous content it held for her. She lapsed into silence so long that her father noticed and remarked on the fact.

'My head aches a bit,' she said.

'The favourite excuse of femininity when she can't have all her own way?' Mark's smile robbed the words of any sting, nevertheless, they expressed his scepticism. 'Bed's the place for bad headaches, I'm afraid.'

To Linzi's surprise the child made no protest. There was a touch of high colour flushing her face and Linzi got up and went to her, touching her forehead gently, to discover it was quite moist and heated.

Mark looked at the small, listless picture she made and did not hesitate. He carried her upstairs and put her to bed, where she refused any supper, shuddered at Sharon's suggestion of hot milk, and asked for orange juice.

'My throat's a bit sore—well, not quite sore,' she amended hastily, 'a bit tickly.'

'I'll go and get it,' Linzi offered.

'I wonder if I should call the doctor,' Mark said worriedly.

'I shouldn't. Not tonight. You know what children are; temperatures flaring one minute; demanding to go out the next.'

Thus Sharon was calmly dismissing his concern as Linzi closed the door. 'What does she know about children? She hasn't any of her own,' Linzi murmured disgustedly to herself as she ran downstairs, forgetting that she herself belonged to that same childless state she deemed so lacking in experience of child welfare.

She found some orange squash, mixed it and added ice, and took it upstairs. Gilda drank thirstily, told them not to worry about her, and settled down with every appearance of going straight to sleep. They hovered in the bedroom, looking down at her, and presently she opened her eyes.

'Put the light out, please.'

Mark did not respond instantly. He put curved fingers against Gilda's cheek, then said: 'One of us will stay with you for a while, darling.'

'I don't want anybody to stay with me, Daddy,' she said clearly. 'I just want to go to sleep.'

Mark glanced at Linzi and sighed. 'We'll look in later on to see if you're all right, but if you're no better tomorrow we're going to call Doctor Deal.'

Gilda nodded soberly and closed her eyes again. Mark turned off the main light but left a small rose-shaded lamp burning on the dressing table. When they returned downstairs he suggested coffee, but both Linzi and Sharon shook their heads to this and the drink he then suggested.

Uneasy silence followed. Mark was plainly worried and indisposed to make small talk. Presently Sharon exclaimed: 'For goodness' sake, don't look so morose, Mark. She'll be all right in the morning, you'll see.'

'I hope so,' he said heavily. 'She's had more than her share of pain this past year.'

Later that evening it looked as though Sharon's casual assurance would be borne out. Linzi tiptoed into the adjoining room, last thing before she settled down herself, and found Gilda sleeping sweetly. Linzi felt her brow with a featherlight touch, found it fairly cool, and listened to the steady, soft breathing for a few moments before going back into her own room. She slept lightly, waking several times, but there was no sound from the small sleeper, and in the morning Gilda announced that her head felt a lot better.

'I told you, didn't I?' said Sharon triumphantly, coming in on a wave of frothy lemon négligé which parted over long slender legs as she sat on the bed and didn't do such a competent job of covering the rest of its glamorous owner.

Mark's gaze shifted back to Gilda. He nodded acknowledgement, although Linzi thought she detected a trace of reluctance in it. 'How about breakfast?' he asked his daughter.

She looked back at him with wide, enigmatic eyes and shook her head. 'My throat's still a bit tickly, Daddy.'

Mark did not waste any more time. He went downstairs to telephone the doctor, leaving Sharon staring exasperatedly at the young invalid. Linzi ignored her and leaned over to plump up the child's pillows, then gathered up the glass left from the through-the-night drink and the morning tea things. She smiled at Gilda, murmured, 'I'll come back soon, darling,' and went from the room. Sharon suddenly decided to follow her. She said, 'Just a moment ...' and Linzi turned.

'Do you think she's sickening for something?' Sharon asked abruptly.

Linzi regarded the other girl steadily. 'That's for the doctor to find out.'

Sharon gave an impatient gesture. 'Well, I don't. I think she's playing us along. And Mark's spoiling her to the point of being ridiculous. She was always a precocious child, but she's ten times worse now.'

'Is that surprising?' Linzi asked coldly. 'When a child of Gilda's intelligence suffers a physical handicap of the nature she has you can't expect any other reaction—from either parent or child.'

'What do you mean?'

'Simply that it's human nature for any father to want to indulge a child, to attempt some recompense for its loss. And it's quite natural for a child who has lost the normal outlet for purely physical high spirits to seek other ways of expression. In Gilda's case,' Linzi went on quietly, 'books and her personal relationships with people make up her world. She isn't precocious; but she is extremely clever. She's also frightened of the future.'

'And what exactly is that supposed to mean?'

'That Gilda needs all the love and understanding we can give her.'

'Wrapping it all up in psychology?' There was a contemptuous curl to Sharon's lip. 'Baby her, and make her even more conscious of her own importance?'

'It's too late for babying.' Linzi forgot her exasperation with the other girl, and her sigh held infinite sadness. 'You can't talk to Gilda now as though to a child. Gilda has lost her childhood.'

Holding the tray very steady, Linzi turned to make her way downstairs, leaving Sharon staring after her with narrowed eyes. When she reached the hall she glanced up.

Sharon still stood there, looking strangely out of place in her exotic chiffon négligé against the age-darkened oak carving

108

of the panelling and the great triple stained glass window against which she was outlined. Her face was thoughtful and the hardness in her blue eyes hinted at the nature of her thoughts as she watched the slender figure with the tray. Linzi felt a shiver tremble across her shoulders and abruptly she broke the contact with that hard blue gaze.

Her falling glance encountered other eyes, misty with sadness captured in paint over a century ago. The Lilac Girl's gaze seemed to be seeking her, almost as though they tried to warn, and with another of those unexplained tremors Linzi hurried across the hall. Suddenly she felt as though she had made an enemy.

The doctor arrived at ten, diagnosed a chill, gave precise instruction, and ordered the young patient to stay in bed.

'No antibiotics?' queried Sharon.

The doctor raised heavy curly grey brows. 'I don't think so. Her wee throat's quite clean. I'll see her tomorrow, and if she takes care she should be as right as rain by Monday.'

'What if it doesn't rain on Monday?' asked Gilda.

Doctor Deal looked solemnly at her over the top of his spectacles. 'You see, you're mending already, young lady.'

'Hm, who's a little fraud?'

The teasing note in Sharon's tone hadn't rung quite true, and the doctor swung round to her, his benevolent expression vanishing. 'Would you be referring to the patient, young woman?'

Sharon's mouth tightened. 'We had no wish to bring you out needlessly,' she said tartly.

'No call to a child with a temperature is ever a needless one.' With that he stumped out of the room, leaving Sharon somewhat discomfited.

Mark hurried to see the doctor out and arrange a time to call for the prescription. When he came back he said sharply to Gilda: 'When did you first feel off colour?'

'Yesterday morning—when I woke up.'

'Why didn't you tell me?'

'I didn't want to spoil anything.' Gilda made little ruffles in the edge of the pink nylon sheet. 'I knew you'd planned to take Aunt Sharon out to lunch and if I said anything you might not go.'

Mark's lips compressed. 'You might have been quite ill.

109

Don't ever do that again, do you hear?'

Gilda took a deep breath and smoothed out the ruffles. 'I didn't feel terribly bad, Daddy. It was just like one of those colds that sort of won't come out. Do you know what I mean?'

'Of course we know what you mean, darling.' Sharon sank down on the side of the bed and put her arm round the child. 'But you should have told us. As if missing a lunch date mattered! We would have stayed in with you all day.'

She looked up at Linzi, and the sweetness vanished from both her expression and her voice as she said: 'But I can't understand why Miss Shadwyn failed to notice anything wrong. You're with her most of the time. Supposing it had been something serious?'

Linzi was painfully conscious of Mark's eyes turning towards her as he straightened. The blatant accusation in Sharon's expression was bad enough, apart from the unfairness of it, but if Mark should believe that she had somehow failed in her trust . . .

'Miss Shadwyn isn't a nurse,' he said flatly. 'One of us should have noticed.' But still the glance he gave Linzi as he went from the room seemed almost as disappointed as Sharon's was condemnatory.

She tried to tell herself that it was not entirely unfounded; she should have noticed that Gilda was not her small, vivacious self the previous day, but then Gilda had been subdued and easily downcast ever since Sharon's arrival. Also, Gilda did tend to be volatile in her disposition, and she was adept at disguising things—when it suited her purpose, Linzi reflected, unwilling to admit how much the loss of Mark Vardan's good opinion could hurt.

Sighing, she tried to banish introspection and set about the more practical business of making Gilda's stay in bed as comfortable as possible. Gilda seemed to have decided to be a model patient, and while it soon became obvious that the cold 'that sort of wouldn't come out' was now in fact coming out extremely vigorously, judging by the fast emptying box of paper hankies on the bed, she did not complain of her throat and managed to eat a fair proportion of the dainty meals Linzi and Mrs Brinsmead prepared specially to tempt her appetite.

The centre of living shifted automatically to the child's bedroom that weekend, and she was rarely left alone. She was undeniably spoilt, and Sharon, after persuading Mark to run her through to Scarborough on the Saturday, brought back a carrier bag filled with sweets, comics, a jigsaw puzzle, and a large expensive box of talcum powder complete with a huge blue puff.

'To help disguise that poor little red nose, my poppet,' she laughed, as she watched Gilda unwrap the gifts.

Sharon was undoubtedly generous towards the child, Linzi had to admit, and yet Gilda showed no more than the polite amount of enthusiasm as she thanked the donor. Her father brought her flowers, and Linzi, unable to get to the shops herself, contributed a luxury box of face tissues which she had not yet had occasion to open for herself. Nanny Tarrance came to visit, and Andrew arrived for a few hours on the Sunday and came straight up to the house to see the invalid. Even Cedric landed that weekend and promptly went hurrying to the village before he paid court to the 'princess'. Perhaps not so strangely, his contribution of the biggest iced lolly the fridge could yield proved the most popular offering, and Gilda licked away happily between sneezes and showed none of her former haughty annoyance at the pert Cedric's use of her father's pet name for his daughter.

By the Monday morning Gilda was much better and her temperature was down to normal. The news that Sharon would have to return to London the following day afforded her considerable relief, and the phone call that Mark took from Alayne, confirming her arrival some time late Wednesday afternoon, added a further fillip of reinvigoration.

Not for the first time Sharon betrayed curiosity about the American girl. Mark had told her something of the facts, but Gilda herself had maintained a stubborn show of indifference. Now, faced again with Sharon's, 'But who *is* she? It's all very well for her to turn up here and announce that her family tree started here and can she come and stay here while she has a look round—most Americans like to claim ancestors here, especially from a county family—but you've only her word for that.'

Sharon took a deep breath, by now convinced of her own theory. 'She might be anyone. Not even an American. It could be a trick.'

'What on earth for?' Mark looked amused. 'What would be the point of her coming here at all?'

'Oh, Mark darling!' Sharon's mouth curved with attractive exasperation. 'This has worried me for ages. You don't seem aware of the fact that this house is packed with antiques, and the way the market has gone in the past few years you're

111

sitting on a fortune. I do believe you don't even know what you have got here. Or its value.'

'I'm not exactly blind, you know,' Mark said equably, 'and one of the last things my grandfather did before he died was to have all the doors and windows fitted with extra security fittings, after a burglary over at old Colonel Winter's place made everyone nervous for a while.' He sighed, and his expression saddened. 'As far as that respect is concerned I'm not worried. This past year made me revise my sense of values.'

Sharon bit her lip, then said more quietly: 'All the same, Mark, you should think of these things.'

'Alayne is not a thief,' said Gilda clearly.

They all looked at her. 'I didn't say she was,' Sharon countered.

'Yes, you did. You meant the same thing.'

'Gilda . . .' Anger flashed in Mark's eyes. 'Apologise!'

'I won't!' Spots of high colour glowed in the child's cheeks. 'She meant it! She said it could be a trick. She meant that Alayne might be coming here to see what was worth stealing. Isn't that what you meant, Aunt Sharon?'

Linzi stood silent, aghast at Gilda's defiance and the dark anger gathering on Mark's face. Sharon began to murmur, biting her lip, but with a gesture Mark silenced her. He looked down grimly at his daughter.

'Unless you apologise instantly I shall cancel Alayne's visit.'

The stricken look on Gilda's face stabbed at Linzi's heart. She held her breath, saw the struggle that was going on in the child, and took an unsteady step forward.

'I mean it,' Mark repeated. 'Because Sharon's suggestion could easily be true.'

'Of course it could,' Sharon put in. 'You must learn not to trust strangers.'

'Alayne isn't a stranger.' Tears were sparkling on Gilda's long black lashes now. 'She belongs here. I know!'

'What nonsense!' Sharon was unable to conceal her scorn any longer. 'Someone you met for about five minutes—I never heard anything so ridiculous!'

'I'm waiting, Gilda.'

Linzi could bear it no longer. Of all of them, she was the only one who had sensed something of the strange affinity between Gilda and her Lilac Girl. She could never begin to explain it, but that did not mean it did not exist, and she could never credit Sharon's careless, worldly-wise suggestion

112

with a grain of truth. She moved to Gilda's side.

'I've also met Alayne,' she said quietly, 'and I'm prepared to stake my reputation on her integrity. Until it's proved otherwise I feel Gilda's loyalty is not misplaced.'

'Until it's too late, you mean,' Sharon sneered.

'I think Gilda owes her loyalty to her own, before strangers,' Mark said curtly.

Linzi sighed, knowing that coin must yet be turned. She sat down on the edge of the bed and touched Gilda's hand. 'That's true, you know.'

Unwilling Gilda looked at her, at the steady gaze that willed the child to forget pride and indignation and say the one small word that would resolve the distressing situation. At last Gilda sniffed and swallowed hard.

'I'm sorry,' she mumbled, and burst into tears.

'I should think so,' Mark snapped, and stalked out of the room.

After a momentary hesitation Sharon followed, leaving Linzi alone with Gilda.

She let the little girl weep for a minute or so, then pushed a clean tissue into her hand.

'It's no use antagonising your father as well as Aunt Sharon,' she advised gently. 'It just isn't worth it.'

'Grown-ups always win,' Gilda sniffed. 'They can say anything they like about other people, but if I say what I think it's always wrong.'

A sad and ancient fact of life, Linzi thought wryly. If only adults would keep their memories a little longer and temper inconsistency with understanding.

'You mustn't accuse adults of anything,' she said softly, 'even if you believe it to be true.'

Gilda blew her poor little red nose hard. 'No, but grown-ups do it behind people's backs instead of saying it to their faces.'

Another sad, but undeniable truth. Linzi smiled faintly. 'Never mind. Now cheer up, you want to be better when Alayne comes.'

Gilda nodded, but there was no lightening of the woebegone little face. 'Daddy's simply furious with me now,' she observed sadly, then, with a surge of indignation, 'It's all *her* fault. She always spoils everything!'

'Oh, darling, you mustn't say that.' Linzi studied the child with troubled eyes. 'She is your aunt, and your father——'

'She's not my real aunt,' Gilda interrupted. 'She'd have to

113

be Daddy's or Mummy's sister, and she isn't. She's Mummy's cousin. It isn't the same at all.'

The nature of Sharon's relationship with Mark was clear at last, in one respect at least. Of the other respect Linzi did not care to think, let alone surmise over. But Gilda had no such inhibitions.

'And she wants to marry my father. That's why I hate her. Because she'd be my stepmother and live with us all the time and everything would be *awful*! A-and we'd have to go back, to live in the flat again, and—and Daddy would g-go away again a-and——' The broken utterances became incoherent as Gilda dissolved into tears once more.

Linzi reached down and gathered the thin, trembling shoulders into her arm. Gilda turned her face against Linzi's shoulder and her body trembled convulsively.

'I—I don't mind if Daddy *does* want to marry someone else, but I don't want him to marry Aunt Sharon,' she sobbed. 'That's why I made him come here with me, because I thought she wouldn't bother to come all this way—she hates the country—it bores her.'

Linzi stroked the dark tumbled hair, and her own heart grew heavy. 'I know, darling,' she murmured sympathetically. 'I know how you feel, you want your father to be happy again. But you can't arrange his life for him—as you can't arrange anyone's life. He has to make his own decisions, as he thinks best, both for himself and for you. And if he wants to choose Sharon for his wife you must try and accept that. It doesn't mean that he's going to love you any less, and perhaps if you tried to be more friendly to Sharon you'd both be much happier.'

'You're on her side.' Gilda pulled away. 'I thought you understood!'

'I do, but you have to try to understand other people's point of view,' Linzi said quietly. 'Have you ever considered the possibility of Sharon being a bit scared of you?'

'Of me?'

Surprise at this idea dried the tears abruptly, and Gilda stared back unbelievingly.

'Yes, because a lot of adults can't get through to children. They want to, but there's a barrier they can't overcome.'

Gilda subsided back on the pillows. After a moment or so of reflection she nodded. 'I know what you mean. Mrs Mead —she's my godmother—once said she couldn't talk my language now that she was getting old, and I couldn't think what she meant, but now I think she meant the same as you.' Gilda paused. 'But I'm still scared ... I wish ...'

Linzi sighed softly. Useless to give the child the reassurance she so desperately sought, to confirm that the instinct, which though merely a child's, unerringly echoed her own. Sharon wouldn't bring happiness into their lives, but if Mark loved her nothing Gilda could do would keep her out ... Linzi forced a smile and hugged Gilda gently for a moment. 'I'll bring you your facecloth and wash those tears away. I don't know what the doctor would say if he came in now. He'd think we weren't looking after his patient very well, I'm afraid.'

'I'm better now. Do you think he'll let me get up today?' Gilda asked after she had sponged and dried her face, and Linzi had tidied her hair.

'I hope so.' Linzi fastened the red ribbon in place and returned the brush and comb to the dressing table. 'Shall I have my morning coffee in here?'

'Yes, please.'

'Would you like some?'

Gilda nodded, her smile breaking through again, a bit shaky, it was true, but sufficient to ease Linzi's heart.

Mark and Sharon did not return, and to Gilda's hesitant query on her return with the coffee tray Linzi said vaguely, 'I didn't see them. I expect they've gone into the garden—it's quite a nice morning.'

Gilda appeared satisfied with this surmise and did not seem to worry unduly when about half an hour elapsed without her father coming back to see her. But when Linzi got up to take the tray downstairs Gilda said in an offhand tone: 'If you see Daddy downstairs ask him to come and see me after lunch, please.'

Linzi nodded and gave the required promise, then, the door almost shut behind her, Gilda called urgently: 'Will you bring my legend book next time you come upstairs, please?'

'Where will I find it?'

'In the small bookcase, or ...' Gilda screwed up her face with frowning concentration, 'in my cupboard in the lounge. The bottom half of the bureau with glass doors, behind the big settee. It's called *Legends of the World* and it's very heavy.'

'I think I'll be able to stagger upstairs with it,' Linzi smiled.

There was no sign of Mark or Sharon when she went down,

although Mrs Brinsmead was crossing the hall, having just speeded her son on his way with a dour, 'Now watch yourself on that road, boy,' as she closed the door. She stopped and smiled quite affably, however, at Linzi, and made to take the tray from her hands.

'I'm sorry you've had all this tray-carrying to do, Miss Shadwyn, but Annie hasn't been in for three mornings—I think it's this same bug Miss Gilda's had—and I've been a bit pushed.'

Linzi refused to relinquish the tray. 'I'll do these—I don't mind in the least, Mrs Brinsmead. I haven't much else to do.'

It was only the work of minutes to deal with the tray, and reset it in readiness for Gilda's lunch, earning a friendly thank-you from Mrs Slaley, who was involved with preparations for lunch, then Linzi was free to seek the tome Gilda required.

Mark and Sharon must have gone out, she reflected as she crossed the lounge to the bookcase, although it was unlike Mark to be missing for any length of time without leaving word—unless he was still furious with Gilda. She banished the thought; he adored his daughter too much to remain estranged from her for very long. And under the agonising intensity of childish emotion, Gilda was well aware of this.

This flash of knowledge brought a wry smile to Linzi's mouth as she scanned the shelves without success and turned her attention to the cupboard section which formed the base of the big old glass-fronted bureau. This proved to be packed with Gilda's treasures, probably because it was more comfortably accessible to her from her wheelchair. There was only one way to unearth one particular item from the hoard, and that was a wholehearted delve from one's knees.

Linzi got down on the carpet and patiently began the search. There were old games, discarded dolls, a teddy minus one eye but undoubtedly much loved in his youth. A box with a broken lid spilled childish baubles and an exquisitely cut scent jar of pink crystal which still gave up its drift of long-used perfume, and amid them all were books, some of which had obviously belonged to generations of youth long before Gilda's time.

The book of legends was almost the last thing she came to, pushed to the back, under the softness of a white and silver brocade evening bag. Linzi looked at it, and caught her breath as she smelled that same perfume again. She knew it had been Lucille's, and that she should thrust it back where

116

she had found it, but something made her open it and slowly examine the contents.

There was a tiny mirror, a fifty-pence piece tucked behind it, a jewelled lipstick, a lace handkerchief with the initial L embroidered in pink and blue garlands in one corner, and a green cloakroom ticket numbered eighteen. Not enough to convey a very telling picture of the owner, the most beautiful woman Andrew had ever known ... Without realising she did it Linzi turned the cloakroom ticket over and saw the scribbled numbers on the back. A telephone number? Lucille's own, or ...? But how had the ticket not been given up when the wrap it tallied was claimed? Linzi shook her head over the small mystery and started to tuck the things in exactly as she found them. She was snapping the bag shut when she heard Mark's voice.

Linzi froze with guilt, the silvery bag suddenly clenched in her hands. Then in the space of a second she realised several things. That he had come into the room, that Sharon was with him, that she must not let him find her with his late wife's evening bag in her possession—and that they couldn't see her! The big chintz-covered settee effectively screened anyone kneeling as Linzi was kneeling beside the heavy mahogany bureau. Panic rushed through her; she had to put the bag back, then stand up quickly and make her presence known. And then as she reached forward into the cupboard she heard Sharon exclaim sharply:

'Don't try to evade me, Mark. We've got to settle this nonsense. The girl is totally unsuitable. She——'

'Her qualifications were excellent,' Mark broke in, and there was the sound of the door being closed. 'We must give her a fair trial.'

'Fair trial! Oh, Mark, all this business about someone young enough to understand Gilda, to share her fantasies and gently stroke her out of them—it won't *work*. I can see the change in Gilda in the few weeks since last I was with her. She's become precocious to the point of insolence, and all this Lilac Girl nonsense!' Sharon's voice rose and quickened. 'Linzi's encouraging her, and she's clammed up. Both of them clammed up. Don't think I couldn't see it. I could. Neither of them had the slightest intention of letting me into their secret.'

Mark's exclamation at that was partly amusement, partly exasperation. 'Sharon, aren't you imagining things now? They have no secrets.'

117

'I'm not so sure about that,' Sharon responded tartly. 'If Gilda *has* to have a private teacher you should have kept Miss Timms. She was older, a much more experienced teacher, and a disciplinarian.'

'But unfortunately she decided the job was too lonely. She decided to go back to general teaching.'

'That was what I was afraid of right at the start, and why I was against the whole idea. However,' Sharon's deeply drawn breath that expressed her annoyance was clearly audible to the dismayed girl behind the settee, 'it shouldn't be too difficult to find someone else of Miss Timms' quality.'

'But Gilda likes Linzi,' Mark said quietly.

'Because Linzi obviously lets her have all her own way. Naturally she likes Linzi.'

It was Mark's turn to sigh heavily. There was a rustle, then a soft plop, as though a folded newspaper was tossed on to a chair. At last he said slowly: 'I want to leave the matter as it is at present. I must. It isn't fair to Gilda, and she must have a chance to settle down, to adjust, and forget.'

'You're making a mistake.' Sharon's tone was filled with persistence. 'You have to face facts, Mark. This isn't good for Gilda. She still needs discipline, school, other children, for her own sake. Basically she's such a sweet little girl—don't risk spoiling her.'

'I'll think about it,' he said wearily.

'Besides,' Sharon's voice softened, as though she sensed a weakening in him and sought to press home her advantage, 'you have to think of the future, your own future, Mark. You have your life to live, a little happiness to find. Some day we have to start making plans ...'

There was a silence, Linzi wanted to put her hands over her ears, lest she hear something that might strike anguish into her heart. But nothing could blot out imagination, the mental vision of Sharon's slender voluptuous body swaying its temptation towards Mark, her arms stealing readily about his neck, her red mouth inviting ... Linzi clenched her hands until the nails bit into the palms and wished she was anywhere in the world but this small section of rose-flowered carpet on which she was kneeling.

Then Mark said softly: 'Just give me a little time, and be patient with Gilda ...'

'Haven't I tried to be?' Sharon whispered.

'Yes,' his voice was low, 'and I appreciate all you've done for us—I'm a brute to take it all for granted.'

118

Sharon laughed softly, as though she were well satisfied. 'You're many things, Mark, but never a brute. All you need is someone to look after you.'

Mark made no response to this, but Sharon must have seen nothing in his mien to challenge her new mood, for she laughed again and obviously glimpsed herself in the over-mantel mirror before she exclaimed: 'Heavens! Look what the wind did to my hair—I'll have to do something about it before lunch.'

She murmured a brief excuse to her host and hurried to the door. Linzi held her breath, waiting until Mark should follow. But the click of the closing door did not come. A board creaked underfoot, telling her he was moving, then two sharper sounds came as his steps left the carpet area and reached the narrow strip in front of the window where the carpet did not cover the broad, polished boards. He had picked up the newspaper, and was tapping it against his hand, and she knew he was standing there, musing, turning over his thoughts on the conversation Linzi had so unwittingly over-heard.

If only he would go!

The room was so still and so silent she hardly dared breathe, and then she sensed him turn away from the window. What if he decided to sit down? She might be a prisoner till lunch time if Mark decided to peruse his morning paper in here instead of his own sanctum. She waited for the creak of the board by the window, and heard instead a sharp exclamation, then a gasp that convulsed her with horror.

'What——! *Linzi*!'

Mark stood by the end of the settee, staring down as though he couldn't believe his eyes. Trembling, stiff with cramp, she scrambled to her feet from the surround of the cupboard's contents.

He prodded the heap on the floor with his toe. 'What *are* you doing down there?' Then something very like horror flooded his own face. 'How long——? You must have been there while——'

Linzi's mouth moved, but the words wouldn't come. She shook her head desperately, backed a step and stumbled, then stammered: 'A book—a book Gilda wanted. I couldn't move —there wasn't time. You came in and started talking—I couldn't stand up when she started to——'

'You were listening!'

'No!' She put out her hand, unable to bear the accusation,

119

the distaste in his eyes. 'I'm sorry, Mark—I didn't want to! Oh——!' She closed her eyes. If only she were a million miles away. 'I'm sorry,' she repeated.

Suddenly she knew she was going to break down. Without realising what she was doing she thrust the heavy book blindly into his hands and averted her scarlet face.

'Please ... forgive me ...' she stumbled past him and fled from the room.

CHAPTER EIGHT

FOR days after that unfortunate occurrence meetings with Mark became agonies of embarrassment for Linzi. She could not forget it, no matter how she tried to put the incident out of her mind with the reflection that worrying about it wouldn't make her feel any less discredited in Mark's eyes. She hadn't intended to eavesdrop, but she had, and nothing could alter that fact.

What must he think of her?

Her face flamed every time the painful question tormented her, which was very frequently, and poor Linzi spent a good amount of time the next few days with her head bowed to hide those betraying tides of guilt.

Gilda, however, was happy again. The doctor called after lunch on Monday and said she could get up, and provided the weather remained fine and dry she could go out the following day. On the Tuesday morning she suffered Sharon's parting embrace with commendable affability and waved goodbye as the car slid away. Mark had decided to drive Sharon to York to catch her train, thus saving her having to travel from Scarborough to make the connection with the London train. When the car was out of sight Gilda rubbed her hands gleefully.

'You don't want to go out this morning, do you? It's a bit windy.'

Linzi shook her head.

'And we haven't got to do lessons this morning?' Without waiting for an answer Gilda rushed on: 'I mean, if I were at ordinary school I wouldn't be going back the minute the doctor let me get up, would I?'

'Gilda, you're a minx.' For the first time in twenty-four hours Linzi felt like smiling. For this she was ready to be indulgent. 'I think we can allow a couple of days of convalescence. But mind, we must get back to work on Thursday,' she warned.

'But Alayne'll be here.'

'I know, but we've lost a week already,' Linzi reminded her. 'We must keep to the morning schedules at least, I'm afraid.'

'Oh dear!' Some of the glee evaporated. 'It means neglecting a guest. We can't, Linzi.'

'Alayne will understand,' Linzi said with unwonted firmness, 'if we explain.'

Despite Gilda's dissatisfaction with this decree Linzi intended to keep to it. The memory of Sharon's blunt assertions still hurt, even though they should never have been overheard. It was no use being too easily won by the child's pleas. Weakness wouldn't help the progress of her education, which had suffered enough already, as Linzi was gradually discovering. In some subjects—those she liked—Gilda was in advance of her age, but in others she had lagged behind. It was Linzi's responsibility to ensure that those gaps were closed, and the term was more than half over already.

But she had not bargained for Gilda's wilful determination, and rapid seizing of the opportunity to 'get round' her father during the bedtime session that evening—during which a joyous reconciliation of father and daughter had obviously taken place. So Linzi was somewhat taken aback by a peremptory summons from Mark next morning.

'What's this about insisting on the school routine while Alayne's here?'

Stung by his brusque tone and hurt that Gilda should betray her this way, Linzi attempted to explain, only to have her reason brushed aside carelessly.

'A few more days aren't going to make much difference. Let her have a break. She can start again when Alayne goes.'

'Very well.' There was nothing else she could say if he chose to overrule her authority. She stood stiffly, then, as it seemed the brief interview was ended, turned to leave.

'There's one other thing . . .'

She waited, a tiny panic seeding in her heart, growing. What was coming?

'I want the west wing closed again. I've——' Her slight gasp stopped him. He looked sharply at her, then went on: 'I suppose I'll have to wait until this American girl has been and gone—having allowed Gilda to issue the invitation—and let her see over the house, that being one of the prime reasons for her visit. Not that I believe for one moment that she'll prove to have the remotest connection with the house or anyone who ever lived here,' he interjected brusquely. 'But this must be the end of it all. Once she's gone, I want to hear no more of this Lilac Girl business.'

The burgeoning panic changed to dismay. Gilda would be brokenhearted. Surely he knew how much her small secret world meant to his daughter?

As though he had read the protests shaping in her mind he said sharply: 'Gilda is retreating too much into the past. It's unhealthy. She has to learn to live in the present and look to the future, and I'd be grateful if you would refrain from encouraging her any further in this silly preoccupation.'

There was a hard note in his voice, giving the impression he did not trust her to follow his wishes. She said quietly: 'I agree that Gilda is more fascinated by this house and its past occupants than she might have been if she hadn't been crippled. But there's another aspect you've failed to take into consideration, Mr Vardan.'

'And what might that be, Miss Shadwyn?' he inquired coolly.

They were back to the icy footing of formality. She forced herself to meet the glints of arrogance in his dark eyes.

'You are a musician. You would not have attained the height you reached in the musical world unless you were possessed of a great sensitivity, imagination, and emotional depth as well as technical skill. You could scarcely expect to father a child totally devoid of those qualities,' she finished steadily.

For a moment she thought his anger was about to break forth. Then his mouth curved with a brief, unwilling smile. 'You flatter me,' he mocked, 'but it makes no difference. I decided long ago that Gilda would have nothing to do with the art world, as long as I had a shred of influence in her life. It renders one too vulnerable to the hurts of living. Simplicity and a less demanding existence may prove less exciting, but they're infinitely easier on the emotions.'

'Happiness and unhappiness spring mainly from the effect other people have on our lives,' she responded quietly, 'not from our choice of job. And forcing a child into preparation for a job not its own choice will cause a great deal of unhappiness. However,' she sighed, 'I shall respect your orders, though I'll be honest, I'm not very happy about them. I'm

122

afraid Gilda will be dreadfully upset.'

'It won't be for long.' He turned on his heel and stared down at the leaping fire with a brooding gaze. 'I've thought it over and come to a decision. Sharon is right—it was a mistake to come here. We can't go on living this never-never existence. I must get back to my work, and Gilda must find a more normal way of life, among other children. I'm taking her back to London immediately after Christmas and Sharon is making arrangements to get her into this school which has special facilities for handicapped children. It's the only way,' he said bleakly.

'Does she know?'

'Not yet. And for heaven's sake don't tell her. I intend to wait until we get back and then drive her down to see the school. When she sees it, and the other children, and the activities they're encouraged to take part in, I'm hoping she'll realise it won't be the horrible existence she firmly believes it to be at the moment.'

There was little she could say, nothing she could do; obviously his mind was made up. Sharon had won.

The divulgence lay like a guilty secret on Linzi's conscience each time she saw Gilda smile, and beneath it was the new, numbing knowledge she had to face; not only the end of her own job, but the end of a friendship which had become very precious to her. For Gilda would soon forget. There would be no place for Linzi in Gilda's life once Christmas had passed—and no place, no matter how small, in Mark Vardan's.

She was thankful for the advent of Alayne. For it meant that Gilda was less likely to notice the forced element in Linzi's gaiety and perhaps seek with childish persistence to fathom its cause. But Gilda lived through that Wednesday strung to the highest pitch of excitement. When at last the sleek opulent Lincoln roared up the drive and halted at exactly three minutes past five Gilda could scarcely speak coherently.

'She's here!' she squealed. 'Daddy! Linzi! Look—open the door! Hurry!'

The car had scarcely ceased to quiver before Alayne sprang out. She poised for a moment, a joyous smile radiating her face, her arms outstretched, almost as though to greet the ancient fabric of the house, then she ran forward as Mark opened the door.

Gilda nearly tumbled out of her chair in reaching up for Alayne's embrace, and the next few moments were given up

123

to the excited incoherencies of greetings.

Was it by chance or purpose, or simply that the colour was her favourite, that brought Alayne in a pale lilac dress of linen and a light car coat of soft, fine-spun heathery wool?

Linzi was watching Mark, and she saw the perceptible start he gave at his first sight of the American girl. Later, when Alayne stood under the great portrait and smiled at them all, the same surprised look flashed into his eyes and continued to linger for quite a while afterwards. Alayne herself was a little taken aback, and her vivacious features sobered when she stepped away and turned to stare up with awestruck eyes at the picture.

The resemblance was uncanny, and a silence encompassed them all. Then Alayne took hold of the heavy antique locket that swung from a chain about her neck and slipped the chain free. Without speaking she opened the locket and put it in Gilda's hands.

They stooped to see, even Mark, and Gilda gave a cry. One of the miniatures in the locket was the same as the portrait's head, and the other was of an older woman, her hair dressed high in the style of the period, whose eyes held that same mist of infinite sadness.

'Is that her mother?' exclaimed Gilda.

'We think so. The miniatures seem to have been done by the artist, and there is a strong resemblance—same eyes, same curve of the lips—although so many of the artists of that time painted those full, curvy lips on their subjects.'

'Where did you get this?' Mark asked.

'It's the family heirloom. This was the surprise I mentioned—I guessed I'd better bring my own little piece of history, to kind of convince you, after you told me all about that portrait. I called my mother and asked her to mail it, and she was horrified. What if it got lost, or the Customs impounded it? And then she called me back the next day and——'

'*From America?*' Gilda's eyes widened.

'All the way,' Alayne laughed, 'to tell me she was coming over.'

'Here?'

There was no sad mist in the blue eyes sparkling at Gilda. The American girl laughed again happily as she nodded. 'Actually she'd planned to make the trip with us, then my father said wait till next fall and we'd all make that big vacation trip to Europe we'd promised ourselves so long. But

124

Aunt Louella was set on making it this year and she wanted me to come along with her for company—Aunt Louella can never go far without a handmaiden—and so the parents said, great, we'll pack Joel—my young brother—away to summer camp and have that peaceful twosome right where we honeymooned nineteen years ago. And now Mom's had her second honeymoon and her big trip as well. She flew in Friday, left this, and went on to join Aunt Louella. They're coming back at the weekend and I'm hoping you'll let them visit—I'll fix them at a hotel, of course, I couldn't dream of imposing on your hospitality,' Alayne rushed on breathlessly, 'but they're longing to see the place—Aunt Louella's convinced now, and we're hoping to piece together a bit more of the story, and——'

Mark held up his hand, checking her. 'Hadn't we better get your baggage in?' His smile held the kind of warmth that made the interruption a charming gesture. 'When did you eat?'

'This morning. I rushed round to do some shopping and just stopped for a coffee at noon. I was so eager to get here.'

'You must be starving.' Again that smile of charm over his shoulder as he turned to go out to the car. He seemed to have taken an instant liking to the newcomer, Linzi thought, trying to ignore the stab of something very like envy as she went to help with the considerable number of packages and bags that filled the rear seat of the big car.

Gilda watched the settling-in process with unconcealed impatience. She would have revelled in an uninterrupted exchange of personal histories with her new friend, and Alayne herself had been almost as carried away with enthusiasm, to the exclusion of such mundane things as a refreshing shower and change after her long drive and a meal. But Mark was firm, and by the time this was all over it was dark, the curtains drawn and a lovely log fire leaping and sparkling, and, after they gathered to drink coffee in the cosy room, there was no hope of a sojourn in the Lilac Girl's real domain, much to Gilda's disappointment.

'It'll be something to look forward to tomorrow, honey,' Alayne consoled, her eyes tender as she looked at the wistful child. She turned her gaze to the adults. 'Isn't it sad the way we forget the urgency and spontaneity of childhood as we grow up?'

'But think of the effect of uncontrolled spontaneity on adult society,' Mark responded lightly. Glints of amusement came

125

into his glance and he added: 'Although I'd say that saving something to look forward to the next day was an infallible sign of a still youthful temperament.'

Alayne laughed joyously, and in the soft radiance of the standard lamp near her chair she looked very young and very lovely. A stab of envy told Linzi that the warm magnetism of Mark Vardan's regard had a great deal to do with Alayne's glow. *Do I look like that in those rare moments when he directs that charm to me?* she wondered sadly, and tried to steel her heart against its own emotion. He seemed to have taken to the American girl at first sight, and Linzi could not help wondering if he remembered Sharon's unpleasant insinuations. What did he think of them now that he had met the subject of them and was able to form his own judgement?

For herself, Linzi's first impression of and liking for Alayne remained unchanged. Alayne's uninhibited friendliness was irresistible, and already she had proved to have a generous nature.

She had brought gifts for them all. A lacquered musical box which delighted Gilda; a scarf of cobwebby sapphire silk for Linzi which had been selected with unerring taste to tone with Linzi's eyes and fair colouring; there was a giant box of candies which was for the house in general, and a paperweight in the form of a small silver-gilt metronome for Mark.

It had quite astounded him, and was a further indication of Alayne's thoughtfulness in choosing a gift both apt and useful for someone she had never met.

After a very short time she was at home in Hillcrest House as though she had always belonged there. There was something almost uncanny about that air of belonging, although not in the least in an eerie sense, and Linzi knew instinctively that Mark Vardan was aware of it even though he made no mention of it.

He came with them the following morning when Alayne was shown over the house, Gilda solemnly taking on the office of guide. And when Gilda decided that a special afternoon tea should take place that afternoon Mark, a little to Linzi's surprise, joined the invasion of the kitchen to make preparations. She was not the only one to notice and secretly shudder as he selected a particularly dangerous-looking knife to carve thin neat slices of ham for sandwiches. Linzi stayed silent, but Alayne shivered and grimaced:

'Mark, please be careful! Your precious hands ... I hate

126

to see artistic hands risking injury. Let me do that.'

He completed the carving of a perfectly shaped slice, then looked at her. 'No. Women hack meat. I've never yet known a woman who could carve either a joint or poultry without mangling it.'

'But we cut it up to eat it,' said the irrepressible Alayne.

'Certainly not.' Mark wielded the weapon again. 'And remember, that even if the woman is allowed more of her own way than is good for her by Uncle Sam, you're not at home now, ma'am. You're in England now.'

'Where the man is master of the domain?' Alayne laughed, and Gilda's hand went to her mouth to hide a giggle as Mark replied: 'Exactly.'

For once Mrs Brinsmead had failed to betray tight-lipped disapproval when Gilda ordained that the best china should be used, and Linzi helped the housekeeper to wash the delicate floral tea service Gilda had chosen after a frowning inspection of the store cupboards.

'That was my grandmother's favourite set—it came out about three times a year—so don't you dare break one, young lady.' Mark directed a warning glance to his daughter, which left her quite unabashed.

She was supervising the laying out of the trolley, consulting Mrs Slaley as to the risk of the array being insufficient to satisfy the appetites of four people.

The cook raised her arms despairingly. 'There's enough to feed the village there, Miss Gilda—and you've forgotten the cream baskets.'

'Angels on Horseback,' Gilda corrected, taking the plate of cakes Mrs Slaley held out. 'There's no room left.'

Somehow a space was made on the laden trolley, teapot and water jug were filled and placed on the lower tier, and Mark himself wheeled the trolley along the lengthy route from the warm, homely kitchen to the evocative, eighteenth-century atmosphere of the lilac drawing room. There, Gilda presided over tea, Mark switched on the third bar of the electric fire he had brought in earlier in the day, muttered that he hoped the ancient wiring would stand the strain, and everyone pretended that the atmosphere wasn't just a little bit shivery and that efforts to date to refurbish hadn't yet quite banished a fusty air of long disuse.

Alayne voted the tea the most delicious she'd ever had, and then, after a little silence, Mark said:

'I don't think my daughter's patience will last much longer

127

—shall we try and reconstruct the history of the Hylcrece family?'

'You don't know much of it, Daddy,' Gilda told him with childish scorn. 'They died out long before we got the house.'

'That's where you're mistaken, my pet,' he said evenly. 'My grandparents were very interested in the house when they became the owners, and they did a great deal of research, through old records, and several local histories in which the house and the family were mentioned.'

'You never told me,' Gilda accused.

'I didn't think you'd be especially interested. In Sir Richard Hylcrece, for instance, whose daughter had the temerity to fall in love with a Lancastrian and had to be hastily married to a more suitable connection, some forty years her senior, who used her so ill that the unfortunate girl administered a potion of hemlock and yew, or something equally noxious, whereupon suspicion fell on Sir Richard and the girl was forced to confess to save her father, then take her own life— the Hylcrece family rarely survived to a placid old age,' Mark interjected dryly. 'And then there was Edward Hylcrece, who died on Bosworth Field, the day before his wife gave birth to a stillborn son. That was the end of the Yorkist Hylcreces. A distant cousin became heir to the estates, and for many years everything came their way, even an earldom, until insanity entered the family. From then on misfortune dogged them. A fire destroyed the east wing in 1600, three male deaths in rapid succession further weakened the line, and in the 1750s the seventh earl incurred so many gambling debts that a major portion of the estate had to be sold.'

'Daddy, get to the time of the Lilac Girl,' cried Gilda.

'I know little more of her than you,' he responded patiently, 'except that she was the only surviving child. There were two brothers, one of whom died in infanthood; the other drowned when he was ten. When she was about seventeen, in 1823 or thereabouts, the Earl decided to close the house and remove the family to the Worcester estate. They did not return north for over two years, and when they did the daughter was not with them. She had contracted consumption and was in a Swiss sanatorium, where she died a few months later, or so the locals who dared to inquire were told. The Countess rarely left the grounds and seemed a changed woman, and there were rumours that she and her husband were bitterly estranged. She died a few years afterwards and the Earl remarried, with almost indecent haste, a girl half his

128

age. He was desperate for an heir, but his young wife proved to be barren, she hated the house and the countryside, and eventually she persuaded him to take a town house. Various rumours of scandal filtered north; the young Countess was blatantly deceiving her husband; he in turn had taken a mistress. However, within two years of his remarriage the Earl was a widower again—his wife was one of the early victims of the epidemic of Asiatic cholera which hit England in 1831. He did not marry again, and from all accounts embarked on a life of debauchery which did not prevent him living to the age of eighty.

'That was the end of the Hylcrece line,' Mark went on, his gaze resting on Alayne's eager young face. 'The house, and what little else remained of the estates, passed to a distant nephew who made a valiant attempt to restore the decaying house to something of its former style. At the turn of the century it passed to his two daughters, who never married and lived out their drab lives in about three rooms with one old servant. And its next owner was my grandfather, who bought it and restored it for his retiring years.'

'And he found the portrait, and the mark on the wall behind the other one that fitted it exactly,' Gilda broke in, impatient of the account of the other Hylcrece ancestors. 'And some of the rooms on the top floor were piled with old lumber and pictures that had lain there for ages, and in an old chest there were clothes and things that had lain there for centuries.'

Mark's brows lifted.

Gilda interpreted their movement as one of surprise at her statement. She nodded vigorously. 'Oh, yes—Mummy once mentioned them. I think she was talking about an awful lot of rubbish that wanted clearing out of the attic and she would have to see about. But that was before I got to know about the Lilac Girl properly.' Her face sobered with regret. 'If I'd known I wouldn't have let Mummy throw them away. Just think, one of those old dresses might have been an actual dress that she wore!'

There was a short silence. Mark's expression visibly altered, became closed in. He said evenly: 'I don't think your mother did much clearing out of attics, Gilda. Not to my knowledge. The task would be too vast. Those attics have been the repositories for the unwanted junk of nearly three centuries of Hylcreces.'

'You mean they may still be there?' Alayne exclaimed

129

excitedly.

'It's probable,' he said slowly. 'My grandfather did dispose of a lot of the furniture in the downstairs rooms which displeased him—in those days nobody wanted to know about it. The vogue was for chrome and glass and tubular styles then; the present craze for antiques didn't start until many years afterwards.'

'You could be sitting on a treasure trove!' Alayne cried.

'So everyone seems convinced,' he said dryly. He looked at the two eager faces on which the same pleading question hovered, and leaned forward to put his cup and saucer on the trolley. 'I think we'll take a look—if you're ready to brave the spiders.'

'Now, Daddy?' Gilda squealed.

'As soon as Alayne and Linzi have finished tea.'

'I've finished,' Alayne said promptly.

'And Linzi's been finished for ages,' said Gilda, before Linzi could reply for herself.

But Gilda's hopes of discovering the old chest which might have contained what they sought proved unrewarded that afternoon. It took quite a long time to assemble torches and the enormous bunch of ancient keys that belonged to the house, although no one knew where exactly they fitted, and to transport Glida up to the attic floor. By this time it was almost dark, the long corridor was shrouded in dust and spiders' webs, and none of the keys seemed to fit any of the massive old locks on the solid doors. Mark succeeded in opening· one, which proved to be a large cupboard. Apart from some crumbling, mildewed old books and a packing case with a motheaten red curtain in it, there was nothing remotely like what they sought.

From the landing end of the corridor, sitting on the light cane chair which Linzi had carried up for her, Gilda watched and listened. Linzi walked back through the gloom to where the lonely little figure waited impatiently. It did not take much stretch of imagination to guess at the frustration of the child who was forced to watch the fumbling efforts of the adults while she yearned to be with them experimenting feverishly with the age-blackened iron keys.

'I think we're going to have to wait till daylight tomorrow,' she said, with a sympathetic smile.

'I'm afraid so,' confirmed Mark's voice from behind. He put the keys and the two torches into Alayne's hands and turned to gather Gilda up into his arms.

130

Linzi picked up the chair, and as she did so Alayne exclaimed: 'Where does that lead?'

Mark looked over his shoulder, and Gilda's head craned to see.

Alayne was pointing at an arched recess in the gloom at the far end of the landing. Without waiting for his response she ran along and up the two stairs in the recess. 'There's a doorway to somewhere through here—may I explore?'

'Yes . . .' Mark set his burden down on the top stair of the flight and followed the American girl. She was fitting keys into the lock one by one, her lower lip caught determinedly under small white teeth. At about the fourth attempt there was a clicking sound and the key gave under her hand. Linzi shone the torch, then Mark said, 'Let me—the door may be stuck.'

With a creak of protest it gave, swinging open into a cave of blackness. Ancient shapes loomed greyly in the probing rays of the two torches—a broken chair, massive old pictures stacked against one wall, a chipped ewer and a bowl so covered with dust its big floral pattern was scarcely discernible. A wicker birdcage lay on its side on top of a hooped trunk, a dressmaker's dummy loomed eerily into view, causing Alayne to give a stifled cry of shock, and everywhere there were old books and cobwebs. Alayne recovered and giggled nervously, then her face sobered and she lifted the cage off the trunk. She fumbled for the hasps, swearing softly as she dropped the bunch of keys, and Mark said, 'Leave them,' when she turned to pick them up.

The trunk wasn't locked. Like the door, it creaked stiffly as she raised the lid. Linzi bent closer with the torch, feeling the excitement of something which did not really touch her own life quicken her heartbeat, nevertheless. There was a tray fitted in the trunk, with tags to lift it free. The old material felt dry and frayed as Linzi helped to lift it out, and for a moment she felt a stab of disappointment, suddenly sure that the trunk was going to be empty. But her instinct had played her false.

The forlorn little mementoes were still there, exactly as Mark had described in his mother's words, that very first evening in the library when he had told Linzi so vehemently: *I loathe this place . . . I'd be happy never to see it again . . .*

For an instant she remembered only those echoes, and his face dark with bitterness. That night seemed so long ago, and she had come to know little more of Mark Vardan, or the reason for that bitterness in the intervening weeks. She looked at him, seeking in the shadowy planes of his features a hint of his true feelings as he watched Alayne reach down to the reminders of a bygone age.

Alayne's hands touched them almost reverently, lovingly, with the same sense of fascination he would have condemned instantly in his daughter. But there was no sign of cynicism or impatience in his expression, and he was silent, until Alayne held up a silver handmirror and leaned towards him, rubbing at the blackness of over a century's tarnish which filmed the embossing on the handle and the ornamental chasing on the back. She caught at Mark's hand, directing the torch beam at the mirror.

'Look!' she whispered. 'Can you make it out? The initial? Is it——?'

He bent his head closer, and suddenly a small shiver ran through Linzi. The sharply etched shadows of the two heads, one so dark, one misted with its fair ethereal nimbus contrasted against the outline on the wall behind, seemed to have retreated through time's door. Linzi wanted to put out her hand to touch Mark, to convince herself that he was still there, warm flesh and blood, to bring him back before the sad little ghost drew him away for ever.

She caught at herself; that was Alayne, whose vibrant personality and husky accents were very much of today's new world, and that dark lean profile belonged to a very real man who possessed a more potent power to stir her senses than any shade from the past, a man whose cynical scorn she could well imagine should he ever guess at her flight of imagination.

Then he said softly: 'I think it's an E. It's difficult to tell until——'

'It *is* an initial E.' Alayne clasped the silver mirror to her heart and her eyes were aglow with triumph. 'It *is* hers. I know!'

'How do you know?' Mark asked in the same soft voice.

'Because her name was Elena.'

The thin little tremor passed over Linzi again. She seemed to hear the name echoing over and over again through the silence. *Elena ... Elena ... Elena ...* as a soft voice whispered down through the years, seeking, needing ... And then a child's cry shattered the silence, plaintive, impatient, a little scared.

They had forgotten about Gilda.

* * *

132

Mark called out instantly and ran to the door. He said, 'We're coming, princess—and we've found them.' He hesitated, half turning back, as though to re-enter the garret, then checked.

'Let's get back to reality. Do you two girls think you could manage to drag that trunk downstairs?' Without waiting for their reply he added: 'If it's too heavy don't bother—I'll come back.'

But it wasn't very heavy.

There were leather handles on the trunk, one at each end, and Linzi and Alayne carried it down to the first floor landing where Mark and Gilda were waiting. They took it into Gilda's bedroom, and there, after they had exclaimed and mused over the trinkets, and tenderly unfolded the faded, brittle silk dresses of lilac, grey, and lavender blue, Alayne sat on the floor, her slender legs curled under her, and fitted the missing pieces into the story of the Lilac Girl.

'She didn't die, not then,' Alayne said softly, 'nor did she ever go into a Swiss sanatorium. She fell in love—with the last person her father would ever consent to her marrying. She fell in love with her groom, and because she couldn't keep her love secret the Earl dismissed the groom and moved the family to Meads, their other house in Worcester—it isn't there now; I went to try to find it, but it had been made into a girls' school in the '80s, and demolished after the school closed. There's a supermarket and a bank on the site now,' Alayne explained ruefully. 'But to get back to Elena ... she was desperately unhappy, and they wanted her to marry a cavalry officer, a young man from a good but impoverished family who was willing to add the family name to his own so that it wouldn't die out. Elena hated him, and then the groom followed her down to Meads. There was a dreadful scene, and that night she eloped with him. They went back to Yorkshire, to a farm by the sea near Whitby, and were married.'

Alayne paused, and her blue eyes were pensive. 'It must have been a very strange life for her, living in a tiny farm labourer's cottage, having to carry every drop of water from the pump in the yard, and bake her own bread, after being used to the luxury of a great mansion and servants to wait on her. But I guess she was happy at first, until she found she was pregnant. Then she wanted to see her mother, whom she missed dreadfully. But when she found enough courage to send a message to her mother there was no reply, except for a curt missive from the Earl's lawyer informing her that from the moment she deserted her home and married without his

133

consent she forfeited all claim to her inheritance. All he allowed her was her white pony and the proverbial shilling. She never saw her home or her parents again.

'She called her son James, after his father, but when he was still a tiny mite her husband walked out one morning and never returned. It was said that he'd hoped to feather a fine nest for himself, and that he'd fully believed that her parents would relent as soon as they heard about the birth of their first grandson.'

'How do you know all this?' Gilda demanded, her expression rapt.

'I'm coming to that in a minute,' Alayne said, her mouth curving a little although her eyes were sad. 'There's one more link to make. Elena was too proud to try to trace her husband. I think she realised that he was a weak, worthless type—also, it wasn't so easy to trace a missing person in those days when there wasn't all the official documentation of individuals that we have now, and she was too proud to beg help from her parents. Fortunately, the couple at the farm were good kind country people and they took her in, offering her a home if she would help in return for her keep and that of the child. However, the minister of the parish was very concerned about her, and when the child was about four she was offered a good post with a lady and gentleman with whom the minister was acquainted. It seems they had quite a large family, and one of the little boys was blind. This family was emigrating to Nova Scotia, and they were looking for an English girl to take with them, to help look after the blind child and be governess to the others. Of course Elena had had an extremely good education, and as they were quite amenable to the idea of letting her bring her little son she accepted the post and set sail with them about six weeks later.'

'Didn't she see her mother at all before she went?' Gilda asked.

Alayne shook her head. 'We don't think so. There are bits missing in the story, bits we'll never know because they're lost and——'

' "We"?' Mark spoke for the first time since Alayne had begun her story, but despite the familiar lift of his brows his voice was gentle, and Linzi knew that he had accepted this strange link, as she had; knowing without doubt that this modern-day Lilac Girl from far across the seas was indeed a

134

true link with the sad girl in a portrait nearing two centuries old.

'Elena stayed with them for almost ten years,' Alayne continued in her soft husky voice. 'Until she caught a chill one very severe winter, developed pneumonia, and died when James was thirteen years old. The night before she died she tried to tell him the truth about his birth and his lost heritage, and begged him to try to get word to her mother, to tell her that her daughter had never forgotten her and never ceased to love her. But she was too weak to tell him it all, coherently, and it was not until many years later that he visited England and managed to trace people who remembered and could fill in some of the missing pieces. All he had was this locket, the cruel letter from the lawyer, and Elena's diary. He discovered that the Countess had died before Elena had left England and no one had been allowed to inform her. Apparently she had heard the news of the birth of her grandchild and had actually tried to go and visit her daughter, but the Earl had prevented this and she had died very soon afterwards.'

Alayne paused to take a deep breath, then went on rather unsteadily. 'James did trace his grandfather, and what he found confirmed your account, Mark. He found an evil old man, sodden with wine and riddled with the sickness of debauchery, and for the only time ever in his life he wanted to kill another human being for the misery he had caused a fine, good woman and an innocent girl. None of Elena's letters had ever been allowed to reach the Countess; he had destroyed them all and persuaded her to believe their daughter neither cared nor regretted her action. When James returned home to Boston he renounced all loyalty, and such few ties as still remained to him, to his homeland.'

'He had been settled in Boston for some time?' Mark queried.

'Yes, since he was aged twenty. He stayed in Halifax for a year after Elena's death, then became restless with the somewhat rigid pattern of a devout household. He was very conscious of not belonging by right, and sensitive about receiving charity, even though he remained in touch with the family for many years afterwards. So he set off to seek a job, without any notion of what his especial talents might be or how he might best utilise them. After a couple of years he worked his way down the eastern seaboard and fetched up in a Maine shipyard, where he stayed for four years, then he realised

that the wealth lay in the cargoes the ships carried, and——'
Alayne stopped abruptly and shook her head laughingly.

'I must leave Great-great-grandfather James's story till another day,' she said ruefully. 'How he came to start his business in Boston, how he married Sophie, who painstakingly wrote down the story he told her years later when he came back from England, because if Sophie hadn't done that and told Grandy Louise when *she* was a little girl we might never have known the story. Because that was the one and only time old Gramp James talked about it. He didn't think it was romantic or intriguing like Mom and I do. He just hated it all, and his grandfather most of all.'

There was a long silence, then Gilda said in a suspiciously gruff little voice, 'So you are! I knew it the moment I saw you.'

'Knew what?' Alayne smiled tremulously.

'That you were the Lilac Girl, and that you had to come back.' Gilda looked down at the silver mirror, then stretched out her hand. 'May I look at the locket, please?'

Silently Alayne slipped the chain over her head and put the heavy gold locket into the child's hand. She stood there, looking down while Gilda turned the locket over and studied the engraving on the back. It was much worn, the outline of the crest blurred, and the initial not instantly isolated from the curves and loops of embellishment which made up the engraving. But it was there, and with a sigh Gilda put the locket and the mirror into her father's hand.

'It's the same,' she said. 'The patterns and initials are the same. Alayne belongs here. She's come home.'

Suddenly the tears ran down Gilda's face, and impulsively Alayne stooped and put her arms round the child. 'Don't cry, precious,' she entreated, 'even though it's because of a funny kind of happiness. I—I feel a bit—kind of watery-eyed myself,' she sniffed ruefully.

Mark stood up, and after a moment he cleared his throat and gently slipped the locket and chain over Alayne's head. The silver mirror he held out to Gilda, but did not immediately relinquish it as Gilda groped and brushed her knuckles across her eyes at the same time.

'Are you going to keep this, darling?' he asked quietly.

'Keep it?' She stared up at him and a strange questioning glance passed between father and daughter before a sudden comprehension and decision was exchanged in that same strategic moment of silence.

136

Then Gilda shook her head. 'I think they belong to Alayne. I think they all belong to Alayne.'

'No!' Alayne looked from father to daughter, and made a quick crossing movement of her hands, palms outwards. 'I'm not going to take your treasures. I didn't come for that.'

'We have the picture. We have her home. We have everything else,' Gilda said simply, and pushed the silver mirror into Alayne's hands.

And now Alayne looked very near to tears. She bowed her head, and Mark slowly put a hand on Alayne's shoulder and cupped his other hand round Gilda's dark head.

For long moments no one moved. Linzi stared at the tableau—the child sitting on the elegant Sheraton settee, the girl at her side, the tall man in the centre, behind, looking down at them with a rarely glimpsed tenderness in his face, and a painful construction rose in her throat. Suddenly she knew what it felt like to be an outsider.

In those moments, for Mark Vardan, she might not have existed.

CHAPTER NINE

THE days of Alayne's visit began to speed by, each one—to Gilda, at least—seeming to pass more quickly than the one before, until the time drew near for the arrival of Aunt Louella and Alayne's mother.

Mark refused to hear of their going to a hotel, but Mrs Brinsmead received his order to prepare two rooms with scarcely veiled hostility. To Mark's, 'Get whatever help you need from the village—it shouldn't be difficult, just for one week,' the housekeeper responded: 'I'll see what I can do, sir, but I'm making no promises.'

Alayne, who by this time was long past the 'guest' stage and fast becoming a family intimate, had already sized up the difficulties in running a home of the proportion of Hillcrest House with a skeleton staff. She had also, with some amusement, slipped into the way of being nice to Mrs Brinsmead, because should the housekeeper decide to leave it would be very awkward without her and might be very difficult to find a replacement who was suitable and didn't object to the isolation.

'This is why I suggested fixing Mom and Auntie at the

Grange,' Alayne confided. 'Five miles is nothing, I could run them back and forward myself in a few minutes. But Mark insisted. He said it's time we woke the house up.' She sighed softly. 'Isn't he a sweetie? I'm trying my damnedest not to fall for him. Wow! But I guess you know all about that,' she whispered ruefully as the "sweetie" walked in person into the room at that moment.

Linzi merely nodded. Where Alayne was concerned she was torn between two conflicting emotions. It was impossible to dislike the American girl or resist her sheer, genuine good nature; but when she saw Mark obviously succumbing to that warm, vibrant personality she could not help wishing Alayne had not become so closely bound up in their lives. If they'd never gone on that picnic of destiny with Andrew ... She tried to push the thought away when it came, dismiss it with the scorn it deserved, for when she remembered the happiness Alayne had brought into Gilda's sadly restricted life she felt ashamed of those selfish lapses into envy. For that was what they were; and Mark Vardan was not for her, so why not face it? It didn't matter that once he had admitted that she was an attractive girl. She just didn't have what it took to transform him from the cynical, withdrawn man she knew into the man he became in Alayne's company. A sweetie! Despite the hurt in her heart she could not repress a smile as she wondered what Mark's reaction would be to that particular appellation.

'I've sent an S.O.S. to Nanny Tarrance,' he was saying. 'I'm sure she'll help out.'

'Do we need anybody?' Alayne asked firmly. 'Heavens, what is there to getting a couple of rooms ready? And why two? I guess you could hold a ball in my bedroom. They can share one room, and I reckon I could shake it down in an hour—half if Linzi will help me.'

'Of course,' Linzi said instantly.

'Don't shake too hard,' Mark said with humour. 'Down may be literal!'

Alayne giggled and jumped up. 'Come on, let's start while I'm feeling strong.'

It took a little longer than her optimistic reckoning. The room Sharon usually occupied held quite a few of her personal possessions, and the two big rooms overlooking the front of the house, as selected by Mark, had not been used for years. The signs of the recently installed central heating had not yet been properly cleaned away, there were raw new

138

wood and plaster patches here and there which stood out garishly against faded paper and time-dulled paint, but the carpets and furnishings, although old, had a rich quality which responded readily to a cleaning attack, and Alayne was crazy over the heavy red velour drapes with their great ruched pelmets and long silken ropes with huge tassels to pull the drapes open or shut.

'I know they're going to be thrilled to be staying here, in a real old English house,' Alayne enthused as she wielded the vacuum vigorously. 'I told Mark the other day he should open it to the public, but he laughed and said it didn't quite come up to the stately home class. Well, I think it does. I think it's a gorgeous old place,' Alayne prattled on. 'But somehow I get the impression he doesn't care for it at all. He says Gilda loves it here and that's why he stays. Do you think maybe it has something to do with losing his wife? Unhappy associations?' Alayne prompted delicately.

So Alayne too was curious. Linzi sighed as she replaced the dainty Dresden shepherdess she had just cleaned so carefully. 'Something like that, I think. I haven't been here very long,' she said slowly, 'so I don't know very much about the family.'

'No? You surprise me,' exclaimed Alayne. 'I'd gotten the impression you'd been here for ages, almost one of the family. So maybe you don't know this Aunt Sharon. Is she the family ogress?'

Linzi could not help laughing. There was much she might have imparted regarding her personal impressions of Sharon, but she kept her own counsel and merely said dryly: 'You've been talking to Gilda. The ogress is about five foot nine, red-headed, and her statistics may be vital but I imagine a man would describe them as divine.'

'I see.' Alayne drawled the last vowel thoughtfully. 'A case of beauty in the eye of the beholder, perhaps. Or, strictly speaking, skin-deep, huh?'

Linzi shrugged slim shoulders and continued her dusting. 'It would depend on the beholder, I think.'

'Exactly.' Alayne giggled. 'I shouldn't, but I love a good scratch occasionally.' Abruptly her face sobered and her mouth hardened slightly. 'She wants to send Gilda to some school the poor little kid doesn't want to go to—leaving the field clear to nail the man.'

Oh dear, she *has* been talking to Gilda, thought Linzi, remaining silent.

'I guess I've got my own ideas about that,' Alayne said slowly, 'and if Mark will give permission I'm going to take Gilda back home with me. I know a surgeon who might be able to do something for her. In fact, if he can't, I doubt if anyone can. He's the tops, specialises in children.' Alayne paused and looked steadily at Linzi. 'Please don't tell Gilda —I'm not sure how she'll take to the idea. But I mean to do something. So maybe the best thing is to let Mark think it over first and then get her round to the idea.'

Gilda to go to the States! Inwardly Linzi gasped. Alayne was certainly a go-getter, and she meant every word of it. But would Mark give his consent? And what would Sharon say? Suddenly Linzi knew that in the American girl Sharon would meet her match at last. There was a satisfaction in the thought...

The vacuum roared into life again as Alayne returned to the job in hand, and the two girls put the finishing touches to a room now bright and welcoming. The old house suddenly seemed to be filling with an air of excitement, as though indeed, as Mark had said, it were awakening from a long spell of sleep.

Nanny Tarrance sensed it the moment she stepped in the door that afternoon and looked about her with curious and wondering eyes. She admitted quite honestly that she was curious about the newcomer and inclined to take with a pinch of salt the discovery of Alayne's ancestry.

'It's true, Nanny,' Gilda assured her mischievously. 'Just wait till you see.'

'Can't wait, my lamb. There's work to be done,' said Nanny briskly, taking off her coat.

But Alayne appeared at that moment, running downstairs and hesitating at the foot lest she was intruding.

Nanny Tarrance's eyes widened and she murmured something under her breath, giving a small, astonished shake of her head.

'Didn't I tell you?' Gilda whispered triumphantly.

There was more incredulity when the visitors arrived and Gilda, who had assumed a distinctly proprietorial air towards Alayne, took charge of telling the story and presenting the evidence, and with the flair of a drama producer concluded with an instruction to the amused Alayne to take up her pose beneath the portrait of her ancestor so that the likeness could be fully comprehended.

Aunt Louella had come prepared to be sceptical, but even

she was convinced.

'I mean,' she waved a beringed hand, 'anybody could have picked up that old locket in a curio store, and any girl with blonde hair could have put on a semblance to that tiny little painting in there—they can do anything with make-up these days—and claimed to be a descendant.' She laughed and patted her blue-tinted coiffure. 'Of course I don't belong to this famous old family with true-blue British blood in its veins—I only married into it, like Carrie here. New Jersey's always been our home, and nine generations has sure diluted our original Dutch blood.' She paused to take breath and glanced up again at the portrait. 'Yes, now I've seen her beside that picture ... yes, I guess I'll believe anything after that!'

Her sister, Alayne's mother, was a quieter, slimmer edition of the ebullient Aunt Louella. She was a music-lover in the genuine sense of the word and once the subject was broached discussed it knowledgeably with Mark, in contrast to Aunt Louella, who, her niece teasingly informed them, was a blatant celebrity-hunter, quite regardless of the particular talent concerned.

Despite this Aunt Louella proved great fun and easy to know during the four days the visitors spent at Hillcrest.

Andrew, who had a few days' break that week, was invited to join a day's outing to York and a meal at night which the American ladies were insisting on hostessing.

'You must, Andrew,' said Alayne, laughing. 'Think of poor Mark at the mercy of *five* females!'

Linzi watched him anxiously, half expecting him to refuse or plead a prior engagement. He had made it all too plain to her what he thought of Mark Vardan.

But Andrew grinned and bowed to Alayne. 'I'd be delighed—but we'll still be hopelessly outnumbered.'

'Charmingly outnumbered,' Mark corrected, smiling.

Was he aware of Andrew's dislike? Linzi wondered. But how could he be? He scarcely knew the younger man, who had never made an effort to further the acquaintanceship, despite his kindly aunt's long association with the Vardan family. But whatever the personal opinions of the two men towards one another neither betrayed any indication of animosity. Alayne changed all that, Linzi reflected, trying not to notice that Andrew had hardly acknowledged her own presence since his arrival with a large basket of mushrooms Nanny had asked him to call for on his way from town. It must be wonderful to have that special élan, Linzi thought. That way Alayne had of charming the opposite sex without being either coquettish or ingratiating, and her sense of humour that was so infectious.

She was unaware of the wistfulness in her eyes as she watched Andrew talking to the American girl. She caught the words 'Red Manor' and saw Alayne shake her head. Mark said something and moved away, and Andrew looked disappointed. Had he asked Alayne if she was going to stay on for the gala? Or had Mark arranged to take her?

Linzi's mouth quivered. The thought of Alayne as his partner, of Mark taking her in his arms ... She caught at herself impatiently and looked away, straight into Mark's eyes. He raised his brow a fraction, and colour flashed in her cheeks. He took a step in her direction, and then Aunt Louella came hurrying down the stairs.

'Well, is everyone ready—hope you're not all waiting for me!'

Mark stopped, and whatever he might have intended saying remained unsaid. Andrew begged for ten minutes to hurry down to the lodge and change into something a little more befitting than the ancient cords he was clad in at that moment, and the company began a leisured move out to the cars.

The weather stayed fine, if sharp, enabling the visitors to indulge in four packed days of sightseeing. The fact that the holiday season was over made no difference; in fact, Aunt Louella announced that she much preferred it that way. 'No automobiles fender to fender all the way. No queues everywhere and double dues.' And the colours of the countryside had a depth and a difference that were fascinating. They shot reel after reel of film, including lots of indoor shots of the house as well as personal pictures of Gilda and Mark.

On their last day they drove to the coast, across the Fylingdales moor, past the three great scanners of the early warning station which lay like giant white golf balls on the rolling expanse of wild moorland, and down to the old part of Whitby, where the indefatigable Aunt Louella climbed the hundred and ninety-nine steps to the abbey—and swore she counted two hundred—accompanied by Andrew and Alayne, while Mark, Linzi and Mrs Redmand took Gilda along the harbourside where they watched a timber boat unloading, until Gilda said she felt cold and they returned to the cars to await the others.

There was just time before dusk to make the detour a few

miles south to the quaint old town of Robin Hood's Bay, where Aunt Louella set off firmly down the steep hill which was barred to traffic, undeterred by the prospect of yet another long ascent of steps on the return journey.

'I must see it,' she said. 'Did you know that the sea actually rushes up the slipway at the bottom there, and once a ship's prow went through the inn window? And a whole street full of houses fell into the sea one stormy night?' She buttoned her jacket against the keen wind and clutched her guide book firmly. 'You can wait for me in the car if you haven't the strength.'

'Someone must stay with Gilda,' said Alayne. 'The hill looks too steep for her chair.'

'I'll stay with Gilda,' said Linzi.

After a hesitation Mark decided to accompany the others, and Gilda and Linzi remained in the warmth of the big comfortable Lincoln, watching the greyness gather across the North Sea. The sun had vanished an hour ago, and the flurries of wind against the car were reminders that winter was not far away.

For quite a while Gilda was silent, her eyes thoughtful. Then she sighed. 'I wish Alayne didn't have to go away tomorrow.'

'Is she definitely going back with her mother?' Linzi asked idly.

'I think so.' Gilda frowned. 'It depends on a phone call she's going to make tonight when we get home.'

Linzi stayed silent. Alayne seemed very much in command of her own destiny; obviously there was a further plan under way and when it was working out as required Alayne would make one of her blithe announcements and no one, not even Aunt Louella, would succeed in diverting the course of that plan.

The gulls came wheeling in from the sea, to settle on chimney pots above the ancient red pantiled roofs and scream their raucous communications. There was something fascinating about the cry of a gull, Linzi thought idly, and wondered how the old sea legend had originated. Were they the souls of the seafarers whom the sea had claimed down the centuries? Some said a sailor would never kill a gull ... Linzi shivered at the morbidity of her thoughts. She glanced across the deserted car park and observed: 'We're the only car here.'

There was no reply. Gilda's expression was faraway and her eyes remote. Suddenly, as though jerked back to reality, she turned her head.

'I was just thinking ... I wish Alayne would fall in love with my father.'

Linzi started violently. With an effort she controlled her voice. 'Do you?'

Gilda nodded. 'And if Daddy were to fall in love with her and marry her it would be perfect.'

'Would it?'

Gilda was too preoccupied with her train of thought to notice the catch in Linzi's voice. 'Yes, because it would make it all come right. As though it were meant. She would be back home properly, her real home. Don't you see, Linzi? It's as though the Lilac Girl had another chance of happiness. As though she got everything back that she lost. I think she would be happy to know that Alayne was going to live here. It's the way it would happen in a storybook.'

'But things don't work out that way in real life,' Linzi said in so sharp a tone that Gilda recoiled, startled by the curt response.

The child's shoulders drooped and she clasped her hands together as though they were cold. 'I suppose not,' she said tiredly. 'But if Daddy did decide to get married again there's no reason why he shouldn't marry Alayne, is there?'

Stung by compunction, Linzi shook her head. 'No reason at all,' she said sadly.

The gulls were in flight again, long curving loops over the grey sea, and their mournful cries struck an answering echo in Linzi's heart that was like a pain. Perhaps the spark of love between Mark and Alayne was already alight. Gilda's idea was not in the least impossible. For perhaps her intense fascination with the subject of the portrait was to prove to have been a strange sense of foresight.

Perhaps it was all ordained.

The house seemed sad and silent after the visitors had gone.

November dawned, bringing a chill damp and mist. For three days it persisted, white, clammy, depressing, imprisoning the great house and its occupants.

Mark reverted back to his more sombre self, immersing himself in his work and leaving the care of Gilda almost entirely in Linzi's hands. They saw him at meals, and the bedtime hour remained unchanged. but his responses were taciturn, and obviously his composition was occupying all his attention. Very often Linzi got the impression that Mark was scarcely aware of anything she happened to say to him.

Andrew went back to university on the Monday; Linzi wouldn't see him again until the day of the Red Manor affair, and even Gilda admitted that there was little else to do but lessons.

She was remarkably cheerful, however. The result of Alayne's telephone call to London the evening before her departure had been entirely satisfactory to Gilda, if not entirely so to Mrs Redmand and Aunt Louella. But it did not come as a surprise to Linzi.

Alayne had decided to remain in England until the New Year. The phone call had told her that her request for a work permit had been granted; she was going to take a temporary job in a big department store for the six-week pre-Christmas period. And she was coming back to Hillcrest for Christmas.

'And then I might, *might* be going to America in the spring,' Gilda announced gleefully. 'Won't that be super?'

Linzi tried to be enthusiastic, but her own heart was further burdened by this latest development. There had been no mention of the possibility of Gilda seeing the American specialist Alayne had mentioned, and Linzi kept silent. Mark would broach this himself to his daughter when he deemed the time was right. At least there was no further talk of the boarding school for Gilda, and Linzi could only hope, for Gilda's sake, that whatever decision might finally be made it would be the best one for the child's future and her happiness.

Of her own future Linzi did not care to think. But soon she would have to talk to Mark Vardan. If he was not going to require her services from the New Year onward—and whatever happened, whether Gilda went to school or to the States, it seemed unlikely that Linzi would be required in either event—she would have to find another job. But she felt strangely reluctant to approach Mark, and when an occasion did present itself she found herself ignoring it. She could not banish the memory of that night when he had first transported her into a heaven of newly discovered delight, only to bring her crashing back into despair with his warning to stay away from him. Nor would she ever forget the embarrassment of being caught eavesdropping. Sometimes, when she encountered Mark's glance, she imagined he too remembered, and wished the unfortunate incidents had never happened.

At the end of the week Gilda decided to interest herself in the matter of Linzi's appearance for the Red Manor gala night. After some thought Linzi decided to send home for her dress rather than buy a new one. The white and gilt creation languishing in her wardrobe at home had been worn only once, on the occasion of a visit to Glyndebourne with Ian; it had been extremely expensive, and now it did not seem to matter that it marked an unhappy memory, and that she had vowed never to wear it again.

When it arrived with the Thursday morning post, and she unfolded it from the mass of tissue in which her mother had so carefully packed it, she found she was echoing Gilda's gasp of delight, and could even smile wryly at the memory of her tragic self, shutting the dress away with her other mementoes of memories of Ian. She had believed she would never love again, never remember without heartache. Well, she still had her heartache—but for a totally different cause! Had she been in love with love? Perhaps. If only she could persuade herself that in a few months, away from the dark lodestar Mark Vardan had come to represent, she might find her heart breaking free.

'Try it on,' Gilda urged. 'I'll shut the door.'

As she spoke she propelled herself with that surprisingly quick speed to the door, pushed it shut, and swung her chair to face Linzi.

They were in the lounge, and a bright cheerful fire was sending its warm glow out, and impulsively Linzi slipped out of her skirt and pulled her blue sweater over her head. In a trice she had donned the white dress, rather anxiously smoothing its lovely flowing folds down over her hips and fastening the gold links of the belt to reassure herself that it still fitted—how awful if all this wonderful Yorkshire home cooking had wrought a certain undesirable effect!

But it hadn't. The gold belt still encircled her slim waist with ease, aiding the clinging nylon georgette to mould her slender curves to their most attractive advantage.

'Linzi, it's super!' breathed Gilda. 'Have you got proper dancing shoes?'

'They're here as well.' Linzi fished the dainty evening sandals out of the box and slid her toes under the criss-cross of delicate gold-straps. 'And I had my hair on top when I wore it to the opera. Like this.' Suddenly excited at the de luxe feel

146

of a dress in which she knew she looked her best, she held her hair bunched high with both hands and twirled round in the centre of the room.

'It's lovely,' Gilda sighed again. 'I wish I could go with you.'

'Perhaps you'll be able to go to lots of gala dances when you're older and the doctors cure your back,' Linzi said softly, beginning to free the zip at the back.

Fortunately it did not stick, but as she eased the dress off one of the tiny gilt clips that shaped the halter neck caught in her hair, bringing a small 'Ouch!' from her as she tried to free herself. She was still struggling when the door opened and Mark Vardan walked in.

He stopped short, exclaiming at the unexpected sight of the slender girl with flushed face, bent awkwardly in bra and lace mini-slip while she held the voluminous white folds of the dress in the crook of one arm as her fingers sought to part a trapped tendril of hair and the halter clip.

She did not hear him enter, but she heard his exclamation and looked up. Fire rushed into cheeks already pink with exertion, and Gilda cried: 'Help her, Daddy—she's caught in something!'

Linzi tried desperately to hold the dress in front of her, and Mark backed away.

'I don't think Linzi wants my help,' he exclaimed, his hand going back to the door edge behind.

'Don't be silly, Daddy,' Gilda said quickly. 'You know each other—and I can't reach from here.'

He stopped as she moved forward. 'No, keep the wheels of that chair away.' His mouth compressed. He turned to Linzi and firmly moved her hands away. 'Stand still.'

She clasped her arms across her breast and felt sure that she must be scarlet all over while Mark gently worked the little tangle of soft hair free. She dared not look at his face, and it didn't ease the situation at all when Gilda, surveying her father's efforts critically, remarked: 'If there was a fire in the night you'd have to see Linzi in her nightie, so there's no need to be shy now.'

'Be quiet, Gilda.' Mark stepped back. He held the dress out awkwardly. 'I'm sorry—I didn't expect a trying-on session. Is this for the Red Manor affair?'

'Yes ...' She was feverishly struggling into her sweater, seizing her skirt. Why did he have to walk in at that precise moment?

147

'Put it on again! Let him see!' cried Gilda.

'I—I'm dressed now. And it'll have to be pressed.' She pushed her hair back, hardly knowing what she was saying, and almost snatched the dress from him. 'I must go and put it on a hanger.'

She gathered up the long box, pushing the waves of white tissue into it, looked blindly for her shoes and realised she was still wearing them, and snatched up her casuals. *Why* did the advent of Mark Vardan reduce her to a state of near-delirium? Simply because he'd caught her in her slip?

Gilda said cheerfully, 'Never mind, you'll see her dress on the night—you're still going, Daddy, aren't you?'

'Yes.'

He had his back to Linzi now as she made for the door. As she reached it thankfully and manoeuvred her armful of things to draw the door close she heard Mark add:

'That's what I came to tell you. I've just had a phone call from Aunt Sharon—she's going too.'

'Aunt Sharon!'

'She's coming tomorrow, until Monday.'

Gilda received the news with predictable disgust.

'I thought the winter would keep her away—at least till Christmas,' she groaned. 'I should have thought there were plenty of dances she could've gone to in London without coming all the way up here.'

But Mark isn't in London, thought Linzi. She felt flat and dejected, unable to whip up any excited anticipation for the Saturday affair, and she was beset by the doubt that Andrew was no longer looking forward to it with the same enthusiasm of several weeks previously, when he had been so anxious to secure tickets before they sold out. But that was before they had quarrelled over Mark, before he had accused her of falling in love with Mark ... before he had described through the golden haze of boyish love the woman who had been Mark's wife...

As ever, the doubts began. Had all the rumours of Lucille Vardan's infidelity been untrue after all? Was it Mark's own cold, uncaring selfishness that had driven his wife to seek consolation in another man's arms?

Linzi tried to push the tormenting questions out of her mind. She would never know now; it was doubtful if anyone

148

ever would know the truth. She could only cling to the one guiding factor; that of the love and loyalty of a child for her father. In Gilda's eyes her father was the centre of all devotion; that in itself, for Linzi, had to cancel out whatever else he might be, in his relationship to his late wife, to other women, to herself ...

Sharon arrived late on the Friday evening, driving up this time instead of coming by rail. She greeted Mark intimately, embracing and kissing him apparently without care for the two unsmiling onlookers in the background, then hauled an enormous dress box out of the back of the car.

'My dress—wait till you see it! It's a dream. From Paris, and not officially released yet,' she informed them exuberantly.

'Linzi has a gorgeous dress as well,' Gilda told her coolly.

'You're going too?' Sharon favoured Linzi with a cool smile. 'But not with ...?'

'Uncle Andrew's taking her—he's had the tickets for ages.'

'Oh.' Sharon made no further comment and turned a brilliant smile to Mark. 'I'll just get this on to a hanger, then I'll be with you—I'm longing for a drink.'

After dinner she and Mark withdrew to his own sanctum, after Sharon had announced that they had some business to discuss. Whatever the business might have been its nature remained undisclosed, however, and at breakfast next morning Sharon appeared to be in a very amiable humour, making more fuss than usual of Gilda and singling Linzi out as the recipient of a detailed account to date of the French fashion boutique she was running so successfully in town.

Mark did not take much part in the conversation. He looked thoughtful, worried almost, and as Gilda had retreated into her 'anti-Sharon' shell it was left to Linzi to keep a semblance of sociality going for the visitor.

At the end of the meal she was surprised when Sharon said unexpectedly, 'Have you a few moments? Let's pop up to my room. I've something for you.'

Puzzled, Linzi could not do anything else but agree, and found herself being presented with a crystal flacon of scent in a gold and white velvet box. It was exquisite in perfume and presentation, and of the kind that costs the earth, and she found difficulty in hiding bewilderment.

She looked at it helplessly and shook her head. 'For me?'

Sharon held up a graceful white hand and smiled. 'No— no thank-yous, please. I'm going to be honest with you, darling. This is a kind of peace-offering.'

'Peace-offering?' Linzi's brows narrowed.

'Yes.' Sharon's smile was winning now. 'I'm afraid we didn't exactly get off on the same foot during my last visit, and I sort of got the impression that you didn't like me very much. That made me defensive, a bit——' she waved her hands, 'a bit edgy with you. But now—well, I'm sure I'm mistaken, and I'm sure that you want to do the best for Gilda. That's the whole crux of the matter, isn't it? We all want what's best for her, poor little poppet. So I decided I must try to straighten matters out so that there are no more misunderstandings. Because I do realise how much you mean to her—oh, yes, you've gained quite an influence over her in the short time you've been here—and I'm sure you have her interest at heart as much as Mark and I have.'

Linzi inclined her head, her gaze steady on the other girl's face.

'So that's it!' Sharon moved slim shoulders in a deprecating shrug. 'I just wanted to say that if I seemed unfriendly in any way it wasn't meant to be personal, simply that I'm deeply concerned about Gilda. All forgiven?'

'Of course.' Linzi accepted the explanation without doubting its sincerity and tried to visualise herself in the other girl's place. To be strictly fair, it had to be admitted that Sharon had tried to do a great deal to help her young niece, and it must be hurtful to find good intentions met by determined dislike from the object of one's well-meant efforts. If Gilda's reaction to herself had been of a similar nature she would have felt very much the same when seeing the child respond affectionately to someone who was almost a stranger in comparison.

'I knew you'd understand.' Sharon's smile was brilliant now. She paused, glancing down at beautifully lacquered nails, then looked up again, her expression becoming serious. 'I'm sure Mark won't mind if I tell you how much he has come to depend on you, where Gilda's concerned. He needs your help as much as he needs mine. No man should have to cope with the problems he has. No wonder his career has had to be set aside.'

Sharon sat down at the dressing table as she finished speaking and touched the comb to her hair. She frowned at the result, and murmured, 'I don't think this damp moorland air exactly improves one's hair-do, does it?'

Plainly the interview was at an end, and the unspoken inference was perfectly clear. Linzi returned downstairs and found Gilda waiting patiently in the lounge.

Suddenly she felt like a traitor.

Andrew arrived in good time that evening to collect Linzi.

He looked different and quite startlingly handsome in evening clothes, and as his eyes lit with admiration at the sight of her she was suddenly glad she had taken extra pains with her appearance.

'We'll see them there?' His look was meaning. Plainly he had no wish to join up with Mark and Sharon for the evening.

'I expect so.'

She knew he was anxious to be away, but she hesitated, feeling she should tell Mark she was on the point of leaving. Then Mark appeared at the head of the stairs, still in dressing jacket over his evening trousers. He leaned over the carved rail.

'Don't wait for us—Sharon isn't ready, and I want to see Gilda settled for the night before I leave.'

Linzi nodded. 'By the way, I've just reminded Mrs Brinsmead to take Gilda's cocoa and biscuits up at half-past nine.'

'Thank you.' Mark sketched a small salute of acknowledgement and turned away.

The drive to Red Manor took about forty minutes and as the weather had decided to behave with circumspection Linzi was able to step out of the car without the spoilsport bother of wraps and scarves and avoidance of mud-splashes. The Red Manor was indeed a lovely, old-world manor, swathed in red ivy and surrounded by well-laid-out grounds. The gardens and the building were attractively floodlit, and an ancient creeper-clad fountain played on the terrace in front of the main entrance. Obviously great care had been taken to retain all the original beauty, and the interior panelling, among other features, had been carefully restored.

In the reception hall, which gave on to a cocktail lounge and an oak-lined bar, Linzi noticed the beautiful old vaulted ceiling and fine carved oak corbels around which concealed lighting had been set. An elderly man with a quiet air of authority who was standing a little to one side stepped forward and smiled at Linzi.

'Yes, it's Jacobean—you approve of our efforts?'

'Very much.' She smiled shyly. 'I was afraid, after seeing

151

the outside, that it might end there.'

'And the space age of decor begin?' The elderly man laughed, and introduced himself, then continued to chat in a friendly way as he showed Linzi and Andrew into the cocktail lounge and procured them drinks of their choice. A moment or so later he smilingly excused himself, but paused by the door to speak to a younger man who looked to be management. The younger man glanced towards Linzi, nodded and hurried away, to return almost immediately with a vellum-bound book embossed in scarlet and gold. He bestowed it on Linzi, with a small bow, and 'Mr Drisedale's compliments.'

The name of Edwin Drisedale had not conveyed anything to Linzi, but now, as she looked at the expensively produced book of the history of Red Manor and gave a gasp of surprise as well as pleasure, Andrew gave a soft whistle.

'I shall have to watch you tonight, I can see.'

'What do you mean?' She forgot her drink and opened the book curiously. 'Isn't it beautiful?'

'A most exclusive souvenir. I doubt if they've dished those out to all and sundry,' Andrew said dryly. 'You mean you don't know who that was?'

She shook her head.

'Only the owner! Of a few breweries here and there, a chain of hotels, the odd property or so in the city, and other interests too numerous to mention,' Andrew informed her in the same dry tones. 'He's supposed to be a bit of a philanthropist on the side, and the preservation of the environment is his latest pet concern. Which is probably why this place hasn't been spoilt in the sacred cause of commercialism.' Andrew stood up. 'Shall I go and put this in the car in case you mislay it? Then we'll go in to dinner.'

While Andrew was gone she looked round, seeking a glimpse of Mark, but there was no sign of the tall dark man who would stand out in any crowd, even one filled with many distinguished figures and opulently gowned women as was the gathering for this special occasion. It was not until she and Mark had almost finished a memorable meal in the huge dining room which overlooked the floodlit terrace and the lake at the rear of the manor that she saw Mark enter with Sharon at his side, escorted by Mr Drisedale.

Sharon looked breathtaking, in a silver and crystal creation that left bare her lovely shoulders and creamy throat, and glittered with every movement, enhancing the brilliant sheen

152

of her burning copper hair. Her poise was superb as she took her place beside Mark at Edwin Drisedale's table, and Linzi's heart contracted as Mark made a small courteous adjustment of his chair when Sharon sat down gracefully.

I might have been sitting there, if only ... Linzi whispered soundlessly, then felt so ashamed of the thought that she turned to Andrew and tried to smile.

But he did not return the smile. Indeed he curled warm fingers over her hand. 'Don't look like that,' he whispered.

She made a small despairing movement of her head that failed utterly as a denial.

'Haven't you forgiven me yet?'

'What for?' Her voice was unsteady.

'You know what for, and you know why,' he said huskily. 'For saying a lot of things I shouldn't have said that day. I tried to persuade you to question personal loyalties when I didn't have the right.' His clasp tightened on her hand. 'I was too late, wasn't I?'

There was a catch in her throat that all the champagne in the world could not banish, and suddenly she could not bear the thought of an emotional scene with Andrew, dear as he had become.

Gently she drew her hand out of his grasp. 'Of course I've forgiven you—there was nothing to forgive. Look, isn't that Tony Tristam over there?'

Andrew transferred his attention to the direction she indicated and nodded. 'The boyo himself—but not looking quite so magnificent in the flesh, methinks. The bags under his eyes are real, though.'

'And who says women are the bitchy sex?' Linzi reproved. 'For that you can ask him to autograph my programme for me.'

'Not likely! You can ask him yourself. Come on, let's dance.'

It was certainly a gala affair in the ballroom, with favours, balloons, spot prizes, a cabaret of famous performers compered by the handsome Tony Tristam, who was too experienced an entertainer to betray the fact that he was joined just a shade under the influence of the champagne bounty that was flowing like water that evening.

Andrew met several people he knew and to whom he introduced Linzi, but the evening did not burgeon into vitality for her until the moment that Mark threaded his way through the crowd and invited her and Andrew to join Sharon and himself for a drink.

Sharon was sparkling, patently having a wonderful time, and a moment or so later Edwin Drisedale joined them, bringing with him his daughter, a tall girl of about seventeen with dark hair and a merry smile. Her name was Carol, and she and Andrew discovered during the course of the conversation that they had a mutual friend at the college she was going to the following year, and still discussing the unknown friend they took to the floor. Edwin Drisedale claimed Sharon for the same dance, and at last Linzi was alone with Mark.

His eyes asked if she wanted to dance, and she put her glass down on the alcove table. He danced superbly, as she had known instinctively he would, and for the moment it was enough to be held in his arms, drifting in that strange, isolated intimacy that music and dance can bring on a crowded ballroom floor. Then she became aware of the silence between them. She stole a look up at his face and saw that his expression was remote, and the small spell of magic deflated like a pricked balloon. Of course he had merely asked her to dance because of politeness; he could scarcely have done otherwise. A quivering sigh ran through her, and suddenly she realised he was looking down into her face.

'You've never forgiven me, have you?' His mouth was unsmiling, hardly moving as he spoke.

She almost exclaimed: *Not you as well!* to the echo of a word so recently on another man's lips, even as she knew she could never make the same trite response to this man.

'I doubt if it matters whether I forgive, or am forgiven,' she said flatly.

'I see.' His mouth set in a thin straight line and he stared coldly past her, continuing to dance in silence.

Linzi bit her lip and wished, too late, that she had left the bitter little retort unspoken. The silence seemed to chill, and Mark's arms slacken, as though they were reluctant to go on guiding her till the music ended. Desperately she searched for something to say that would break the impasse, anything to take that grim, remote hardness out of his eyes.

'Mark, I'm sorry . . .'

'What for?'

'I—I didn't mean——' She stumbled, tried to correct her step, and he said in the same curt tone:

'You didn't mean what?'

'That—that——' She stopped abruptly, catching sight of a

154

man gesticulating at the edge of the floor. When the man saw that he had caught her attention he began to thread his way towards them. Her hand slid down Mark's shoulder, gripping his arm. 'Mark, I think someone wants . . .'

At that moment the man reached them and touched Mark's shoulder.

'What the——!' Mark spun round.

'I'm sorry, sir.' The man stepped back. 'But you're wanted on the phone. The lady said it was urgent. I think you'd better take it, sir.'

'Lady?' Mark's brows drew together, and his arm slid away from Linzi's waist. 'Who?'

'She didn't give her name, sir. Something about a little girl . . . She seemed upset. If you come this way . . .'

Mark did not wait. With a jerked, 'Gilda!' he almost ran from the floor, heedless of indignant looks from a couple with whom he collided. Sudden fear darkened Linzi's eyes and she hurried after him, pushing past the dancers and the people sauntering and talking along the wide corridors.

For a few moments she lost sight of him, then she saw the open doorway of an office richly carpeted in crimson, and Mark with the phone in his hand. She saw the colour drain from his face and the shock in his eyes. Then he dropped the receiver on its rest and came unsteadily towards the door.

'It's Gilda. She's gone! *She's missing!*'

CHAPTER TEN

GILDA missing!

It was unbelievable. It couldn't be true. How could it happen? Linzi asked herself over and over again during the nightmare race back to Hillcrest. How could a little crippled girl simply vanish into the night?

'I don't understand it!' Mark kept repeating, his foot driving the accelerator flat to the floor. 'The woman must have made a mistake. She must be dreaming. Gilda can't have gone. It's impossible. Unless . . .'

His lean features set into a pale mask of anguish, and his unspoken fear communicated itself instantly to Linzi. Had Gilda been kidnapped? She dared not voice the fear, trying desperately to convince herself that it was all a nightmare, that those stunned moments when Mark turned from the

155

phone to recount Mrs Brinsmead's frantic message had never happened. It had to be a mistake...

But the forlorn hope was swiftly quenched when the car roared up the drive and the figure of the housekeeper was outlined in the bright rectangle of light at the open door.

Mark leapt from the car. 'What happened? How did——?'

'I don't know, sir.' The woman's hands clenched on the air. 'Oh, I'm so glad you came—I didn't know what to do—whether to——'

Mark brushed past her, to rush across the hall and take the stairs two at a time. Mrs Brinsmead looked as white as death, and it was left to Linzi to close the heavy door on the cold night wind that swirled into the house. For the first time since leaving Red Manor she realised that they had left the others behind and it was possible that Sharon and Andrew did not yet know of Mark's abrupt departure. When he had shouldered past Linzi after that startling announcement she had stood for a moment, stunned by shock and disbelief, then without thinking she had raced after him, straight outside without a thought of collecting her wrap, and had almost fallen into the car as he started to drive off. Now she stood irresolute, knowing she should telephone the other two, yet every instinct forcing her to follow Mark. The need to see for herself won and she sped up the stairs to where light streamed from the open door of Gilda's room.

Mark appeared there, like a man who could not believe the evidence of his own eyes. 'She's not there! But how? Tell me how?'

She looked past him, at the big familiar room with its pastel shades and its dainty furnishings, at the settee with the three dolls, their wide china blue eyes staring vacantly under silken lashes at the empty bed, the bed that had been slept in, plainly, but where the tousled, turned-back clothes revealed only a rumpled pink sheet and two frilled pillows slightly askew.

Linzi ran to the bathroom, saw the light burning in its emptiness, then threw open the door that led to her own room. The light burned there, too, where Mark had already looked in the frantic minutes he preceded her. She opened the wardrobe doors, the cupboard, found them exactly as she left them, and ran back into Gilda's room to find him pulling back the window curtains.

He swung round, his eyes demented with fear. 'Her dressing gown's on the floor here, by the bed.'

Linzi picked it up, folded it without realising her hands did the motions, and saw him stoop to snatch up the small, furry blue slippers that still lay side by side on the floor by the bed. He stared at them, then dropped them and shook his head. 'I'm going to phone——'

Mrs Brinsmead caught up with them, appearing at the bedroom door. She said, 'I've looked for her, Mr Vardan, in there, and Miss Shadwyn's room. I thought she might have tried to get to the bathroom, because I was late in——'

'What time was this?' he cut in.

'Just before I phoned you.' Mrs Brinsmead wrung her hands. 'She was all right when I brought her cocoa up at five to nine. You see, there was a play I was waiting to see on television, so I asked her if she minded having it a bit earlier, just before it started, and she said no, and that she was feeling a bit tired and she'd read the thing her Aunty Sharon had left for her and she was——'

'What thing?' Mark snapped.

'One of those brochure things.' Mrs Brinsmead showed a flicker of surprise that he should question this at such a time. She crossed to the bed and drew a slim, glossy brochure the size of a small magazine from the shelf in the bedside cabinet. She held it out. 'It's for the special school you're sending Miss Gilda to after Christmas. She showed it to me—there's a picture of the swimming team and the two children who entered the special sporting events they have for paraplegics. She was having a little bit of a cry to herself, but I told her she'd beat them all if she really put her mind to it, and she said yes, she'd try hard, and,' Mrs Brinsmead paused unhappily and looked at Linzi, as though for some assurance that she wasn't to blame, 'then she said I hadn't to bother sitting up if I didn't want to, because you and Miss Shadwyn had promised to look in when you got home and if she was still awake you would tell her all about Red Manor and what Tony Tristam was like.'

Mrs Brinsmead sighed, and avoided Mark's stare as she went on more slowly: 'So I went back downstairs and watched the play. It finished at ten, and then I meant to get up and make myself a cup of tea and a bite to eat, and go up to get Miss Gilda's supper things. But I picked up the evening paper to glance at the headlines, and I must have dozed off, for the next thing was I heard the clock strike eleven. I don't know how I came to do that, I don't usually——'

'Never mind,' Mark said impatiently. 'Didn't you hear anything? Anybody breaking in, or prowling round, or any suspicious sounds? Damn it all, you must have heard something, woman.'

'I didn't,' she said vehemently. 'It was like I told you on the phone. I put the kettle on for my cup of tea and while it was on I went upstairs, quietly, because I thought she'd be asleep and I didn't want to disturb her. Her little bedside light was still on and then I saw the empty bed. Just as it is now. I couldn't think what had happened, and I said, "Gilda, where are you?" and she didn't answer. Then I thought she'd wanted to go to the bathroom and tried to get there by herself because there was nobody to help her—she did once, you remember, Mr Vardan? Rolled out on to the floor and tried to crawl and drag herself along, and you came in and found her on the floor and she was crying.'

'I remember.' Mark's eyes clouded. 'And then . . .?'

'Well, nothing.' Mrs Brinsmead shook her head hopelessly. 'She wasn't in the bathroom, and I looked in Miss Shadwyn's room, and I didn't know what to do. I mean, how could she be anywhere else but here? She couldn't be downstairs, poor lamb, I didn't know *what* to do, so I ran straight down to the phone and called you.'

'I'll phone the police.' Mark strode from the room, leaving the housekeeper and Linzi to stare at each other with wide, frightened eyes.

The same question loomed, unanswerable. What had happened to Gilda? How could she just vanish without leaving any apparent trace? Then Linzi exclaimed aloud, 'Her clothes!'

She opened the wardrobe, checking quickly along the rack of garments. Mrs Brinsmead joined her, drawing out each pair of shoes in turn. She straightened.

'Her brown shoes aren't here.'

'Neither is her pink dress—the angora wool one.' Linzi whirled round. 'Look in the drawers, see if you find anything else missing. I'm going to see if her brown gaberdine is still downstairs.'

Linzi hurried away and found that the coat was indeed missing from the hall coat rack. She turned breathlessly to find Mark crossing the hall.

They both began speaking at the same time, then Mark stopped, letting her exclaim her discovery. He nodded grimly. 'The police are coming. They wanted to know if there's any sign of a break-in. We'd better start searching, but hadn't you ...?'

He stopped with a gesture, and Linzi became aware of her now incongruous-seeming attire. She turned away.

'I'll change as quickly as I can, then I'll help you.'

All the time she was stripping off her evening clothes and thrusting into more sensible slacks and pullover Linzi's brain was trying to find answers. But she kept coming back to the same fear; that Gilda had been kidnapped. The dreadful possibility was not unfeasible; it must be fairly widely known that Mark was a wealthy man and that he was devoted to his only child. Gilda would be helpless to resist, and even if Mrs Brinsmead had not been dozing it was unlikely that she would hear anything from her sitting room with the television going full blast. Even if a cry for help had been allowed to escape the child ...

Linzi felt sick and frightened when she hurried downstairs. Suddenly the house had become filled with foreboding and she was aware of its dark vast ramble of unused rooms and corridors. She longed for Mark's nearness, the reassurance of his strength, and then when she found him in one of the big storerooms beyond the kitchen quarters her heart ached at the sight of his taut worried features.

The longing to give comfort was intense, but how could she give anything but the empty phrases of hope? He brushed past her, his hand flicking out to check her when she would have switched off the light.

'I'm leaving the light on in each room as I check—but there isn't a sign so far.'

When she looked at the great bolts and locks on all the outer doors, the securely fastened windows, some of which, in the store-rooms, the gunroom, and the old sculleries, were either barred or showed the unmistakable seal of disuse in cobwebs, Linzi began to feel their search for an intruder was wasting time. She wanted to rush outside and look for people to ask if they had seen any sign of a little girl ... If only the police would come ...

They arrived in a very short time, even though it seemed an eternity to Linzi, and then all the explanations had to be recounted again. Linzi fretted with impatience while the young detective questioned Mark. At the mention of Red Manor he frowned.

'You say she's crippled. Did you leave her here alone?' His look and his gestures seemed to accuse and encompass the whole of the lonely old house.

'My housekeeper lives in.' Mark's voice was thin. 'Gilda is never left alone.'

The detective nodded, then told his companion to have a look round while Mrs Brinsmead repeated her account. At Mark's request Linzi went with the constable, covering first the section of the ground floor she and Mark had already searched. The constable did not make any comments until they reached the vast old drawing room with its shrouded furnishings.

'Do you never got lost in here?' He smiled faintly at Linzi. She shook her head and closed the door.

He glanced round, then pointed to the door at the far end of the passage. 'Where does that lead?'

'Into the other wing. We don't really use it.'

He tried the door. 'We'd better have a look. Have you the key, miss?'

Linzi went to get it, and for a moment thought that Gilda must have hidden it. After a hurried search she located it in one of Gilda's many boxes of 'treasures' and hurried downstairs again. But the secret wing gave up no secrets, nor any indication of what had become of the missing child. Back in the library the detective sighed and said: 'Upstairs now,' and Mark groaned.

'This is going to take hours, sergeant.'

The detective looked sympathetic. 'We must, sir. You see, it seems logical to rule out the possibility that she played a childish prank and hid from you. You say she's unable to walk, and that she's a sensible child, therefore wherever she went she had to be carried. But we have to make sure she isn't still in the house.'

'She might be,' cried Mrs Brinsmead. 'Maybe she can't cry out to let you know . . .'

Mark made no further demur and the upper floor was thoroughly searched, all the window fastenings carefully examined, without any trace of what they sought.

They returned downstairs as Sharon and Andrew arrived.

Sharon looked furious, but she quickly calmed down when she discovered what had happened. 'We didn't even know you'd left,' she cried, 'and nobody could tell us why. We knew something must have happened, but I never dreamed it was . . . this.' Her hands fluttered and she went to him. 'Oh, Mark, try not to worry too much. We'll find her—I know it. I would sense it if—if anything dreadful had happened to her.'

The young detective did not appear unduly impressed by this demonstration of feminine intuition. He put the photograph of Gilda which Mark had supplied carefully into his notebook and walked to the door.

'We'll do everything we can, sir. Now we've got this description. You'll let us know immediately if you hear anything at this end?'

Mark nodded bleakly, and the two policemen went out to their car.

'Are you all right?' Andrew had come silently to Linzi's side and put his arm round her shoulders. 'This is a shock.'

She nodded, close to tears now that the reaction was setting in. 'I'm sorry I ran off without telling you, but when Mark got the message I just came with him, without thinking.'

'I understand.' His arm tightened. 'Come and sit down. You can't do anything at the moment.'

'We can search the grounds,' Mark said, disengaging himself from Sharon's hand on his arm. 'At least we'll feel we're doing something.'

Andrew went with him, armed with torches, and the two girls huddled on chairs in the kitchen, sipping the hot tea which Mrs Brinsmead had made. The silence of despair descended as the long minutes dragged by, and when the phone shrilled they all started, eyes wide in faces drained of colour. Linzi moved first, running along the passage to the open door of the library. Sharon was close behind her as she lifted the receiver with a trembling hand.

'Who is it?' demanded Sharon.

Linzi hardly heard her. The voice at the other end was almost the last one she expected to hear—the light, soft drawling voice of Alayne, now husky with puzzlement as she asked for Gilda.

Linzi told her unsteadily, biting her lip as the distressed response came over the line. Then it was her turn to gasp at Alayne's startling message.

Gilda had telephoned her an hour ago.

'I was out—I've just got back—but Janie was in the apartment and she said it was definitely a child's voice. She thought the name was Gerda at first, then she remembered my telling her about you all, and was sure it was Gilda. But in the middle of it all those darned pips went and the line went dead. Janie waited for the number to ring again, but nothing. I know it's late, but I had to call back. I couldn't imagine what would set her to call me at that time. It was nearly eleven, Janie thinks, though she didn't think to check the time,' Alayne paused. 'If only I'd stayed home! Mark must be out of his mind.'

'He is.' Linzi's knuckles shone white as she gripped the receiver. 'She didn't tell Janie where she was, or what had happened?'

'No.' Alayne's worried sigh came over clearly. 'Just that she wanted me, and where was I, and what time would I be back. God! If only I——' Alayne paused, and when she spoke again her voice was more controlled. 'Tell me, is there *anything* I can do? Shall I come up?'

Linzi shook her head, uncaring that it was a futile gesture which couldn't be seen. 'We're waiting to hear from the police. Mark and Andrew are searching the grounds. But it's dark, and—and——' Her voice broke and she swallowed hard.

'I understand. Now listen, I'm going to clear this line. Tell Mark I'm praying for her, and please let me know the minute you hear anything. I don't think I'll be going to bed tonight,' she concluded wryly.

Linzi put down the phone and hurried from the room, ignoring Sharon's detaining hand. She did not want to stop to recount the gist of the interchange between herself and Alayne; all she wanted was to find Mark and tell him that his daughter was apparently alive and well at eleven o'clock that evening.

But the question still remained; where? It was impossible to trace the call, the police said, although they had immediately put a call round the local exchanges to see if any operator remembered putting through a call to the London number. But they were afraid it had been made STD from a callbox, and the child had not had sufficient change to extend the call—if it *had* been Gilda.

They read the same doubt in each other's eyes: how could it have been Gilda?

At a quarter to one Mark phoned the police station to see if there was any news. It was a vain hope, and the chill of despair engulfed them again. Mrs Brinsmead suggested more coffee and Mark grimaced. No one could face coffee, let alone food. Andrew went down to the lodge to let Nanny Tarrance know what had happened and tell her that he was staying at the house in case there was anything he could do to help. She

162

thereupon insisted on coming back with him, and there were six worried people sitting in Mark's library, frustrated by their sheer helplessness to do something constructive. Mark and Andrew wanted to drive out and scour the countryside, but Sharon and Linzi, for once in agreement realised the futility of such an action. For where did they begin? How could they knock on every door? How could they keep in touch? And if a call came from the police how would Mark and Andrew be contacted quickly. The emergency call which had gone out before the late news bulletin would alert a tremendous number of people; perhaps one of whom might have seen or heard something to provide a clue to the where-abouts of the missing child.

At one o'clock Mark begged the two girls to go and rest, but neither could bear the thought of trying to sleep, and a little while after this it began to snow.

They watched from the window, the slow, thin drifting fall which gradually thickened into a soft curtain of white. The chill fingers of winter seemed to close round the house, their icy dominance penetrating the walls despite the warmth within and the glowing fire in the library.

'This is all we need!' Mark groaned. 'Even the damned weather——'

The jangle of the phone cut into his words. With two strides he reached it, and in the sudden hush as he picked up the receiver Linzi hardly dared breathe.

They watched his face, trying to read hope in the clipped monosyllables of his responses, then a sigh that was a physi-cal pain ran through Linzi as he exclaimed:

'Thank God! I'll get over there right away and——'

He stopped. A frown knit his brows, and his lips moved, shaping protests he seemed unable to voice until the person at the other end stopped speaking. Then some of the tension went out of his shoulders. 'Very well—but I could save him the journey. It's a filthy night.' A pause, then, 'And she's safe? Unhurt?'

There was the faint crackling response, then Mark fumbled the receiver back on to its rest. He pressed his hands down on the desk top, supporting himself, his head bent, for a few moments before he slowly straightened and turned.

'She's safe.' Strength seemed to have drained from him. He crossed to the drinks cabinet and splashed spirits into a glass, then gave a gesture which was an invitation to anyone who wanted a drink to help themselves. No one moved, and he sank into a chair, taking a gulp of his drink. 'She's with a Doctor Whyndale at Sheriff Wold.'

'Where?' exclaimed Sharon.

'Sheriff Wold. It's a small market town about twenty miles from here. No,' his breath expelled in a long sigh, 'don't ask me how she got there. There's a lot I don't understand, but apparently this doctor is much concerned about her. He's insisted on bringing her back himself.'

'At this time?' Sharon looked amazed.

Mark shrugged wearily.

'Who is this Doctor Whyndale, anyway? And how did she come to be at this place, wherever it is?' demanded Sharon.

Mark got up and paced across the room, ignoring her questions. He stopped at the window and peered out into the darkness. 'I wonder how long it will take?' he muttered worriedly.

No one replied, and after a short silence Nanny Tarrance touched Andrew on the shoulder and whispered something to him. He nodded and they stood up. Nanny went to Mark's side and said gently: 'We'll be going now, laddie. You'll be better without a lot of folk fussing around when she comes home.'

'No . . .' Mark shook his head.

'Yes,' said Nanny firmly, 'I think the bairn'll be wanting her daddy and nobody else. If you need us we're not far away and you've only to ask.'

With a glance round and a softly spoken goodnight she went from the room, and after a hesitation Andrew followed, pausing to put his hand on Linzi's shoulder and say his quiet goodnight to her. She returned it unsteadily and watched him go. Already the gala occasion at Red Manor seemed to have happened in another time, long forgotten, and the present stood still, waiting . . .

The headlights' wash of radiance and the soft swish of tyres on the thin icing of snow came exactly thirty-five minutes later. The portico light and the hall lights spilled from the house and clearly illuminated the big Daimler limousine drawing to a halt at the door. Mark ran out as the car stopped, and Linzi clenched her hands so hard the nails bit into her palms. The cold wind cut through her pullover, but for the moment she was not conscious of the cold, or of Sharon huddled into a fur wrap and shivering at her side.

A big man in a sheepskin jacket and country cap was coming round the front of the car, speaking briefly to Mark, and then opening the rear door. He put out one hand, checking Mark's move, and reached into the car.

A moment later Sharon gave an incredulous gasp, and Linzi's hand fluttered to her throat. Then tears stung into her eyes and spilled over.

For, supported between Mark and the stranger, Gilda came towards her. *Walking.*

The thin drift of falling snow flecked Gilda's hair, and her feet left small black imprints in the white coating on the gravel. Linzi and Sharon fell back as the two men and the child entered the outer hall, and then Sharon recovered from amazement. She ran forward and seized the child's hands.

'I don't believe it! You're walking! Have you been a fraud all this time?'

The child's face closed and her hands wrenched out of Sharon's grasp. She did not speak, but there was total rejection in every line of her slight body. Then her mouth crumpled and with a cry she turned blindly to her father.

He swung her up into his arms, cradled her head against his shoulder, and uttered a shuddering sigh that was an unashamed sob. 'Darling baby,' he murmured brokenly. 'Is it true?'

Her head moved convulsively against him, and he whispered: 'But why, my precious? Why did——?'

'I'm sorry, Daddy, I don't know. But I had to—because you were going to send me away—and marry Aunt Sharon, and I knew you didn't want me.' She gulped and fastened thin arms fiercely round his neck. 'When she gave me the book thing about the school I thought it was all true that Mummy said about you, that you didn't want us, and when I broke my leg I heard you say to the doctor, "She *will* walk again?" and he said he hoped so but they weren't sure of the extent of the damage, and then I knew I wouldn't because it was a punishment for what I did when I tried to make Mummy go back to you instead of going to the airport to go away with Uncle Bart and the car crashed, and it was my fault because I pulled the wheel and——' She couldn't go on for the sobs that shook her whole body, and Mark's face wore the expression of a man who had glimpsed hell.

He covered her brow and the tangled hair with kisses and held her close, murmuring to her, trying to soothe her.

165

Beside Linzi, the big grey-bearded man sighed softly under his breath. 'I knew it,' he whispered. 'It was a cry for help. This is why I felt I had to bring her back myself and see her father.' He took a step forward, and at the same time Mark turned. The look he directed at them was hard, but his voice was tender as he said:

'No, you won't be going to that school, my precious, nor will I be marrying anyone who doesn't love you as much as I do. We'll be going back home soon, and you'll go back to your own school, and see Jane and Caroline and Mandy again, and we're going to forget all this, for ever.'

He drew a deep breath. 'Too many people have tried to tell me what to do best for my own child. In future I'll be grateful to be left to make my own decisions.'

Sharon's mouth opened. 'If you mean *me*, Mark, I've only tried to help.'

'I'm aware of that, and I'm grateful. But now . . .' He turned towards the stairs, holding his burden as though she was the most vital part of his existence. 'Gilda is going to learn to walk again—I think we both are.'

CHAPTER ELEVEN

LINZI slept late the next morning, after lying awake long after silence at last enfolded the old house. Now, roused by Mrs Brinsmead with a very welcome cup of tea, she saw that it was nearly ten o'clock and felt as though she had only just closed her eyes.

The housekeeper drew the curtains, letting in pale liquid winter sunlight, and announced that the snow had gone. She turned and surveyed Linzi. 'Mr Vardan said you had to have your sleep out, but I thought you wouldn't want to sleep too long—gives you a headache, doesn't it?'

Linzi nodded, sipping the tea gratefully. Her head did feel heavy and her eyes gritty from a very late night, the events of which were all rushing back into her memory.

'Last night was a bit of a turn-up for the book, wasn't it?' remarked the housekeeper, as though she had read Linzi's thoughts. 'Fancy that imp running away like that! Did she ever let on to you that her legs weren't as bad as she would have us believe?'

Linzi shook her head. 'I still can't believe it.'

'Well, I reckon her father's trying to get to the bottom of it all this morning. They went into the library as soon as they'd finished breakfast, with that doctor. Seems he was a very important nerve specialist before he retired. Trust that minx to run into somebody like that—another man to dote on her!'

Despite the trace of lip service to disapproval of Gilda's startling waywardness, there was admiration of the child's exploit in Mrs Brinsmead's face. She stood by the window for a moment, plainly disposed to stay and chat, then observed idly: 'Wasn't it lucky we got the big room done out for Alayne's mother and aunt? I was thankful for it last night when Mr Vardan insisted that the doctor stay overnight instead of driving back in the snow. It didn't take five minutes to slip the fresh sheets on and put out a couple of clean towels. But men don't think, do they?'

Linzi ate her biscuit and agreed that they didn't, and Mrs Brinsmead went on:

'Still, I didn't mind at a time like that. It was very good of him to look after Gilda and bring her home. There's no knowing whose bad hands she might have fallen into at that time of night.' The housekeeper stifled a yawn and made for the door. 'Mr Vardan must be tired—he sat up all last night beside her. She wouldn't leave go of his hand, even when she fell asleep, bless her. He was still there, looking all cramped and tired, when I went in at half-past eight.'

Mrs Brinsmead reached the door, opened it, then closed it again. '*She's* packing—says she's afraid of getting snowed up here and the Christmas rush starting in her boutique.' Mrs Brinsmead smiled meaningly. 'I reckon there's at least one person in this house that won't be sorry if she doesn't come back.'

With another meaning look, to which Linzi had to content herself with a mere raising of her brows in response, Mrs Brinsmead departed. She had never been so human, Linzi reflected wryly as she got out of bed and pattered to the bathroom.

By the time she was dressed and had finished breakfast it was nearing eleven. There was no sign of Gilda and her father, or the child's Samaritan of the night, nor did they emerge when Sharon came down with her bandbox and the case which held her ball dress. She left them in the hall and marched along the library corridor, to emerge a few minutes later with Mark. He carried her things out to her car, she said

167

a cool goodbye to Linzi, and drove off without a backward glance. Mark paused, inquired if Linzi had had her sleep out, and returned to the library.

He looked dreadfully tired, drawn and heavy-eyed, but quietly happy, Linzi thought as she wandered into the empty lounge. Last night must have been a tremendous shock to him, to find his daughter missing, then to discover that she had regained the use of her legs, to the extent of running away from home, apparently without ever giving a hint of this to anyone, least of all the one person who should have been told, himself.

And how had she got to the place where Doctor Whyndale had found her? How had he found her? And what had she meant in that heartbroken outburst about causing the crash which had ended her mother's life?

These were questions to which Linzi had no answers; answers which perhaps only Mark and Doctor Whyndale would ever know.

Linzi pushed the puzzling elements of the whole business out of her mind. They were no concern of hers; soon, when Mark took his daughter back to their home in the south and Gilda returned to her old school, to pick up the threads of a normal, little-girl life while Mark reconsidered his musical career, there would be no place in their lives for Linzi. Hill-crest, and the Lilac Girl, would recede into the past, probably to become a forgotten memory. Suddenly she had a feeling that the house would rapidly lose its fascination for Gilda, and as Mark had stated so vehemently his dislike for the old place it was quite likely that he might decide to sell it. And this time, if Andrew's friend still wished to go ahead with his scheme to turn the house into a holiday home for handicapped children, there would be no abrupt cancellation of the sale. *That must have been when he had the reconciliation with Lucille,* she whispered soundlessly, *and then, little more than a year later, it all began again, to end in tragedy . . .*

The trend of her thoughts were more than she could bear, and abruptly she turned away from her unseeing contemplation of the November-grizzled garden. She remembered Alayne, and wondered if, in the turmoil of the previous evening, anyone had thought to let her know. The American girl would be worried; she had plainly become very devoted to Gilda during the short time they had known one another. Linzi went out into the hall, to the little panelled recess where the other phone was, and dialled the London number. She

168

knew that Alayne was unlikely to be in at this time of the day, but the porter of the block of flats where she was staying would pass on the message of Gilda's safety at the first opportunity.

Doctor Whyndale left soon after this, regretfully refusing Mark's invitation to stay for lunch but accepting with obvious pleasure an invitation to dinner one night the following week.

With a dry, 'And no more hitch-hiking with strange men, young lady,' and a pat on the cheek to Gilda he took his leave.

'I'll see to that, don't worry,' Mark said stringently. 'And now,' he regarded her anxiously, 'I think it's time you had a rest. We'll bring your lunch on a tray, then you must rest until teatime.'

But Gilda had no intention of going to bed and she was quite adamant about it. Although she was very pale, with great dark circles round her eyes, Mark weakened, admitting he hadn't the heart to insist on obedience.

'She's spent long enough in bed and in a chair this year,' he said in an aside to Linzi, which Gilda patently strained her ears to overhear. He bent and brushed gentle fingers down her cheek. 'Just don't overdo it, and don't develop a cold from your night-raking, please, darling.'

'I won't, Daddy,' she promised blithely, 'I'm too happy.'

It was obvious that whatever doubts she had cherished regarding the genuineness of her father's devotion had been resolved, and also the real or imagined guilt that had lain secretly on her young conscience for many months seemed to have lifted.

After lunch she curled up on the big chesterfield in the lounge and decided to make her confession to Linzi and Nanny Tarrance, who had popped up to see with her own eyes if the rumour already circulating the village was really true.

When Gilda got up and walked unsteadily round the settee, then curled up again and looked proudly at her, Nanny Tarrance's eyes were moist.

'But when—how did it happen?'

'Oh, a bit ago,' Gilda said, somewhat evasively.

'A bit ago! And you never told anybody?'

Gilda pulled a face, betraying that she was becoming a little weary of this question. She picked at a fraying break in the arm of the settee cover and mumbled, 'I couldn't—I wasn't sure.'

'Well, I don't know!' Nanny wagged her head, then looked at Linzi, as though to say: What do *you* make of it? When there was no helpful theory forthcoming Nanny turned a shocked expression to Gilda. 'And so you ran away to prove it. Whatever for?'

'I don't know. I just had to.' By now the frayed spot in the cover had quite a little fringe. 'Daddy knows now, and he's forgiven me. Doctor Whyndale was super—he wouldn't let anybody be cross with me except himself.'

'Oh.' Nanny weighed this somewhat smug statement, and waited for further elucidation.

'He gave me a lift. I never thought he'd stop when I held out my hand just outside your house, but he did. Then he wanted to know what on earth I was doing out alone at that time of night, and I said I'd missed the last bus—it goes at quarter to ten and it was about ten to then. And he said how did I know he was going my way, and I told him I wanted to go to Malton and this road leads there eventually. And then he said he wasn't going to Malton but Fernbridge, a tiny village outside Sheriff Wold. I was beginning to get scared because I was sure he didn't believe me. He started asking me who I was and which school I went to, and what did my father do, and had we lived here very long, and was I in the habit of stopping strange cars for a lift and what were my people thinking of to let me come so far away by myself to visit a cousin. So I asked him to put me off in Sheriff Wold and I would phone my father and he would come and pick me up, and he said no, he would take me home himself if I gave him the directions.'

Gilda paused for breath, avoiding the eyes of her listeners. 'I was really scared by then, and all funny and shaky, and I told him I'd rather he didn't because my father would be mad if he knew I'd stopped a strange car for a lift. I asked him to drop me in the town because a friend from school lived there and I could say I'd stopped off there to see her on the way home.'

Linzi closed her eyes despairingly, imagining the fear of the child and the plight her reckless action had led her into.

Gilda went on, 'He said he didn't believe a word of it and he was going to stop at the next phone box and phone my people himself. We were coming to some traffic lights and I prayed they would turn red before we got to them. They did, and I said he needn't bother and thank you and this would be fine for me, and I got the car door open and got out. My legs felt awful, all watery as though they weren't there, and he shouted after me, but the lights changed again and he had to drive on, because of the cars hooting behind. I ran round the corner and there was a transport café still open. I bought a cup of tea and sat behind two big lorry drivers so that I was out of sight of the door, and wondered what I should do. Then I saw my diary in my bag and remembered Alayne's new number was in. There was one of those open phone booths in the café and I couldn't reach very well, but one of the drivers dialled for me and said, "Blimey—kids are getting sophisticated these days, ringing their pals in London, just like that!" But Alayne wasn't there, only somebody called Janie, and then the pips went and it wasn't worth putting any more money in. I thought Alayne would tell me what to do next.'

'Oh, darling!' Impulsively Linzi got up and went to sit on the arm of the chesterfield. Firmly she removed Gilda's busy fingers from the task they were unconsciously so busy on and murmured: 'Leave a bit of that cover intact, pet.'

'I'll mend it—I'll go and get my sewing box.' Gilda was about to suit action to words, but Linzi put out a restraining hand.

'Presently. Tell me how you met Doctor Whyndale again?'

'He came back to look for me. He hadn't been able to get me out of his mind, and then when I got up in the café my legs wouldn't work and he had to carry me. But he was so kind he made me cry, and I couldn't help telling him about Aunt Sharon and my problem about Daddy not going away again because of me, and he never said anything all the way to his house, except that I hadn't to be scared any more and he'd help me all he could. But after I'd had some malted milk and chocolate cake he said I'd have to go back to get everything straightened out the proper way, and he'd have to ring the police but it was a mere formality, because Daddy would have been so frantic with worry he'd go to them straight away. Then he said he would take me home himself, and suddenly I wasn't frightened any more.'

There was a silence. It seemed she had nothing more to add, and Linzi knew instinctively that she was not going to answer any more of the questions that Nanny Tarrance might ask. There was a worried look on the older woman's face, and a strange blend of concern and speculation in her eyes. Suddenly Linzi recalled an impression gained weeks ago that very first evening she arrived at Hillcrest, and looking at Nanny

171

Tarrance now she knew it had not been a mistaken one. Now, as then, the old woman was troubled by something she was holding back—holding her peace . . .?

As though she sensed this Gilda uncurled her thin limbs and set her toes to the floor. She stood up slowly and took an unsteady pace forward. She paused, and held out her hand. 'Come with me, Linzi, please, I'm going to walk to Daddy.'

She was very shaky those first few days, but with the resilience of youth she gained strength surprisingly quickly. It was still a wonder, and a mystery, and the child continued to hold her own counsel as to the exact moment she had made the momentous discovery that she could walk again.

The approach of Christmas seemed to occupy her thoughts most of the time now. Lists of presents were written, agonised over, and torn up in favour of new ones. Her savings were counted over and over again, and the choice of a gift for her father a cause of much concentrated thought. The matter of his own gift to her was one for almost as much speculation, but he remained utterly impervious to all hints and all the devious cross-questioning his daughter was capable of. She wanted a bicycle. And so did several thousand other youngsters, was all she could prise out of him.

Those were bitter-sweet days for Linzi. The sound of Gilda's happy laughter and her scampering feet brought a joy so intense it still brought a lump to her throat. But through it all was the knowledge she shrank from facing. One morning, the day after Doctor Whyndale had dined with them during a wonderfully happy evening, she knew she must not defer any longer the decision she dreaded. She seized the moment while Gilda was stickily involved in the Christmas-cake-making ritual with Mrs Slaley and went in search of Mark.

She found him copying manuscript and his smile at her turned her heart over.

'Congratulate me!' he exclaimed before she could speak. 'I've finished it.'

'Congratulations,' she said soberly. 'Did love win—or hate?'

'Do you need ask?'

There was a little silence, and then she sensed the inquiry in his eyes was not entirely concerned with his question. She swallowed hard.

'I wondered . . .'

'Yes, now what's worrying you?'

The light-hearted mood he appeared to be in made it even

more difficult to say what she came to say. 'It's about my job.'

'Your job?' His smile vanished. 'Here?'

'N-no, not exactly.' She looked down. 'My new one.'

There was another silence, then he said, 'Well?'

She took a deep breath. 'Obviously you—that is, Gilda—won't need me any more, not when you go back and Gilda goes to her old school. So,' she bit her lip, 'I'll have to think about finding something else in the New Year.'

There was no response. She looked up and saw the old impersonal mask reforming.

'I see,' he said at last. 'You want to leave.'

'No—that is——' She moved her hands hopelessly. 'I don't exactly want to leave, but I fully realise that my job here has come to an end, and with all the excitement I quite understand that it just hasn't occurred to you.'

The tightening of his mouth unnerved her. She went on unevenly, 'It's just that I need to know when—when I'll be free, so that I can look for something else, perhaps a temporary post, until——'

'Yes, I see,' he broke in impatiently, and turned away. 'I had forgotten. Please feel free to accept anything you may find available in the New Year. I hope you'll stay until then, of course. We're having a few people over the holidays, and we'll probably drive down on the second of January. We could give you a lift down, if that date would suit you to terminate our agreement.'

She nodded, unable to speak, and moved blindly towards the door.

'May I say I hope you'll keep in touch with Gilda, and come to visit her, perhaps at Easter?'

She nodded again, and went from the room before the tears betrayed her true feelings. Not to keep in touch with *him*. Not to come to visit *him*, perhaps at Easter. Not to remember ever that once he had noticed her as a woman, as an attractive girl as well as a capable tutor-companion to his daughter. Only once . . .

A curious empty bleakness entered Linzi's spirit now that the matter was settled. She tried not to give in to useless regrets, to recognise that she had taken the only sensible course, and she resolutely fought the reluctance to begin the preliminary moves towards finding a new job. On impulse she wrote to

173

her old headmistress, telling her a little of her life since she left school and of this, her first job after leaving teacher training college. Shyly, she asked for advice, and received a warm and friendly letter by return of post, inviting her to call and discuss the possibility of returning to teach at her old school later the following year. Another letter produced the possibility of a relief post for the spring term at a private school, but required an interview and a decision within the next ten days, and a third letter regretted that a more mature teacher with experience would be required.

The first step had been taken, surely the hardest one towards the break, and each succeeding one would take her a stage farther from an impotent love which had no place in her life. At Mark's request she agreed to say nothing of her plans to Gilda until Christmas was over; by then, he believed, Gilda would be settling down to a more emotionally stable life pattern, and as she entered into the preparations for Christmas she believed she was successfully subduing her own forlorn emotional state. As long as she kept at a distance from Mark, tried not to meet his glance, scrupulously avoided his touch, invoked the strength of pride, and threw herself energetically into trying out every idea that Gilda's fertile imagination could suggest in the way of Yuletide she believed that one day she might start forgetting . . .

By the time the first visitor arrived the house was decked with colour and glitter, all of it contrived by Gilda with Linzi's aid. Huge sprays of holly cut out of green and red paper twined up the staircase, a hand-painted crib lit by a concealed torch and backed by a curtain of dark blue velvet shining with stars was set in the hall, bright mobiles spun gently from hooks overhead, and every dark niche had its colourful touch. Gilda's triumph was a giant cracker some five feet long with shiny scarlet paper and silver stars pasted round its fat middle. A tiny gift for everyone had been painstakingly wrapped and labelled and hidden within, and the only flaw that caused a furrowing of Gilda's young brow was the lack of an almighty bang when the great moment of pulling came.

By Christmas Eve the party was complete except for Alayne, who was driving up during the evening and would not arrive much before midnight. Gilda's godmother, Mrs Mead, and her jovial husband arrived before lunch, bringing a niece and nephew aged twelve and eight respectively, who provided youthful company for Gilda; mid-afternoon brought

174

Mark's business manager, Don Willerby, and his wife, and Andrew and Nanny Tarrance came for supper. During the evening a party of youthful carollers came from the local church, old-fashioned lanterns held aloft on sticks, to sing the old traditional, well-loved carols. The sweet young voices rang clearly on the frosty air, and a hush descended on those gathered to listen.

It came upon a midnight clear ... For a little while the goodness in men's hearts might overcome the hatred and strife of a sick world, to invoke the eternal message of love brought by the Babe born in a lowly stable nearly two thousand years ago.

'If only it could be like this always,' Gilda whispered, her fingers curling within Linzi's, and Linzi echoed the heartfelt sentiment silently. Mark invited the carollers in for glasses of punch, and suddenly the old house seemed vividly alive as it filled with the rosy-cheeked young people. Laughing, Don Willerby borrowed the fluffy scarlet tam-o'-shanter of the youngest caroller and passed it round the company, then peered in for a very rapid reckoning before adding his own 'making-up' contribution and returning it with a solemn bow to the giggling owner. 'I bet we'll beat the other lot with this,' she remarked in an audible aside to the senior in charge, which brought much laughter and the confiding explanation that the 'other lot' were the august of the church choir.

It was a wonderful Christmas, and it went all too quickly. No sooner had the ceremony of the tree taken place, the cries of delight from the recipients of gifts and the anxious, 'Sure you like it?''s from the givers, than it was time for church, then home to the feast and the Queen's message, the enforced rest afterwards and the juvenile business of pulling crackers, paper hats, guessing riddles, and the dismantling of the famous cracker which had been so solidly constructed that no amount of pulling would part it. Gilda got her bicycle—a miniature model in brooch form to stand in lieu of the real one she would select for herself when they returned home, and the gift which thrilled her most was the one from Alayne —an exact replica in antique gold of the locket with the Lilac Girl's portrait which Alayne had had made specially for her.

'I'm so happy,' Gilda sighed when at last she was persuaded unwillingly to bed. 'I kissed everybody under the mistletoe tonight. Did you?'

'Nearly everybody.' Linzi's face was in the shadows as she

stooped to kiss Gilda goodnight. She had seen Mark kiss Alayne, and known the overwhelming temptation to forget all her vows and allow herself to drift where she might be drawn to the sweet salute. But she had taken care to avoid Mark and mistletoe. The joy could only renew the sorrow.

The Meads left the day after Boxing Day, and the Willerbys the following morning. Andrew, somewhat to Linzi's surprise, had departed for Leeds on Boxing Day morning to spend the rest of the holiday with friends, and finally only Alayne was left. She stayed a further two days, taking a final nostalgic look round the secret wing before she travelled north to Edinburgh to spend Hogmanay with her mother's Scottish friends. Then she was flying home.

Gilda cried a little and clung to her before she got into the car, and Linzi was acutely conscious of the ending of a small era which would never come again. It was possible that Gilda would have her holiday reunion with Alayne, and quite possible that Alayne would make a return visit to England, but it would never be quite the same again and Linzi sensed that the child already recognised it would be so, and mourned a little for the loss.

Only two days remained now of the old year, and the hours seemed to fly in the post-Christmas clearing away combined with preparations for the move. Mrs Brinsmead had asked to be free on the first as her husband, who was a seaman, would be returning home the next day and she wanted, naturally, to open their own house in readiness for his homecoming, rather than let him go to his sister's as previously planned.

'He only has a three-day turn-round this time,' she explained apologetically, 'and it would be nice to be home together.'

Mark agreed instantly. There was little left to do except lock up the place, and Nanny Tarrance had invited them to New Year lunch at the lodge. Linzi had a suspicion that but for this invitation Mark would have decided to travel south a day, or even two days earlier.

By New Year's Eve she had reached the point of wishing it was all over. Although, as far as she knew, Mark had still not told Gilda of the parting to come, some of the bleakness in Linzi's heart seemed to find an echo in the child's. She was very subdued that evening and to her father's surprise announced that she didn't think she'd bother to stay up after all to see the New Year in.

'I thought you wanted to be our first-foot,' he commented.

'I did,' she lounged on the library window-seat, 'because of starting to walk again and all that. But Nanny says it's very unlucky for ladies to be the first-foot. It has to be a dark man.'

'I'm not dark enough?' His brows went up.

'Oh, I suppose so,' his daughter admitted, 'but you'd have to come in first.'

Mark heaved a sigh. 'Ungentlemanly, or lucky? I've never been a superstitious person, but far be it that I dispute Nanny's wisdom—or risk allowing any more misfortune into this house. It's had more than its share,' he added bitterly.

It was a sombre note on which to retire and awake to the dawn of a new year that seemed to stretch drearily into a future empty of heart's desire. *This time tomorrow we'll be gone*, Linzi thought bleakly as she walked with Gilda and Mark down to the lodge shortly after noon on a New Year's day bright with pale, frosty sunlight. Mark had scarcely spoken that morning, and she stole a quick glance at him, to see the dark profile set in the taut lines she remembered from that very first meeting at the little stone lodge which was their destination now.

He turned his head suddenly, as though he sensed her regard, and she saw the cold wintry greyness had hardened his eyes as on that earlier occasion. Was it over four months ago? His expression was like that of a stranger, as though those months had never intervened, and she could find no softening of his mouth before she quickly averted her face.

'Don't drag on my arm, Gilda,' he exclaimed irritably. 'You're ten, not two.'

'Sorry.' Gilda, walking between the two adults and linking arms with them, seemed subdued, as though affected by their air of moodiness. She disengaged both hands and with a little skip that still betrayed awkwardness managed to project herself a couple of paces ahead. Mark instinctively put out a hand to restrain and steady, and she shook it off. 'No, you haven't got to help me, anyway. The doctor said I had to try to be independent all the time as well as keeping on with my physiotherapy exercises. Will I be able to go riding when we get home?'

'I see no reason why not, if we can find a reputable school within reasonable distance.' He glanced at Linzi. 'Lucille always flatly refused to let her ride.'

The name of his wife came as a cold shock, despite the dispassionate tone in which it was uttered. It was the first time he had ever referred directly to Lucille in this way, and suddenly the shadow of her lay cold on Linzi's heart. Not only Gilda's mother; Mark's wife, whom he had loved, must have loved dearly or would he have married her? Who had enchanted the youthful Andrew and won from him a loyalty that was still strong, five years of maturity later ...

Their arrival at the lodge gate saved Linzi having to make any reply, and the warm-hearted hospitality of Nanny Tarrance instantly enveloped them. They had to have wine and cake first, for the New Year, and she hoped to goodness that Andrew and his friend wouldn't be late; they were driving from Leeds and expected to arrive by noon, and she didn't want dinner to spoil.

Had Linzi and Gilda not been fascinated by the vast array of cards Nanny had received and which were strung from ribbons on each wall and crammed two deep along the mantelpiece and in every spare chink between ornaments, the sharp sidelong glance from Nanny that accompanied the word 'friend' might have prepared Linzi for what was to come. But she missed that certain glance, and so when the car drew up and Andrew's companion emerged, to be drawn laughing and shining-eyed into the curve of his arm as they hurried up the path, a soft exclamation of surprise escaped Linzi.

It was obvious that the acquaintanceship with Carol Drisedale, begun on the night of the gala at Red Manor, had blossomed into something much closer. Their fingers were still interlinked when they entered the sitting room, and there was a trace of awkwardness about Andrew when he faced Linzi, to exchange seasonal greetings and kiss her cheek.

Carol looked like a girl revelling in love and being in love, and Andrew like a man for whom fate was moving with bewildering and slightly dismaying speed. When the large and leisurely meal was over Nanny began a brisk clearing away, aided by Linzi and Gilda, and Carol, after a soft secretive smile at Andrew, also volunteered her help. But Nanny shook her head, and without any protest Carol sank back willingly into the snug depths of the settee and the warm proximity of Andrew.

'I don't like it.' Nanny closed the kitchen door firmly and dashed wash-up liquid liberally into the bowl. 'He ought to have more sense. She's only *seventeen*!'

178

Linzi took a tea towel from its peg and waited for the first dish to emerge from the steamy froth. She was uncertain of what response to make, of how to persuade Andrew's somewhat formidable little aunt that at twenty-six he would, with sense or otherwise, want to choose his own girl-friends, and how to convince her that Carol at seventeen today was probably more knowledgeable and more mature than many a twenty-year-old of Nanny's generation. She said gently: 'It may not be serious.'

'Serious? It's serious all right.' Nanny was almost attacking the dishes and the snowy lather swirled wildly in the bowl. 'Why didn't he come home once in the whole month before Christmas? Not for a single weekend? Huh! Took him all his time to spare one day at Christmas away from her. He never let a girl take all his free time like this before. And there was I hoping ...'

Nanny drew a deep breath and looked at the slender girl in blue quietly drying the big Willow Pattern dinner plates. For a moment the cold rush of the wind against the steam-glazed window was the only sound, then Nanny sniffed and plunged her hands back into the water. 'Too late for hoping now—not that there ever was any real hope, I'm beginning to think.'

Linzi was silent. She knew very well what Nanny had hoped. *A nice sensible lass like yourself* ... The echo floated back from the past, and brought a surge of anger and despair. Was that all she suggested to people? A sensible person who would fill the bill of their requirements—for someone else? She stacked the plates jerkily, as though their sharp rattle could assert her reality. Not for the first time she was experiencing the strange sensation of being a kind of metaphysical onlooker. So many things had happened during her stay at Hillcrest, to people with whom she had become closely involved, but who despite this had remained totally uninvolved with herself.

And tomorrow it would all be over.

The thought brought panic, and a consciousness of the minutes racing by. The afternoon dissolving in casual sociality, in the tea Nanny insisted on dispensing at half-past four, and more talk that floated round her without making any personal impression, until the moment that Mark said it was time to go, and then they seemed scarcely to have been back in the house for five minutes before Mrs Slaley was saying that the evening meal was ready and it was a cold one and they could

179

have it whenever they were ready.

Mark was silent, abstracted as he ate. Only Gilda chattered away, and Linzi felt that every mouthful would choke her. When it was over there was nothing else to defer the final task—packing.

The little room which had been home for four months looked denuded when the small personal knick-knacks were stowed in her case and only the suit in which she was travelling remained in the otherwise empty wardrobe. She and Gilda each showered and got into their night things, and rinsed out the undies they had worn that day; by morning the small garments would have drip-dried in the bathroom and be ready to slip into cases along with the overnight things.

'That seems to be everything,' Linzi said at last.

Gilda surveyed the open cases, both almost full. 'It's only half-past nine,' she observed. 'It's too soon for bed.'

'It isn't for you, you know.' Linzi walked through into the adjoining room and checked Gilda's wardrobe for anything the child might have forgotten. One silky jumper remained in one of the fitted compartments. She held it out and looked questioningly at Gilda.

Gilda shook her head. 'It's too small. By next summer it won't fit me at all. Shall I go down and make some cocoa?'

Linzi folded the jumper and tucked it into a corner of Gilda's small case. 'You'd better take it with you, though. Now, if you pop into bed I'll make the drinks. Do you want a biscuit?'

'No, thanks—let me go down and make them, please.' Gilda tightened an errant red ribbon that held her thick tresses and looked pleadingly at Linzi. 'I love being able to do things again—please?'

Unable to resist this plea, Linzi agreed. After all, her authority over Gilda was virtually ended now; it seemed pointless to try to enforce it at this late stage. While she waited for the child to return she did a hasty revision of the big dress case which Gilda had insisted on packing herself. The youngster had made a creditable job of it, except for the layer of books which would soon bounce down among the neatly folded garments once the case was moved. She made a separate parcel of them and sat down on the bed, suddenly conscious of weariness, to await Gilda's return.

A full quarter of an hour had elapsed, and she was on the point of going out on to the stairhead to see if there was any sign of Gilda—or sound of a mishap with the cocoa—when she heard the music and stiffened. Unsteadily she stood up and crossed to the window, drawing aside the curtain to look down. The spreading rectangle of amber shone out beneath, touching the wet shrubs with ghostly gleams of brilliance. She pressed her forehead to the cold pane and listened to the melody which was now as familiar as the beat of her own heart. The lovely sweet lyrical theme, and the dark surging undertone. Love—and hate. *Oh, Mark,* she whispered soundlessly.

'Daddy's playing,' came the light child's voice from the doorway. 'I just went to say goodnight to him to save him coming upstairs because I thought he'd be busy packing.'

Linzi nodded, unable to trust herself to speak. She did not want the rich milky cocoa, nor the chocolate biscuits which Gilda had brought; she wanted only to seek her own bed and the darkness, to speed the night away, and the inevitable parting. A clean break ... But she could not hurt the little girl, so she forced herself to eat a biscuit and sip the hot drink, and listen to Gilda's chatter while the sounds of the music whispered and swelled below.

Gilda was disposed to reminisce, of the secret wing, of the picnic with Andrew and the advent of Alayne, of many incidents which now held poignant memories for Linzi. At last she stood up and said firmly: 'Bed, or we'll never be able to wake up soon in the morning.'

She slipped the white quilted dressing gown from the small shoulders and urged Gilda towards her bed.

'I haven't cleaned my teeth!' Gilda seized the dressing gown, shaking her head vehemently.

'Hurry,' Linzi said tiredly.

She tightened the girdle of her wrap and wandered restlessly back to the window. The light still flowed out into the darkness, but Mark had stopped. Then a moment later the melody began, only to falter and die abruptly as so many times before. Three times it was repeated, until the crash of chords choked the tender theme with a dark stormy crescendo.

'I'm ready now.'

She turned blindly to see Gilda standing by her bed. She drew the clothes up over her and tucked them in, then stooped to kiss her as she had done every night for four months.

'Goodnight, darling,' she whispered.

''Night, Linzi.' Two arms fastened round Linzi's neck and pulled her down close. 'I'm glad we're going home tomorrow, but I'm sorry we're leaving here. Are you?'

'Yes.' Linzi couldn't trust her voice to say any more. She disengaged herself gently and reached out to the lamp.

'Leave it on, please. I'm not quite——' Gilda started up. 'Linzi, are you crying?'

'Of course not!' She turned away sharply, before a second tear could follow the one the eagle-eyed Gilda had seen. 'Go to sleep,' she whispered unsteadily, and escaped quickly into the privacy of the adjoining room.

If only Mark had not started to play!

The music had torn down all the painfully built defences she had gathered to her during the past few weeks. But for the music she might have maintained her frail control until the moment of parting, until the finality of stepping out of the car at the door of her home, until the goodbye without even a handshake to make the physical contact which could shatter her emotions.

She had believed the composition complete. He had said: 'Congratulate me,' and she had asked: 'Which won? Love —or——?' and he had said lightly: 'Need you ask?' But the music tonight had not spoken of love. It had torn apart at the same moment of torment as on countless times in the past, to plunge into the torrent of despairing chords which seemed to cry their scorn of any belief in tenderness, in love.

She stood by the neatly turned down bed, unfeeling hands smoothing the soft lilac frilling at the edge of the pillow, then turned to wander listlessly round the room. The open suitcase on the ottoman seemed to mock her, and abruptly she closed the lid on its potent reminder of the morrow. She stooped to pick up a thread from the carpet, paused to stare into her own mood-misted eyes through the dressing-table mirror, then reached sharply to snap down the light switch.

The room was plunged into darkness and she stopped, her mind computing the fact she had not first put on the bedside lamp and busily making the small pattern for her next decision. To stumble across the darkened room? Or put on the main light again so that she could see, put on the little lamp, and return to switch off the main light? But instinct rejected the automatic reasoning minutiae of the brain and drew her to the long ribbon of faint luminescence that shimmered down the chink between curtains not completely closed.

Like a slender, graceful automaton she crossed the darkened room and parted the curtains. A half moon hung lazily, its light pale and winter hard against the midnight blue of night's infinity, and no sound stirred the stillness of the sleeping countryside. She looked down and saw that the light had gone below, and an unbearable sense of loneliness overtook her. She might be the only living being in this dark silence.

She did not know how long she stood there, her soft breath making a thin phosphorescent bloom on the glass, her lightly clad body as yet immune to the chill emanating through old crevices in the window timbers and stealing around her feet. She was scarcely conscious that she was making her farewell now, to the old house itself, to the child sleeping in the next room, to all the people who had helped make up the fabric of this brief part of her life, and most of all, to the man whose presence pervaded her every waking moment, and would continue to do so for a very long time to come.

When she heard the sound of the door opening she felt no fright, only a rush of irritation. She gripped the soft velvet edges of the curtains and sighed impatiently: 'Oh, Gilda, go back to bed, for goodness' sake!'

There was no reply and she swung round.

Mark was standing in the doorway.

CHAPTER TWELVE

SHE sensed his gaze searching the room, and saw his involuntary movement as that gaze reached the window and herself.

'I'm sorry.' His gesture was awkward. 'I didn't mean to frighten you, but——'

'You didn't frighten me.' Her voice sounded unreal in its clarity. 'I thought it was Gilda.'

He reached for the light-switch and there was a flurry of soft steps behind him as he did so. Gilda appeared under his outstretched arm at the same moment as the dazzle of light flooded the room.

'Daddy! She might be asleep! Don't wake——' Gilda's voice petered out as she saw Linzi. 'I didn't—I thought you'd be——' Again the child's voice faltered, and before the look of sudden anger in her father's face she turned before the inevitable order rapped from his lips. He watched her clamber back into bed and then closed the door between the two rooms. He avoided Linzi's eyes as he said grimly: 'She told me you were crying.'

'Crying?' Anger rose in Linzi. 'Why should I be crying?' His shoulders lifted. 'She had no right to say such a thing.'

'Perhaps not. If it was untrue.' His mouth compressed, and there was a weariness in the way he turned, as though to leave. 'I merely had a notion I might offer comfort.'

'Comfort!' Linzi knew she was foolishly repeating his words, but sane and calm responses would not form themselves. Her hands trembled as they caught the girdle of her robe and feverishly tightened it. 'Why should I want comfort?'

'Yes, why?' Again that lift of his shoulders. 'Maybe because Tarrance got under your skin more than you bargained for?'

'Tarrance—Andrew?' A sudden weakness made her want to laugh hysterically. 'You thought——? Andrew doesn't mean anything to me in that way. I don't know why——'

'My impression was otherwise. Totally,' he cut in. 'Today, when you saw him, with that child, you looked as though someone, something, had taken your world away.'

'But I——' Linzi shook her head helplessly, halfway between tears and bitter laughter. How blind could a man be? She turned away, and suddenly Mark took a fierce step towards her.

He seized her shoulders and spun her round to face him. 'Tell me, are you in love with Tarrance?'

'No! I'm not in love with anybody!' She twisted against the strength of his hands. 'Let me go—you're hurting me!'

'I'd like to hurt you at this moment,' he gritted. 'Is this true?'

'Yes, it's true. What do you want me to say? That I love Andrew when I don't? What is it to do with you, anyway?' Hardly knowing what she was saying she forced her hands against his chest in a vain effort to free himself.

'It has everything to do with me.' His hands tightened. 'Linzi, do you have to leave us?'

The question startled her into temporary submission. She stared up into his features and her mouth parted tremulously. 'Of course I have to leave you. How can I stay?' she whispered hopelessly.

'Because I want you to stay.' Inexorably he drew her close to him. 'And at this moment I believe I could make you stay.'

In a moment of passionate madness her whole body became

184

aware of the hard masculine strength of him, reaching out like a magnet to overcome all resistance. She wanted to succumb to that potent attraction, let her senses drown in the intoxication he wanted to evoke in her, but sanity prevailed and she stiffened in his arms.

She bowed her head against his shoulder. 'No, Mark, please . . .'

'Do I still repel you?' he asked bitterly, his arms suddenly slack. 'Because of one foolish moment when I forgot an ancient propriety,' he added wearily.

'Repel? Is that what you think I——?' She felt limp out of the support of his arms, and an ague pervaded her limbs, seeming to drain her strength. She sank down on the edge of the bed and averted her head. 'I'm tired, please leave me alone, Mark.'

A sigh shuddered through him, as though of defeat. 'Why did it take so long?'

She did not know what he asked, and she was too dispirited to care.

He turned away. 'But I know now. I love you, Linzi.'

She thought she had dreamed the words, out of the fabric of her longing.

'I knew how much when I realised we were going to lose you,' he said unevenly, 'even though I'd always vowed I'd never love another woman. Not after Lucille.'

The words and the voice were real, but all their sense not believable. She whispered bitterly, 'Did you love her so much?'

'At the beginning I was enslaved. Then I hated her.' His voice was ragged, almost harsh, then the life went out of it as he added: 'But this means nothing to you. I'm sorry, it was unforgivable of me to try to arouse you with a purely physical emotion.'

He was moving as he spoke, towards the door, to walk out of her life, and she watched from within the frozen trance of disbelief. Then his hand touched the door and she broke free from the spell. She leapt to her feet.

'*No, Mark!* Don't go! Don't——' In the space of her words her feet winged her to him and her hands fluttered, still hesitant, still unsure, while the sombre veil of despair began to dissolve from his features, until he gave a cry to echo her own gasp and opened his arms.

For long moments he held her, his hands convulsive on her back and his lean face warm and hard as it moved fiercely

185

against hers. The joy of enclosing him with her arms was almost an agony, and then he murmured huskily: 'Is this true? Do you mean this? You're not——?'

For answer she gave him her lips, and the sweet pliant curve of her body made him groan softly as he gathered her even closer. Long moment later he raised his head and looked down into blue eyes darkened with the ardour he had wrought.

'I believed you eternally cool, eternally untouchable,' he whispered. 'I still can't quite believe it.'

'Neither can I,' she whispered.

'You'll marry me?'

She inclined her head, still a shade unconvinced that dreams do come true when one least expects them to.

'Very soon?'

'Very soon.' She raised her mouth to his cheek and whispered, 'I do love you, so much.'

'Tell me more.' His touch was gentle now, sensuous through the thin silk of her wrap.

'I always knew you weren't happy, apart from worrying about Gilda,' she said softly. 'I knew you'd been hurt, and I wanted you to be happy, but I never thought *I'd* be able to make you happy.'

'You're making a passable start,' he said on a husky note. 'But why did you avoid me like the plague all these weeks?'

She tangled soft fingers in his hair. 'To save my sanity. You did tell me to stay away from you.'

He sighed softly at the trace of reproach she could not keep out of her voice. 'I had to. I didn't want to risk being accused of trying the old seduction business. A young girl whom I respected, under my roof, and in that respect, under my care. And you were getting under my skin too quickly for my peace of mind. What with that, and Tarrance apparently first in favour, there was little else I could do, other than try to maintain a strictly platonic relationship. But often, when I was alone, at night, and I thought of you ...' Suddenly his mouth claimed her with a fierce hunger that told her more than any words of his longing.

Abruptly he thrust her to arm's length. 'We—that is, I— shouldn't be here, not like this.' The dark warmth in his eyes emphasized the intimacy of the bedroom, and the soft clinging lines of silk that scarcely concealed the filmy night-dress which in turn revealed the slender curves and hinted at the secrets of her body. 'I don't want to leave you,' he said gruffly, 'this is a special time of joy which is unique. There will be many times of supreme happiness in our future together, but none will be quite the same as this moment of discovery. I want to prolong it.' He hesitated, his eyes shadowing. 'There are also things I want to tell you, so that you'll be prepared for any snide little hints you may be given by so-called well-meaning people once we return to London and the news of our marriage is known. And I want you to hear them from my own lips first. Can you slip on a coat or something and come downstairs for a drink?' *Before I have to relinquish you until morning,* his eyes pleaded.

The thought of parting was no more welcome to Linzi, even as she realised the sweet folly of lingering here in Mark's arms. She took from the wardrobe the three-quarter-length camel coat in which she was going to travel the next day and slipped it on over her wrap. It looked slightly ludicrous atop the pastel lilac folds, she thought as she glimpsed herself in the long mirror, and she said so to Mark. But he shook his head.

'You've yet to learn, my darling, that the eye of love sees beyond mere outward show.' Taking her hand, he led her downstairs to the library, where he poured her a drink and then stoked new life into the dying fire before taking the other fireside chair.

His eyes reflective, he said slowly, 'Some will say that I drove Lucille into other men's arms because I cared little for anything other than my career. Others will hint of her affair with a prominent political man and my supposed threat of blackmail to end the affair. Neither is true.'

He paused, and Linzi waited, apprehensive of what she might hear about the woman who had once been the centre of Mark's world. For he had loved her first . . .

'Lucille never loved me,' he said quietly, 'even though she had played the part of the loving but neglected wife until she almost believed it herself. She was a young actress, with that flair for extracting the utmost drama from any given situation which is essential to any performer. Unfortunately she insisted on carrying this talent into our private life. At first we were happy. She used to travel with me, until Gilda was born, when it wasn't suitable or fair, I felt, to subject a tiny child to so many changes of climate, time, and strange apartments. That was when the quarrels began. She wanted our life to go on exactly as before, and she had no qualms about leaving Gilda in the care of whichever au pair girl we happened to

187

have at the time.

'She accused me of wanting to leave her so that I could have affairs abroad, and yet she made no secret of her own conquests. It was a long time before I realised that each of her affairs was a kind of challenge, a test of her power over me, and of the capacity of my love and forgiveness. Gradually I realised that she revelled in the dramatic reconciliations; they were the spice of marriage for her, and with that realisation my love died, until I didn't care how many lovers she took. The last three years of our marriage were a sham, a façade we maintained solely for the sake of our child. Then, two years ago, while I was in the States, she brought her lover here, the innocent Gilda's "Uncle" Bart, and that was when I decided to get rid of the place, offer Lucille her freedom, and try to start afresh. At first she blustered, told me she would take Gilda and make sure I saw as little as legally possible of my daughter, and then when she realised I was serious she suddenly capitulated and for Gilda's sake we began the whole miserable charade all over again. But it was Lucille herself who confided to her closest friend that I had threatened to make public her affair, knowing that her lover would take fright at the first hint of scandal. It was a complete fabrication, of course, but it spread round the grapevine in no time.'

Mark paused and stared sombrely into the flames. 'I still don't know why she did it. I don't blame her, because I don't think she could help herself. She lived for excitement, parties, travel, and change. But she should never have married and had a child. She was too volatile of temperament, too highly strung. But I find it hard to forgive what she did to Gilda.'

Linzi felt her throat constrict. She wanted to go to him, to smooth and love away the dark bitterness of memory from his brow, but she remained silent, to let him end his account in his own time, knowing that after this night it would never be spoken of again between them.

'It wasn't until recently, after Gilda shocked us all, that I discovered the truth behind the accident, from Nanny Tarrance, and Gilda herself. As you know, it happened last March. We had come here in February because it was such a fine, early spring. I had a series of European concerts, the final one in Paris, after which I was coming back here and we were staying over Easter, before I set off on the Australian tour. We'd had the usual row before I left, she didn't want to stay here, and I'm afraid I lost my temper and told her to

188

go where she pleased. But I never dreamed that she'd take me at my word and decide to leave me. Or that she planned to take Gilda as well. She waited until the day before the Paris concert, and then packed up here and told Gilda they were going home, and to meet me the following night. But she didn't know that Gilda had seen the airline tickets in her dressing-table drawer. She didn't tell the child until they were actually in the car, on their way, and you can probably imagine Gilda's reaction. She was panic-stricken, begged her mother to turn back, and in the argument somehow Lucille lost control of the car. It skidded, turned over, and Lucille never regained consciousness.

'They rang the house first, and Mrs Slaley told them I was in Paris and managed to find my manager's London number, then she ran down to the lodge and she and Nanny rushed to the hospital. They found Gilda in a frantic state, fighting the sedatives she'd been given after they'd set her smashed leg. She was clutching Lucille's bag, refusing to let it go, and all she could say was to beg them not to tell me. She was incoherent, still shocked, and with that great gash on her forehead, but she implored Nanny to destroy the tickets. Her one coherent thought was that I shouldn't learn that her mother was going away from me.'

He sighed deeply. 'I doubt if we'll ever know just how much psychological effect this had on Gilda's recovery. All these months she carried the guilty fear that she had caused her mother's death, and there was the subconscious doubt that Lucille herself had instilled, that I didn't really care very deeply about leaving Gilda while I fulfilled my engagements abroad. I'm afraid that Gilda did begin to fear that my career meant more to me than my family, and began to doubt my affection for her. Doctor Whyndale believes it definitely retarded her recovery, and that subconsciously she retained her invalidism once she discovered that I was prepared to cancel all my future tours and stay with her.'

There was a long silence, then Mark said wonderingly: 'Did you have any idea of what was going on?'

'You mean ...' Linzi looked at him, 'that she could walk again?'

He nodded.

'No.' Linzi drew a deep breath. 'I had no idea, only those suspicions, or hopes, rather, that I told you about. The day of the picnic when she moved. And the day in the secret wing when she nearly fell out of her chair and I was positive she'd put out her feet to save herself.'

'I remember.' Mark got up to fill their glasses, then returned to his chair, his eyes reflective. 'It seems her one dream was to walk again, to give me the most wonderful surprise of my life, and quite some time ago she discovered that she could stand unaided, and take a few shaky steps forward. But she was frightened of Sharon, and all her old sense of insecurity, of my not really wanting her, erupted again and kept her silent. She wanted to be sure, and so she kept her secret, until I told her I might marry Sharon. What an idiot I've been!' Mark clenched his hands. 'I believed that Sharon would complete our home again, that she would love Gilda as dearly as she professed to, and that it was indeed the only sensible thing to do. Gilda's flight was an impulsive, desperate protest against the disaster I was about to make of our lives. It certainly succeeded; it also helped me towards reading the truth in my own heart.'

At last he turned and looked into Linzi's eyes again. 'I'm sorry to burden you with all the unhappiness of my past, but I wanted you to know it all first, before ...' He hesitated. 'Am I asking too much of you? To take on the added responsibility of helping me to give her the love and the stability she needs so much?'

Linzi could not bear to see the agony of doubt haunting his eyes. With a choked little cry she ran to him, to be caught and pulled down into his arms, to be kissed with all the heartfelt longing of his deeply passionate nature.

'I never dared to believe I'd find love like this,' he whispered. 'Nor that it would be returned.'

'I thought you were falling for Alayne,' she said in a low voice, pressing her face to his.

He laughed softly. 'Were you jealous? I wish I'd known! No, Alayne has one of those very happy, extrovert personalities which are hard to resist. She isn't like you or me, who hide our feelings for fear of rebuff.' He paused, his fingers tangling in Linzi's hair, then added wryly: 'Gilda had the same bright idea; that Alayne might make an admirable wife for me. Although she's very fond of Alayne, I suspect that it was a case of anyone rather than a marriage of convenience with Sharon. Did you know that she once suggested yourself as a possible candidate?'

'Me?' Linzi's cheeks grew scarlet, despite the fact that there was little need now for embarrassment over young Gilda's matchmaking ideas. 'She didn't!'

'Oh yes, she did,' Mark said wryly. 'Then she informed me that she thought you and Andrew had a special thing going for one another, and maybe I was too old for you,' he added feelingly.

'But not too old for Alayne!' Linzi could almost laugh now at the recollection of her many anguished surmises on that very matter. Then her expression sobered. 'Mark, do you think she'll accept me? I mean, being her teacher is one thing, but becoming your wife and——'

Mark's lips interrupted the doubts. 'I think she'll take full credit, personally. Thank heaven I put off the evil moment of telling her you were leaving us tomorrow. I had vague ideas of saying you wanted to see your family, and then asking you to come back...'

'Oh, Mark, if you knew how I dreaded the parting!' She put her face against his shoulder. 'I thought I would never see you again.'

'Did you, my darling?' He drew her close again, and for a while they were silent, until Mark stirred reluctantly and gazed down into the soft oval curve of the face that lay contentedly against his shoulder.

'I don't want to, my love,' he whispered, 'but we have to say goodnight. Having you in my arms like this is becoming too sweet a torment. So...' his mouth feathered her brow and once again claimed the sweet trusting lips, 'till tomorrow, my dearest heart...'

'And all our tomorrows,' she said softly.

Accept FOUR BEST-SELLING ROMANCES FREE

You have nothing to lose – and a whole new world of romance to gain. Send this coupon today, and enjoy the novels that have already enthralled thousands of readers!

- ✂ - - -

To: Mills & Boon Reader Service,
FREEPOST, PO Box 236, Croydon, Surrey CR9 9EL.

Please send me, free and without obligation, four Mills & Boon Bestseller Romances, and reserve a Reader Service Subscription for me. If I decide to subscribe I shall, from the beginning of the month following my free parcel of books, receive 4 new books each month for £3.40, post and packing free. It I decide not to subscribe, I shall write to you within 21 days, *but whatever I decide the free books are mine to keep.* I understand that I may cancel my subscription at any time simply by writing to you. I am over 18 years of age.

Please write in BLOCK CAPITALS

Name⎯⎯⎯⎯⎯⎯⎯⎯⎯⎯⎯⎯⎯⎯⎯⎯⎯⎯⎯⎯⎯⎯⎯⎯⎯⎯

Address ⎯⎯⎯⎯⎯⎯⎯⎯⎯⎯⎯⎯⎯⎯⎯⎯⎯⎯⎯⎯⎯⎯⎯⎯⎯

⎯⎯⎯⎯⎯⎯⎯⎯⎯⎯⎯⎯⎯⎯⎯⎯⎯⎯⎯⎯⎯⎯⎯⎯⎯⎯⎯⎯⎯

⎯⎯⎯⎯⎯⎯⎯⎯⎯⎯⎯⎯⎯⎯⎯⎯⎯⎯ Post Code⎯⎯⎯⎯⎯

Offer applies in the UK only. Overseas send for details.

SEND NO MONEY – TAKE NO RISKS 9C2